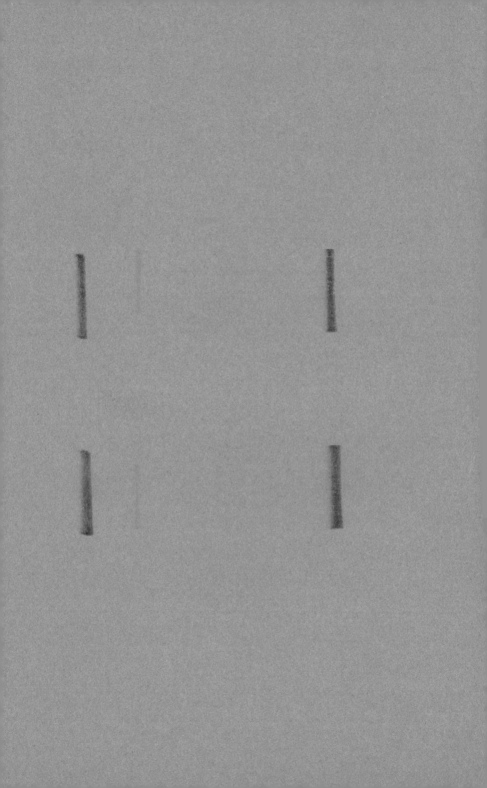

THE DISTURBED GIRL'S DICTIONARY

THE DISTURBED GIRL'S DICTIONARY

NONIEQA RAMOS

carolrhoda LAB

MINNEAPOLIS

Carolrhoda Lab™
An imprint of Carolrhoda Books
A division of Lerner Publishing Group, Inc.
241 First Avenue North
Minneapolis, MN 55401 USA

For reading levels and more information, look up this title at
www.lernerbooks.com.

Cover and interior images: iStock.com/bezmaski (background); iStock.com/
nojustice (drywall); iStock.com/mxtama (textured); iStock.com/ojoel (fungus tub
texture); iStock.com/retrofutur (bathtub); iStock.com/123ducu (concrete texture);
iStock.com/Jag_cz (splatter explosion); Picsfive/Shutterstock.com (notebook).
Foilstamp: iStock.com/Dimedrol68.

Main body text set in Janson Text LT Std 10.5/15.
Typeface provided by Linotype AG.

Library of Congress Cataloging-in-Publication Data

Names: Ramos, NoNieqa, author.
Title: The disturbed girl's dictionary / by NoNieqa Ramos.
Description: Minneapolis : Carolrhoda Lab, [2018] | Summary: Fifteen-year-old
    Macy, officially labeled "disturbed" by her school, records her impressions
    of her rough neighborhood and home life as she tries to rescue her brother
    from Child Protective Services, win back her overachieving best friend after a
    fight, and figure out whether to tell her incarcerated father about her mother's
    cheating.
Identifiers: LCCN 2017004654 (print) | LCCN 2017031962 (ebook) |
    ISBN 9781512498554 (eb pdf) | ISBN 9781512439762 (th : alk. paper)
Subjects: | CYAC: Family problems—Fiction. | Emotional problems—Fiction. |
    Learning disabilities—Fiction.
Classification: LCC PZ7.1.R3656 (ebook) | LCC PZ7.1.R3656 Di 2018 (print) |
    DDC [Fic]—dc23

LC record available at https://lccn.loc.gov/2017004654

Manufactured in the United States of America
1-42212-25774-9/28/2017

TO MIGUEL, MY TWUE WUV!

"DO AS THE BULL IN THE FACE OF ADVERSITY: CHARGE...."

—JOSÉ DE DIEGO

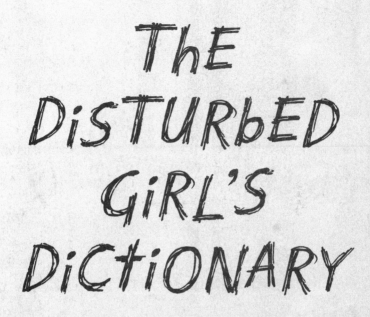

The Disturbed Girl's Dictionary

By Macy Cashmere

For Macy Cashmere

ALWAYS/NEVER

Interjection. Sometimes hated. Always feared.
Never disrespected.

"Still getting radio silence." I scroll down my list of followers. "But she didn't unfollow . . . or unfriend me."

The word *unfriend* makes George tighten the strap on his helmet. (See H for Helmet. George is what you call special. But not to his face if you want to avoid me jackhammering yours.) "Look, look. Alma posted another one of her kids." Alma's got so many siblings and half-siblings and cousins living at her house I lose count.

I hold up my iPad and George leans over, almost tipping his desk. "Yo, see that in the background? The little dude there on top of the fridge!" He scrolls and laughs, slamming into the seat so hard it crashes into the desk behind it. If you sit near George, it's highly recommended you wears a helmet too.

Teacher Man glares at us. He is annoyed because our ignorant asses broke the school firewall again to check social media posts, but we can't even pass a daily quiz. Right now we're supposed to be doing a historical analysis between suffrage and civil rights, but I got to know if my friendship with Alma is history first. We haven't talked in two weeks and I'm in serious bestie withdrawal.

History is the only class the three of us have together anymore. The only reason Alma is in a regular class—and rest assured there's nothing regular about the cray-crays in this class—is because all her other classes are AP and she needs a breather. Alma's not here today though. She's on another field trip in this program called Tomorrow's Leaders Today. (See G for Gifted and Talented.) George and I are not in this program because nobody appreciates our gifts or talents today—or any other day. Currently George is displaying his talent for appreciating my jokes. Every time he laughs he bashes into desks like bumper cars. Any minute he'll start wheezing and get sent to the nurse. George has the asthma.

Me: "Alma always never posts pics of herself. Even her profile pic is of one of her kids. Check it out. This girl is Alma's mini-me. She always never—"

"Macy! George!" Teacher Man is staring us down. "Let's talk about why we cannot use the words *always* and *never* in the same sentence."

"What do you mean by *we*?" I lean way back in my seat. People are always talking like that to me. Saying *our* and *we*.

Our plan for Macy is . . . I think we can all agree that . . . We don't want THAT to happen, do we?

Teacher pops a cap off a black marker and writes the sentence I said on the whiteboard in Caps Lock.

ALMA ALWAYS NEVER DOES THAT.

He's trying to turn this into what he calls a teachable

moment. Like that time he made us proofread all the graffiti in the bafroom.

With a red marker, he crosses out the word *always* and rereads it. He says, "See, *always* is what we call superfluous. It's clutter."

Clutter? Like he knows my life.

"You're pissing me off," I say. I stay seated. I don't get in his face. Yet. I stay in my circle—draw a imaginary one around my desk. (See C for Circle.)

Teacher turns his back. "I hear you, Macy," he says. "I'm sorry you're angry."

"I didn't say I was angry," I shout. My circle is bursting with flames. "I said I was pissed."

The teacher turns on the projector. He's got a PowerPoint with GIFs. He's got Vines. He's got everything but a top hat and a cane. He is ignoring my behavior. This is a time-honored teacher strategy that also royally pisses me off.

I reach into my desk. Take out *History of the American People Volume 1* and clean house. Cross out all the pages about shit that's got nothing to do with me. What's left? Not much. The teacher keeps clicking through his slideshow until he hears the silence of the other kids. Until he hears the slashing of my pen.

"*Macy!*" he whips around, blinking in the light of the projector. "What are you doing?"

I guess he is no longer ignoring my behavior. "Are you angry?" I crack my knuckles. "Or are you pissed?"

If he were a cartoon, smoke would be pouring out his ears. A kid coughs as if he can smell it. "Put the Sharpie down, Macy. Vandalism will not be tolerated. You—"

"Vandalism? I'm not vandalizing any more than you. I'm just deciding which words count and which ones don't. Which words mean something and which don't. That's exactly what you do."

"Macy! You can't argue two plus two is three, and you can't argue that *always* and *never* should be used in the same sentence. You're not in middle school anymore." He slams his marker on the lip of the board. It rolls onto the floor. "I expect—"

Me: "You dropped something."

His nostrils twitch.

Yeah. He's pissed.

"What you're not picking up on is how much is at stake here, Macy. Nobody's gonna give you a lollipop anymore just because you throw a tantrum."

"What did you say, motherfoe?" I throw my desk.

The other kids hide under their desks like it's a tornado drill. Teacher Man pushes the office button. I'm going. Don't even need to give me a lollipop. It's a violation of my civil rights, though. Depriving my ass of a education. I walk out and slam the door.

I sit outside the principal's office and take out the dictionary you're reading right now. (By-the-fucking-way, you're reading this because I'm missing or dead or in a nuthouse, or CPS stole it, and maybe you don't know I'm standing right behind you, motherfoe.)

Back to *Always/Never.* Miss Black, my English teacher, says that to prove your point you have to give many examples. Here's mine: Mothers always never leave.

I remember the first time my mother left. She thought I was asleep, but I saw her packing her bags. I don't know why she left the house that night or what made her come back, but she did. I mean I guess she's got enough reasons to leave, but what I always never get is what brings her back. Is a bad mother the one who leaves or the one who stays even though she should go?

I checked what was inside those bags. In one bag was a ratty old stuffed dog missing a ear. Her honey-bear bong and a dime bag. (And let me share my disappointment that a dime bag don't actually got no dimes in it, believe me.) Pictures of herself at the beach. Queen Helena hair gel. A lock of my brother Zane's hair. (See B for Burner and G for Gas.)

She always leaves a note. It says: *I know you'll never forgive me. But you'll always love me. I know it. I still love my mother. The bitch. (The bitch* is crossed out, but I can still read it through the scribble.) *All my love, Yasmin.*

But she always never leaves. Always acts like those bags aren't still in the back of her closet, waiting. In the morning, I always look for the piece of tape hanging on the front door where the note was. Always find all the empty kitchen cabinets open like she wants us to know there's nothing left for us here. The stuffed dog is back in that bashed-up box of hers. She got it from the group home when she left at thirteen. The bong and the dime bag are back in her panty drawer. The gel is on the kitchen sink where she does her hair when somebody's stunk up the bafroom. The pictures of me on the dresser have never left.

APPLE

Noun. A apple a day keeps the doctor away.
So does not having no insurance to pay him with.

It's lunchtime. This is supposed to be my twenty minutes.

We get 180 school days a year to try and undo what every fuck-up did to us, to themselves, to the fucking planet. But we only get twenty minutes for ourselves. Can you do the maf?

Twenty minutes to laugh our asses off, stead of being told to sit our asses down and shut our mouths up. Even a damn fruit fly got more time to live.

Today I'm sitting in the cafeteria by my lonely-ass self, rolling a apple down the lopsided table I'm sitting at. It falls off the edge and bruises. If Adam offered Eve the apples from my cafeteria, she'd a been like yeah no, thems nasty. I flash back to the day Alma and I stopped speaking.

Alma crunches a apple that I swear has been sitting in the cafeteria since the beginning of school and maybe the beginning of time.

"How can you eat that shit?"

"Please don't call my food shit. I eat it because it's healthy."

"Some people eat bugs because they're healthy. Don't mean I'm gonna eat them."

"But you'll eat that blue Laffy Taffy? That's no better than eating plastic."

I stick out my blue tongue.

"If your tongue looks like that, can you think about what your insides look like?" Alma shakes her head in disgust at my ignorant ass. "I'll grant you the produce here is substandard. But what if I could show you a place where the fruit is better than plastic?"

"Does this involve a field trip?"

"Yaas, queen. Come with me to the supermarket."

Me: *"The Super S? Bwhahaha."* (See S for Super.) *"Can we place a bet?"*

Alma: *"No. Not the Super S. A real supermarket. My mom makes the trek there once a month. The bus fare is expensive, but she has this special card from WIC. It gets her formula and fruit for the babies for free."*

"Wait. A card? Like a credit card? Could I get me one of those?"

"No. It's only for kids under five."

"Dang."

"Anyway, the Tomorrow's Leaders group is going there on a field trip in a couple weeks, to learn about health and rational decision-making and budgeting."

Me: *"So I guess the rest of us idiots is okay sick, stupit, and broke."*

Alma: *"Macy, my point is that you and I can go together sometime."*

But we didn't go there. Because the next day we had the fight.

And the next night I dreamed of a magical supermarket. One where we was outside. Not in a cafeteria that could double as a hospital waiting room. One where you had time to finish a sentence—and your damn food. Where there was nothing and nobody but you and your bestie and you could pluck Laffy Taffy from the trees.

AM

Verb. A verb? Who I am is something I do?
Seems to me who I am isn't much about what I do,
but a whole lotta things that's already done.

Am I disturbed? School says I am. Social worker says I am. Teachers say I am. The paperwork with the words *Individualized Education Plan (IEP)* says I am.

"Maybe we could get some money for this," I hear my mother say, peeling off the IEP paperwork from the kitchen table. She sits down. "Your father got some when he busted his knee moving furniture."

"Cha-ching," I say. I mean, if being crazy is worth anything we'll be billionaires. My mother starts looking it up on her phone.

I grab the paperwork. Look at the photo of me clipped to the top. I shaved my head the day before school picture day, and it itched so bad I had scratch marks in my scalp. Pierced myself so I could connect a chain from my nose to my ear. I like options. Bee-you-tee-ful bitches!

"I still can't believe you did that to yourself," my mother

says, glancing up from her screen. "All that beautiful black hair. I used to love to comb it."

"Yeah, I remember. *Sit your ass down. Stop being a little fucking baby, it's just a knot.* Ah, the memories."

"Shut up, Macy." Her screen sucks her back in.

I read. Paperwork says Last name: MYOFB. First name: Macy Cashmere. Couple of days shy of fifteen. Born to Yasmin and Augustine MYOFB. Current residence no longer a 1980 Ford Pinto. We moved from a car to a no-tell motel to the house we're in now when Daddy got that job as a mover. I remember when Daddy pulled up to the garage. "This time," he said, "when the roof leaks it'll be the rain and not somebody's toilet." Part of the roof caved in like three months later.

Me and Zane used to run through the house with umbrellas when it rained, with my mother screaming, "Stop it, that's seven years bad luck, fourteen, stop!" Once the sun came out while it was still raining, and my mother smiled. She said, "That means a witch is getting married, you know." I liked when she talked like that. And my dad joked, "We had sun showers on our wedding day, right?" And she smacked him, but she was happy.

I look at the bars on our windows and think about my daddy in prison and the last time he's seen the sun.

"I wonder what kind of money that foster family is making off Zane," my mother says. My brother Zane got kidnapped by CPS three weeks ago. "I didn't stay long enough for my foster parents to make money off of me."

I turn back to my paperwork. It says I was born premature. ADHD. Learning disability unconfirmed. Emotionally disturbed. Exhibits compulsive behavior. CPS investigation pending. Life pending. (I scratched that last part in.)

I sniff the paper. Oil has soaked through the packet. It's Domino's. I lick some oil from my finger.

"I hate when you do that shit," my mother says, getting up. "You could've had some pizza."

"You know I'm on strike," I say. "Hunger strike."

"You still gonna be on strike when it's your birfday?"

"Yeah—about that."

"About what?"

"About the restaurant. The big to-do. I'ma pass."

"What? Do you know how much I would've killed to have my mother remember my birfday? Shit, once she forgot me at the grocery store. I went to the bafroom and when I came out she was gone."

"I know you don't have no money for a fancy restaurant. Where'd you get it from? Mr. Guest, right?"

"Macy, you need to learn to appreciate—"

"That's a yes."

"Fine, Macy. Have it your way. And his goddamn name is Sal."

She digs in a drawer and pulls out a square envelope. "In fact, since you're boycotting your birfday, that must include the gifts too." She crumples the envelope into a wad. Stomps off to her bedroom. "Good night!"

"FYI! It's 10 a.m."

I stare at the trash can. Pull out the envelope, out of curiosity. Just to know what the card inside says. *Buy yourself a new sweatshirt. Love, Mom.* A hundred-dollar bill floats to the ground. A hundred bucks. Talk about a sell-your-soul-to-El-Diablo moment. What could that buy me?

I decide to put it away for emergencies. Only then could I use Mr. Guest's money. I tuck the bill in my jeans pocket for now. Rip off the oil spot from the IEP paper and chew on it. It is so delicious.

A feather blows through the hole in the window. I look out. Wait, it's not a feather. Snow!

Looking out the window is like watching television. Only no one can say you haven't paid your bill and they're going to shut it off in thirty days. Nobody owns the snow. Except maybe the junkyard dogs just before dawn.

I picture the snowflakes tasting like the oil spot I tore from my IEP. Some snowflakes taste like pepperoni. Some taste like pineapple and ham. My brother Zane and I used to gather empty pizza boxes, candy wrappers, gutted McDonald's Happy Meals, and play Restaurant. Pretend to eat the food that used to be inside the wrappers. Some of them still had their smells: peanutty caramel, orange-cinnamon. Every once in a while we'd actually find a stray Skittle or something. A few days before Zane got kidnapped (See B for Burners and G for Gas.), we split a Dum Dum some kid dropped. Rinsed it off. He took a lick. Then me. Somehow we got full.

Now I scope out the back of the fridge for old cartons of white rice. Shake the toaster oven. Score! A burnt pepperoni and half a charred crust. Tomorrow's breakfast!

I pull my dictionary out of my backpack. Macy Cashmere's Dictionary. What you are reading right now. (See D for Dear Reader.) I rest it on my lap. I don't want no stains from Domino's pizza oil on it. Now that Alma isn't speaking to me, it's the only part of me that isn't stained. Messed up.

Which is why I need Alma to forgive me. Alma knows who I be. It's more than who I am.

ALL ABOUT YOU

Abstract noun. You Don't Know My Life.

For Alma's birfday, she had a big party at her church hall. At the last minute I dropped the bomb I wasn't gonna go. That's why we ain't talking.

This was our argument:

Me: "You know I'm not that girl."

Alma: "It's my birthday. It's not about you."

Me: "That's why I'm not going."

Alma: "Damn it, Macy! Tell me my best friend is not skipping my party because of what she has to wear!"

Me: "It's one reason. Out of many."

Alma: "God, I think I'd be insulted if you came in a dress. Don't you think I'm better than that?"

Me: "I know you're better than that."

Alma: "So you're coming?"

Me: "No."

Alma did not need some chick in a sweatsuit—AKA me—

sitting in the shadows of her disco ball holding some crumpled card that should have money in it but don't. (I did think about putting Monopoly money in the card. Alma would have laughed. But then I pictured her mother's sour puss. The photos on Facebook—*What's Wrong with This Picture?* being the caption for any photo with me in it.)

"Alma. You deserve better."

"Don't tell me what I deserve."

"Somebody has to. Because you have no idea."

For Alma it is ALWAYS about everybody else.

But not this time. My gift to her was not to go. To make it all about her.

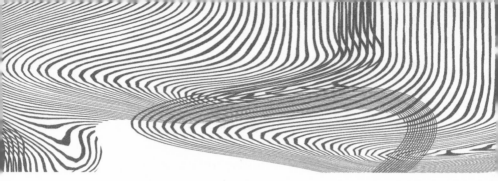

ANNOYING

Adjective. People who eat pizza with a knife and a fork.
I mean fold that bitch and eat like a normal person.

I stand outside and taste a snowflake. Last time I stood outside like this, Alma was with me. You sick of flashbacks already,
motherfoe? If I want your opinion, I'll ask for it. (See D for
Dear Reader.)

"*Alma, ain't you even gonna taste one flake?*"

She shakes her head. "*Do you know how much car exhaust has
been absorbed into those snowflakes? The—*"

"*I never had no trouble digesting snowflakes.*"

"*Well, that's not saying much. God, I remember when you used
to eat glue sticks. Lip balm like it was candy.*"

"*The strawberry ones is the best. C'mon, Alma. Do just one.*"

Alma sticks her tongue out real fast like a frog striking a fly.
"*There. I'm freezing. Can we go now?*"

*Alma proceeds to cross the street toward a construction site full of
burly dudes before I grab her arm and steer her to the longer route.*

"*Girl, you could see the danger in a snowflake, but not in what's* over there?" I flip the finger at the guys already constructing what *Alma's body looks like under her coat. She never seems to know it. When she's being watched—which is all the time. I love that about her.*

"Look! Look at the fresh pile of snow right there. I bet you I could save it in my freezer and make something with it."

"Are you always hungry?"

"Are you ever?"

"I eat."

"You don't eat meat. You don't eat bread."

"It's called vegan."

"It's called annoying."

"It's called self-control."

"Control THIS." I lob one snowball after another and make her taste that damn snow. But she won't retaliate. So I stop. Alma can be so annoying sometimes.

I stick a snowball in my pocket.

Am I hungry? ALWAYS.

ANY DAY NOW

Preposition. Synonyms: That'll be the day.
Don't hold ya breaf. When pigs . . .

My mother is curled up on the couch not paying the bills. I'm sitting on the floor not doing my maf (math. MAF.) homework. "I'm having a guest over," she says.

Me: "Don't you EVER want to be alone?"

My mother: "With a face like this I don't have to be."

"With a face like what? What do you even look like? The only time you're not wearing all that shit"—I point to her makeup—"is in the shower."

"Take a look in the mirror, Macy. I'm not the one who looks like shit. Let me know when you're ready for a makeover. I did make you so I'm in there"—she points to my face—"*somewhere*."

She flips to the news.

"CHILD PROTECTIVE SERVICES SHOULD BE UNDER INVESTIGATION!" a lady on TV shrieks into a microphone. "THEY SENT MY GIRLS TO FOSTER

CARE AND NOW THEY'RE DEAD. YOU TELLING ME THAT'S BETTER OFF?!"

Me: "How can you watch that? Turn it off, Ma."

The news reporter shakes her perfectly styled head at the lady, showing she gets it. The camera does a close-up: "The two girls drowned in a lake on a vacation with their foster parents," the reporter says. "This is not the first death in the foster care system this past year. . . ."

My mother lights up a joint. She exhales and says, "You know any day now, weed will be legal here. Then CPS can't take away kids anymore just because a parent smokes a herbal cigarette."

Me: "I don't know how you can just sit there like that."

My mother: "What else am I gonna do? It's not like I even know where Zane is. I got no choice."

Me: "Didn't CPS say you're supposed to do parenting classes to get him back?"

My mother, exhaling: "It ain't never that simple, Macy. And I mean, I wasn't good at school the first time."

Me, throwing my stuff into the backpack: "This is different. That was for you. This is for him."

My mother: "This from the girl who's failing—I don't know—everything?"

Me: "I'm failing maf. And science. Maybe art. But I'm failing *subjects*. Not"—I lower my voice—"Zane."

My mother: "Oh, Miss Thang got all the answers now?"

Me: "Did you even sign up?"

My mother: "For what?"

Me: "The class, Mom!"

My mother: "I will. The paperwork's on the table. In a minute." A minute passes. Another. . . .

Me: "Any day now, Ma."

My mother: "Okay. Anything to make you shut up." She messes with her phone for a minute. Looks up. "There. It's done."

Me: "When do you start?"

My mother: "Tomorrow."

She goes back to flipping channels. I get up and go to the fridge that was supposed to be fixed "tomorrow." We keep all our food in the freezer now because the fridge died. The freezer's in a death spiral but is still cooling. I grab a orange juice carton I jacked from the school cafeteria. I chug it and throw the container in with the dishes that will be washed "tomorrow." If we buy any soap. "Tomorrow."

A-W-A-Y

Adverb. Synonyms: No way. No how.

George and I are sitting outside the science lab waiting for class to start. We're supposed to have our investigations written up. We're working on experiments. At least everybody else is. My life is a experiment. Every time anything happens there's a explosion. I'm supposed to be thinking about a big question. *Why does this happen? Why does that happen?*

"Hell if I know," I tell George. I carve A-W-A-Y in the wall. A bunch of kids edge farther down the hall. George edges closer to me until I feel his Chewbacca coat against my arm.

"A-W-A-Y!" I shout.

George burrows his head in his coat.

"No, not you, George! Not ever."

He pops his head out. "A-W-A-Y."

"Want to know how it happens?" I ask George. (See E for Even You.)

George's head whips right to left, left to right. He thinks IT might happen now. He tightens his helmet.

Me: "You get called out of class. To the office. The stranger from CPS is waiting there and stands up and asks you to sit down. This isn't the first time. They always try to touch you. They want to high-five or pat you on the back but it's more than that. They come with promises. They come with candy. They ask you questions. They want to know how you're feeling and all sudden you're talking about feelings you never knew you had. They want to know what you eat and how you sleep. When you talk they write things down. They get you warmed up."

George rests his head on my shoulder.

Me: "They're here because somebody called. Somebody was worried. No, they can't tell you who called. So now everybody is out to get you. Everybody that smiles is full of shit. Every adult that whispers is whispering about you, your clothes, your hair, or lack there-fucking-of. You start to notice the stank of your sneakers, even though it never bothered you before."

George smells his sneakers. Coughs. Takes them off. Throws them down the hall.

"When they come to get you it could be any time," I tell George. "Day or night. At home or at school. Right off the street. Once they get you in the car, there's no turning back. They got you. There's nowhere to run. Not to the police. They'll take you right back no matter how much you scream."

Even if they let you go, they watch you. They'll never stop till they take you A-W-A-Y.

I'm tripping hard. (Not on drugs. I *am* drugs. Every disturbed girl is.) They took Zane away three weeks ago, but it didn't hit me until now. It's like I've had amnesia. It's like what the soldiers get, only I haven't been to war.

"They took Zane from the hospital," I tell George even though he already knows. (See G for Gas.) I tell him because I'm telling myself. "At the hospital, I saw some lady crying because her kid was dead. That's how I felt walking out of there without Zane. Dead dead dead and it was all on my head. I should have done better."

"Dead dead dead," George says, lying down on the floor and taking aim with a invisible gun.

"The next day CPS came to get me."

George nods his head, hard, his helmet falling over his eyes. I see it in my mind.

Me to my mother: "Mom, what should I do?"

My mother: "Since when do you want to know what I think?"

Me: "Not now, Ma. They're coming."

My mother: "I don't know what you should do. I know what I would do. But I had friends when I was your age."

"I grabbed my toothbrush," I tell George. He nods. "I ran outside. Didn't even think where I was going. Didn't know where I was till you answered the door."

George clicks his teeth and whistles.

A-W-A-Y. Daddy is A-W-A-Y. For three years. Zane is A-W-A-Y. Maybe forever. I'm so lonely I could die.

They're going to take me A-W-A-Y.

Teacher sticks her head out the door. Sees George in sniper position. Sees me carving A-W-A-Y in the wall. She hits the office buzzer.

They're going to take us away—ha! They're coming to take us away.

23

AFRAID

Adjective. Synonyms: scaredy cat, chicken, punk-ass bitch. (No, not pussy. Vajayjays are like the Hulk, *man*. Why people always gotta say you got balls? Balls? Flick em with a pinky and a guy's on his knees. Vaginas is fearless.)

I'm lying on the couch. It's 3 a.m. The walls are paper-thin, and Mr. Guest and my mother are loud. But the voices in my head are louder.

There's the voice of my daddy bursting in the door. He finds Mr. Guest with my mom and asks me, *How long have you known?*

There's the voice of Zane. The one I've always understood no matter if no one else does.

What scares me the most right now, though—not the voices I hear, but the voice I don't hear: Alma's. That's the only voice that drowns out the noise.

I have to get Alma to forgive me before my head explodes.

And I have a lightbulb. My English teacher, Miss Black, has started this thing she calls Muffin Mondays. She said, and I quote: "I understand many of you have difficulty doing home-work at home, so I'm starting a breakfast club. You show up at seven, I'll bring the muffins. I make them fresh." As in, these are not from Sonic—or Pillsbury even.

My lightbulb is to go get me some of those muffins. And not eat them. I will save them for Alma. She knows how much I been wanting those muffins. More than Tantalus wanted those grapes. Your ass ever heard of Tantalus? Google it, you ignorant motherfoe. Imagine Tantalus finally gets his ass ahold of those grapes he hasn't been able to reach for a fucking eternity. Then instead of eating them he gives them to you? Alma will forgive me then.

This is not my first try to get the muffins, though.

My mother: "What the what? Drive you where? Get to school by fucking when?" (Cue my mother throwing the covers over her head.)

So it's up to me. And I have my best lightbulb yet.

I will steal the car! Genius, right? If I wait until five in the morning, all I have to do is steal the keys from my mother's room, take the car, get the muffins, make up with Alma, and bring the car back by lunchtime. Because my mother—AKA Sleeping Booty—don't even wake up till noon anyway.

Tick tock. Five o'clock. I crack the door. All the air rushes out and all the pot fumes rush in. I reach out to the door slo-mo and twist the knob. If Beyoncé belted out a tune, it would have been quieter. I stand there and wait for my mother to whip out the machete from under her bed and decapitate my ass. The keys wink at me in the dark.

Keys. Not something you really want to be picking up when you're trying to be quiet.

"Bitch, you better back up!" my mother hisses.

I stop, drop, and roll toward the door. See, Señor Health Teacher. I was paying attention.

"Ay, Yasmin, shut up!" from Mr. Guest.

Snores.

My mother don't even shut up in her sleep. She's probably sleep-texting. From the floor I reach up, over, and clutch the keys.

Score! The keys to getting back my bestie are in my hands.

AGAINST ALL ODDS

Adverb. IN A WORLD full of crackheads and stupit asses, Macy must . . .

I lock the door behind me. Even with two sweatshirts on it's cold as hell. As if I'm covered in steaks, a stray German shepherd gives me the eye. But nothing is going to keep me from those muffins. I will step on the gas and reverse on your ass, Cujo!

I duck into the car and throw my backpack on the passenger side. My heart is beating so loud I swear I can hear it as I stick the keys in the ignition. The car roars. Dang it, so loud! I can't gun it, though. I know to let her warm up first. I test out my skills switching between the gas and the brake like Daddy used to do when he'd make the car dance. I got this. I know to turn around when I back up so I don't hit the washing machine or the toilet or the fridge in the front yard. Yes, we got more spare parts than the Jiffy Lube.

The street is clear. YAAS!

I pull out. Everywhere windows are dark. But I feel like every star is a cell phone aimed at me. *Click! Send! CPS: Message received.*

Alma's Voice in my Head: *And you didn't think of this before?*
Me: *Uh. Before what?*

I decide to hunker way down in the seat.

A car pulls up beside me. Shit! The car and me are driving parallel to each other. Mystery Machine in the left lane, me mostly in the right. I slow down. It slows down. I speed up. It speeds up. The car is following me? Shit, I can't see but if I stick my head up it will see me. It stops. I stop. Because maybe there is a stop sign? I wouldn't know because I can't see jack.

Whoever it is, their music is really loud and I can't stand it. I stick my head up.

"FUUUUUUUUCK!!!!!!!!" the guy in the Toyota screams.

"FUUUUCK!" I scream.

He guns it. I try to gun it. The car dies. Nooooooo! It's rolling to a stop. I aim for the gutter. Park right in front of a alley with a dumpster. Good. That way when my stupit ass gets murdered, the killer don't have far to drag me.

There's a car rocking in front of me. I duck down. Out of the rocking car stumbles a girl in a blue wig and not much else. The car drives away. "Hey," she screams. "Wait. My coat!"

Shit. You got to be kidding me. Fucking Odysseus had less shit happen to him. (What the whaaat? Did I read Odysseus? Hell yeah. The comic. Okay, the back cover.)

I don't pray to God. Calling people just when you need shit is not my style. I do hunker under the steering wheel and mess with some wires. Bingo! The car revs up. The heat kicks on. I sit up.

The blue-wigged woman looks straight at me. Walks right toward me, squinty-eyed. I know she can't tell: Girl or boy? I also know that to her skank ass, it don't matter. She steps up to my window, rubbing her shoulders to warm up. I shake my head NO. Skinderella shivers and turns away.

What would Alma do? Yeah.

I pull up and roll down the window. I say: "Yo. Here." I pull off my sweatshirt and toss it to her.

Ho Ho: "Are you wearing a sweatshirt under a sweatshirt?"

Me: "Uh. You ain't one to be talking about nobody's wardrobe, lady."

"Sorry. Shit. Thank you. You don't know—"

"I don't want to know." I go to roll up my window.

She runs beside me and raps on it.

Me: "Don't make me run over your skank ass. No offense."

Ho Ho: "None taken. But. Could you. Give me a ride. I got money."

Cootie money. "Nah."

Ho Ho: "Please! Just to the gas station."

Damn! What would Alma do? Almaaaaaaaa! "Get in."

The smell climbs in my car before she do. I start driving.

"You mind if I smoke?"

Anything will smell better than she do. "I guess not."

She ashes out the window, which has never been opened before. Shit. I hope that window closes.

Ho Ho: "What's your name?"

Me: "Uh. Macy Cashmere."

Ho Ho: "Wow. My name is Velvet! My pimp chose it. How did you get yours?"

Me: "Well. My mom found a Macy's bag on a bus. She was fifteen and pregnant with me. Found a cashmere sweater in it. Thought it was good luck."

Velvet: "Was it?"

Me: "Not for her. But for me—I think it's too early to tell."

Velvet: "Yeah. You mind me asking what you're doing out here?"

Me: "It's kind of a long story. My best friend's mad at me. I'm trying to get muffins for her. And forgiveness. For me." (I don't know why I tell her all that.)

I pull to the curb by the gas station. She starts taking off my sweatshirt.

Me: "Nah. Keep it." (Cooties code red.)

She gets out and then sticks her head in the window. She is a lot younger than I thought.

Velvet: "You go get those muffins no matter what. Against all odds, okay?" She sticks her hands in my sweatshirt pouch and hobbles into the store.

Bye bye sweatshirt. Parting sucks ass (Shakesbeer).

I go to school and park. "No matter what" better be over now.

AGAINST ALL ODDS

The Sequel.

I stand outside. The janitor sees me from way down the hall and comes to let me in. It's even earlier than I usually get here. But Pepe knows to look out for me. (See D for Disturbed.)

"Good morning, Miss!" Pepe says. "You going for the gold again this year?"

I nod. He knows I don't smile. He don't expect me to. The only award I've ever won is attendance. I like to see the teachers' faces when I get the trophy every year. I hold it up like the Statue of Liberty. Alma claps. George cheers. Until he gets faint and has to go to the nurse. George has the anemia.

The other thing I like about getting here early? (See D for Disturbed.) I get here before the principal pulls in. I know exactly what kind of car she drives. I know exactly what kind of car each teacher drives too. I like to say, "Hey, teacher, you just bought the Chevy Equinox, right?" I jingle my sharp, pointy house key when I say it. "Hey, Miss, you got your Dodge Caravan washed?" I like to watch them squirm.

I wave to Pepe as I stroll into Miss Black's room. Just at the moment when her record player needs to switch to the B side. (See L for Love Supreme and P for Pink.)

Miss Black: "Macy! Take a load off. The muffins are on their way. My fiancé is dropping them off." The B side drops. "So you know the deal is—"

"I know the deal. I got me this." I hold up my dictionary. (Which you are reading because I've been held for ransom by ISIS, or sold into slavery by Boko Haram as a undercover operative to rescue those girls they kidnapped like a century ago—because who else is going to?)

Miss Black gives me the eye, and I start writing in my dictionary right away so she knows I mean business. I've had Miss Black before, and she don't play.

The smell of those muffins comes up the hall before Fiancé does. My hands shake. The counselor calls this Reptile Mind. When you're all appetite and no brain.

Miss Black tells Fiancé to lay three on my desk.

Fiancé: "Here you go. I've heard a lot about you, Macy."

Those three fat, hot, buttery muffins he set in front of me—I'll remember the smell till the day I die. I'm about to drool. "No!" I pound my desk, making the muffins jump.

Everybody looks up, then back down at their homework. Miss Black shakes her head, and Fiancé moonwalks to the next desk.

Me to my hand: "No I will not. Will not. Not! Not!"

Then I don't know what happens. Except that my tongue tastes it. My big fat mouth is to blame. One less muffin for Alma.

Me slapping my hands: "No! No! No! Damn me!"

Miss Black: "Macy. Girl." She waves Fiancé off to safety. "Hello? You come with a warning label but not instructions. Start me off on step one."

Me: "Step one. These is for Alma." I rip out a piece of paper from my dictionary and start to wrap up the muffins FOR ALMA.

"Macy. Hold up. Take this." Miss Black hands me a paper bag. I nod. Okay. One for me, two for Alma. That's fair, right? I hold my breaf so I don't smell the muffins. I stuff two into the bag and shove the bag into my sweatshirt pocket. Nothing Alma is going to eat should go into my backpack.

I write in my dictionary till seven forty. That's when Alma gets to school. She got to make breakfast for all her kids so she can't come earlier. I ask to go to the bafroom and grab the pass while Miss Black's third eye crisps the back of my neck. I have to find Alma before it is too late. Reptile Mind feels the muffins against my belly and wants them inside.

I make my way into the restroom for cover, then plan to head to Alma's homeroom. Muffins accomplished!!!!!

ANIMAL

Noun. Synonym: manimal.

I step into the restroom. A second later, I hear a dude's voice:

"We been talking for a week, baby. C'mon. Just a little kiss."

I peek through the crack of the stall door. I can barely see. Some dude is standing over a girl. I hear heads crack. Teeth scrape.

"Damn, girl. You got to do your lips like this."

Two heads press together again. Girl's hands are at her sides. Boy wraps his arms around her. I'm about to check out of their hotel, but stop when Boy lifts the girl up and I hear something that makes my little hairs stand up.

"What?" comes out all muffled from the girl, her face still pressed against his. "Wait! ST—"

I know what ST— means. And I know that voice.

I fling open the stall. Dude's all up on her. His eyes are closed and he's kissing up all over her neck. Her eyes are wide open. She tries to kick him in the nuts but he has her legs pinned good. "Yeah, baby," he says, pretending she's bucking because she's into him.

I shout: "This is your idea of a first date? A bafroom stall? That's nasty. Ain't you never heard of McDonald's?"

He opens his eyes. "What the fff—"

I step aside and Alma runs out of the stall. I step back into the doorway. I'm her rapist-proof vest.

Dude steps toward me. He is tall. On his pimply skin sprout his first scrubby hairs. But he's not taller than any of my mother's guests. I could take him.

"Who the fuck are you?"

I say: "Who the fuck am I? Who the fuck is you?"

Alma whispers behind me, "Maybe you better go." I can tell that she is crying.

Me: "You hear that? She says maybe your punk ass better go."

He steps back and does a once-over on me. "What are you supposed to be?"

"Her bodyguard. What is you supposed to be?"

The conversation is getting what Miss Black calls repetitive.

"Bitch, I don't know what you talking about but you better get the fuck out of here!" He pushes me. I crash into Alma and she flies against the sink.

I gain my ground and raise up my fists. "Bring it!"

From the outside we all hear, "What is going on in there?"

Dude's eyes Jiffy Pop out his stupit crunchy-haired head. I punch him in the jaw and kick him in the stomach. (Didn't I warn you that I'm a black belt in kick-ass? My dad taught me some skills.)

He falls backward into the stall and one hand goes into the toilet. "FUCK!!!"

I grab Alma. "Nothing, Teacher Lady!" I say as we run through the door past her. "Just some shit all over stall number three!" I drag Alma down the hall. "Better call Pepe!"

ALONE

Adjective. The predictable AF conclusion.

Alma and me head to Pepe's closet for a conference.

She closes the closet door and takes a deep breaf.

First I hug her. This is not the first time this shit has happened. Actually, it's how we met when we was twelve. The first time some dude tried to get up close and personal with her on the bus. He stuck his hand right up her skirt. I stuck my foot right up his ass.

Hug over. Now: "Really, Alma? What were you thinking even talking to that animal?"

Alma: "He wasn't like that a week ago."

Me: "They're all like that."

Alma: "Macy, they are *not* all like that."

Me: "They are around here."

Alma: "What are you saying, Macy? That it's my fault?"

Me: "It's his fault and his mother's fault for him being a animal. It's yours for not seeing it."

Alma: "My fault because I don't see the ugly in everybody like you?"

Me: "Look, Alma, I love that you see the good. But don't see it when it's not there. What would have happened if I wasn't in the restroom?"

Alma starts crying. Dabs her eyes with tissue.

Me: "I'm sorry. Sorry about this. Sorry about everything."

We hug again. She lets me go.

Me: "I got something for you. A gift."

Alma: "No, don't give it to me."

Me: "What? Why?"

Alma sighs. "You're my hero, Macy. But I don't want a hero. A hero swoops down. Saves the day. Then leaves. I want a friend. A best friend. A friend who comes to my birthday party. Because what matters to me matters to her. No matter what."

Me to myself picturing Velvet's stank head in my car window: *No matter what.*

Alma: "A best friend isn't only there when everything's wrong. She's there when everything's right. She makes it right just by being there. Macy, I gotta go."

She leaves me in Pepe's closet just like that. The fresh smell of her hair and skin is skunked out by Pine Sol and wet moldy mop heads. I'm alone with a pocket full of muffin crumbs.

ANSWER

Noun and verb. Example: "Ahnsuh me, bitch!"

How will I get Alma back? No matter how many lightbulbs I get, they blow out. I don't have the answer. But I have another pressing problem to think about for the time being: getting the car back home. I cut out during lunch break. Limbo past the principal's office window, slip out the front doors, duck-walk to the car in the lot, and slip in. I wait for a police car to pass, then power up the car. While it warms up, I look all around. Coast clear. I pull the car out of the parking lot and onto the road.

I park the car in my yard and slink out. I see the pipes outside my bafroom leaking, meaning someone is finally up using it and I got back just in time.

Three stray dogs decide that because I have the smell of muffin on me, I must be a muffin. This is good motivation to run very fast. They chase my ass all the way back to school just in time for the bell.

I spend the rest of the day not having answers for anybody about anything. Every place I am Alma isn't. Every time I start coming up with a lightbulb some teacher asks me some stupit shit and I forget what I was thinking. George is out sick so I can't run anything by him. If George honks his fake horn, that means my idea may invite too much police activity. If my idea is pretty good George hunkers down and accelerates. Damn it! I'm out of gas.

When I get home there's a after-school snack waiting for me and some hot cocoa. No, wait, that's just the commercial on the TV.

An hour after I get home my mother comes out the bedroom, connects her phone to the charger behind the couch, and looks up. "So, how was your day?"

"The teacher told me it amazes her someone so smart could act like I do."

"People used to tell me I'm smart. But that was when I was little. Before I went to school. School makes everybody stupit."

"Really, Ma?"

My mother sits on the couch and texts with one hand while flipping channels with the other. "Yeah," she says, "teachers never called on me when I knew the answer. They would wait until I didn't know nothing."

I stare out the window trying to think of a answer about Alma. A prostitute is in our driveway again. I check to see if it's Velvet. No. She's wearing some crazy Disney costume. Two dogs is doing the same thing the prostitute is doing with somebody's dad. I change the channel. In my mind, I make it snow.

The snow blankets everything, the gutted cars, the trash cans, the dogs, the prostitute and someone's dad. Snow car looks like a boat. Snow trash can looks like a buoy. Snow dogs look like fish nobody discovered yet. Snow ho and somebody's daddy look like a mermaid. One boat sails the wrong way down our one-way street. My favorite thing about snow is that it is silent.

Bam! I blink and turn around.

It's the TV. My mother is watching a movie. I aim my finger at the TV like a remote and turn back to the window.

But I can't get a signal. I can't bring back the snow. I can't bring back the silence. Too many noises I don't want to hear: from the dogs, from the man.

Someone's dad zips up and walks to his car. The prostitute is just a prostitute. The trash cans are just trash cans. The cars just cars. One dog is left. It's got to be the bitch.

I look at the bitch sniffing the wind. Looking right. Looking left. Wondering where the dog that did her was at. He probably said he'd be right back. He was just going to take a leak. Bitch looks at me.

"What you looking at?" she says. "Answer me when I'm talking to you! Hello!"

I blink and turn toward the bitch. Not the dog outside, the one on the couch.

"Did you hear me?" my mother barks. "I got a email from your school. There's some kind of family night. The drama department is putting on a play for free." She holds up her phone so I can see the flyer of all the girls in big-ass dresses. "Stupit," my mom says. "They should've told me a week ago. I don't got enough gas."

Gas? I think. *Yes. That could be a problem.*

"How do they expect us to get there now?" she says. "They should send a bus or something to pick us up."

When Yasmin says send a bus she means they should send a bus that has a stop right beside the couch. By "or something" I think she means a magic flying fucking carpet.

Come to think of it, I wouldn't mind having one of those.

When I grow up, I'm going to move to Canada. It snows there every day.

ANSWER 2

Noun. Sometimes there ain't just one.

I'm following my own footsteps like you do in the snow when you don't want anyone to find you. Except I'm not in the snow, I'm in the living room and my mother is stabbing her heel into the floor because she hates it when I pace.

"Stop it, Macy! You're wrecking the floor!"

"*I'm* wrecking the floor?" I point to the hole she is stabbing in the rug. "What are you wearing on your feet? Stilts?" Her heels are like a foot tall.

"Shut up, Macy."

"Since when do you care about the floor? That's like living in a dumpster and complaining about the smell. No offense."

"That's my point, Macy. Let's have a little class."

"Class? You could move a piano and a chandelier in here and—"

"Macy, I don't have time for this!"

She runs to her room to change her shoes. I guess circus

freak was not the fashion statement she was trying to make. I try to think about my problem and not my mother's. But I can't get a lightbulb. I feel like I do when the teacher blacks out the answer and I can just see it underneath the marker. I squint, I'm thinking so hard. Until . . .

DING!

I get a lightbulb and it has something to do with my mother's outfit.

I could break into the drama department and get a fancy dress to wear! I could sing Happy Birfday to Alma in the dress! Then Alma would reset and everything would be like it was before.

My mother comes out her bedroom. Her heels are shorter but so is her dress. "Aren't you cold?"

"I got me some ways to warm up."

"Ew."

"Dancing, Macy. Maybe a little nookie too." She clips on a ponytail. "It's natural."

"The nookie, not the ponytail, right?"

"Shut up, Macy. I'm gonna superglue one of these things to your shaved head in your sleep."

"I'm gonna superglue some clothes on you in your sleep."

Both of us at once: "SHUT UP."

"Just remember to drink water, okay? So you don't get hungover."

"Okay, Mom," my mother says.

"Hey," I say, scoping out her dress. My lightbulb grows super bright: maybe I can achieve my goal without breaking and entering and theft!!! "You got any dresses my size?"

"WHAAAT?"

"Don't get excited. I heard spandex makes a good slingshot."

44

My mother pulls out her spandex dress and snaps it against her booty before she flips me off.

I wait for her girlfriends to pull up before I take my lightbulb to her closet. I slingshot a purple dress at a mouse, but then I get to business. I find a maternity dress in there from when my mother was pregnant with Zane. I try it on.

I imagine Zane in my belly and what kind of mom I was to him when he was here, what kind of mom I would promise to be if he came back. He was a kicker, my mother said. By the time he got out of the womb he'd already earned a black belt. I had to know jiujitsu just to change his diapers.

I stuff a maternity outfit into my backpack. I even find a fake fur. Operation No Matter What is a go!

My mother and her guest get in around four. I hear the dude complaining that he can't get her dress off. Miss Black says this shit is known as irony. I take my traumatized self and their leftover Chinese food to the car. But I can't eat it because it's full of bamboo shoots and also cooties. I offer the lo mein to the dogs. Shove a fortune cookie in my mouth. Pull the fortune out, all wet and half-chewed up.

It says, *You will go far if—*

Fucking figures. I put my backpack with the maternity dress in it behind my head, put the fur over me, and try to sleep for a while.

I must've slept, because the sky is lighter. I hot-wire the car and let it warm up. I'll sit up straight this time. I mean, what difference does it make? Around here fifteen-year-olds got kids. I'm gonna stand out just because I'm driving a car and not a stroller?

I pull the car into the street. A minute later, near the Church's Chicken, I see Velvet. In my sweatshirt. I HEART that sweatshirt. It was my dad's. (All of mine were.) It still has a barbecue stain on it. (All of them do.) I pull over.

"Yo, Velvet. If you're around here at noon I'll trade you this fur for that sweatshirt."

"Oh my gosh, *really*?!!"

"Jesus says to clothe the necked. Peace."

I prepare for my entrance to school. It's hard to squeeze on heels in sweat socks. And even though the dress is a maternity outfit, my hoodie is making it all bunchy. I smooth myself out.

Pepe bows as he opens the door. I bow and he starts to tell me something about a cutesy? but then the principal and assistant principal are homing in on me.

Principal, looking me up and down: "Good morning, Macy. That's quite an ensemble."

Me: "Yeah. Uh. Much assembly was required."

AP: "Is this" (whisper voice) "in the dress code?"

Me: "Dress code got the word *dress* in it, don't it?"

AP: "Macy, how are you going to do PE?"

Me: "I got art today!"

AP: "You have an answer for everything, huh, young lady?"

Me: "Today, yes!"

They let me pass. That's a good choice on their part because I brought a slingshot thong as a weapon and I'm not afraid to use it.

Some dude says to his friend: "Hey, it's the next top model." I knew the slingshot thong would come in handy.

Dude: "My eye! My eye!" He bangs into his friend and accidentally pokes *him* in the eye.

Gandee said a eye for a eye would make the whole world blind, motherfoes. Maybe Gandee did not mean to apply his words to the current situation, but I think it works.

I'm about to make a epic exit from the hall when I stumble on my damn shoe. The shoe catches on my jean hem. Just as I'm about to eat linoleum, I float.

I HEART George.

"Why are you dressed?" he asks.

"I'm going to get Alma back in history class," I say.

He don't ask any more questions. He knows me.

He puts me down and holds my arm like we are about to square dance. Strike that. We do square dance because George thinks that shit is funny. If I don't let him, he'll cry. Now imagine what this shit looks like to the kids watching. But everybody knows that dying laughing will take on a new meaning if I think they are laughing at George. Or if George thinks they are laughing at me.

See, George is six foot six. He could have been a basketball player, except he kept lifting the girls up so they could reach the net better. He could've been a football player, but he kept asking the dudes he tackled if they was okay.

George wheezes and stops square dancing. He pulls out his inhaler and sucks on it.

"You okay? Need to go to the nurse?"

He shakes his head so hard his whole coat shakes. After stuffing his inhaler into his pocket he makes like he's jumping onto his motorcycle and motions for me to jump on the back.

"Okay, Jorge." I climb on. Nothing happens. "George?"

"Hello?" He taps on his helmet.

"Oh. Okay." I put on my imaginary helmet and he rides us to class. We park outside history and walk inside. I freeze and George knows something is wrong. It's staring us both in the face. And no, it's not all the kids pretending they are taking selfies when they are taking my photo instead.

It's the writing on the wall. *Tomorrow's Leaders Field Trip today.*

Alma isn't even in school today. She's at a fancy supermarket thirty minutes and a million miles away, learning about rational decision-making.

George starts to cry.

Teacher Man: "Julio, escort George to the nurse, please."

The tears lower George's blood sugar.

Julio: "Yes. I'll take him to his" (*dealer,* he whispers before coughing and ending with) "nurse."

I bunch up my dress and stare at the words on the right: *Tomorrow's Leaders Field Trip today,* and then the words on the left: *Emancipation Proclamation.*

I emancipate my stupit sweaty self from the dress and heels.

DING! I have maybe the best lightbulb I have lit all week. I will tell the teacher in study hall that I have to poo. I will then proceed my ass to the nearest exit, stuff myself back into the dress and find Velvet. After getting some directions, I will drive myself to the supermarket where Alma is making rational decisions. Alma and I will make up for the field trip we never had!

Operation No Matter What continues, bitches . . .

BARGAIN

Noun. Selling your soul to El Diablo.

"Directions in exchange for a fur coat?" Velvet shouts back at me, lighting up a Newport. She looks both ways like a little kid crossing the street.

On the far corner, some dude in a ninja hooded T-shirt is eyeballing her. "Everything cool? Is that your pimp?" I say as she gets near.

She leans in the car window. "Yeah, he's working me today. No worries, I got it covered. Made an extra twenty last night he don't know nothing about."

Ew.

"So, Macy. I gotta know. Not that it ain't worth it, but what's going on?"

"Remember the fight I had with my BFF? Well, Mission Not Accomplished—yet. We got a deal or what?"

"I'll tell you what. For a free fur coat, I'll take you there myself."

She struts her skanky self to the passenger side and opens the door. Dude in the ninja hood has his hand up shading the sun from his eyes, and he's eyeballing us hard. I let her in, though. The clock is ticking. I can't mess this up.

Velvet looks at me and smiles. If her teeth weren't all fucked up she'd be real pretty. "Maybe you could pull up your hoodie?"

"I get it," I say. "I'm a john. Ew." I do it.

"Just make a left turn at the light like we're going to the motel. Then I'll get you to the supermarket."

I drive down the street and turn left on red. Shit! A bus is barreling toward me. I swerve out the way.

"Honey, right on red! Not left! Pull over!"

I pull over. Which is too bad for the seven squirrels that didn't see me coming. I hang my head against the steering wheel and exhale. Velvet puts her hand against her chest like she's having a heart attack.

"Macy," she says, gasping. "Maybe I could drive?"

"No! It's all good. I get it. Right on red."

"C'mon. What if someone is on the lookout for you? Plus, if you let me, I'll pay for gas." She points to the gauge. She's a observant little skank. I guess in her line of work you have to notice every little thing.

We switch places. She drives funny. Like she turns on this clicker whenever she wants to turn. "Is that what that's for?"

"The turn signal? Yes, honey. Now, how long's your mission gonna take?"

"Alma's there for a field trip. They gotta be back after lunch. I got maybe thirty minutes?"

"How about I get gas and meet you back in front in—"

"Yeah, NO. Get the gas first."

"Wow. You're not shy."

"Nope."

She turns around and pulls up to the gas station.

"So were you gonna steal my mother's car?"

Long pause. "No. But I would have thought about it. That's all. Just a thought."

I like how she was straight with me. She shows me how to do the gas. I like that too.

A couple minutes later Velvet pulls up to the supermarket. I now know what Dorothy felt like when she saw the Emerald City.

I take it all in. "A'ight," I say. "Changed my mind. You wait for me. Keep warm."

"I thought you didn't trust me?"

"I don't." I grab the fur.

"Good luck with Alma," I hear her say. Velvet remembered Alma's name. Damn. For a minute, I feel bad about grabbing the fur. I enter the supermarket through the giant sliding-glass doors. SHINY.

I walk to a section called Produce.

"Macy! What are you doing here?" Alma runs up to me, looking me over from my fur to my sweat-sock-stuffed stilettos. She grabs my hand and holds it like a infant's. The minute she touches me I realize every hour, minute, and second that she hasn't touched me. That no one has. Not like that. I let her pull me along. Because of her softness, because of her warmth, and because if she lets go I'm gonna stuff half the supermarket in my sweatshirt.

Apples. Pears. Something labeled honeydew. Bananas. And—shit, I don't know what that is. But whatever it is, I have to eat it. "Alma! There's FREE samples!"

Alma: "Yes, they're free. But you're only supposed to take one. Breathe, Macy."

In through my nose . . . I suck in the smells of the apple bins. Not cafeteria apples. Apples like you read about in storybooks that is baked into pies and shit. And then I see the signs. Fuji and Golden Delicious and Gala and Granny Smith and Honeycrisp. There are many many kinds all with their special names. I pull away from Alma. Reptile Mind takes over. Alma grabs my sleeve. She knows what is going to happen.

Alma: "NOOOOOOOO!"

Me: "I have to!!!!!!"

I lift a sample lid and gobble up the entire plate, spitting out toothpicks as I go. When I'm done I move on to the bins. I bite a Fuji. I bite a Golden Delicious.

Somewhere in the background someone is yelling: "Suh-cure-ity! *Suh-cure-ity!*"

Someone else is saying, "Macy? What is she doing here?" Someone else: "The school will pay for that. And that. And— Alma! Make her stop!!"

I bite a Granny Smith.

Someone is saying, "Get down from there!" I bite a Red Delicious.

Somewhere someone ties my hoodie sleeves behind my back and pulls. Avalanche!

Field trip is *OVER!!!*

I blink. Cigarettes and gasoline choke me. Damn! We are standing in the parking lot.

Tomorrow's Leaders Today's top banana: "Alma. How did she get here?"

Alma: "I don't know! I had nothing to do with it. But we can't leave her here."

Speaking of my ride, I look around. Just as I'm vowing to hunt her down and kill her slowly, I see her crazy ass waving from the back of the parking lot all incognito and shit.

The school bus pulls up. *Screech!* A store person pushes a cart over to the bus. It is filled with separate bags for each of the students. Alma hoists her powdered milk and vegetables and stuff onto the bus with all the other kids.

She comes back out the bus, pulls me toward the door. I try her patience. I look at Velvet and think about my mom's car. Alma snaps her gum and shakes her head, squinting, trying to see what I'm seeing across the parking lot. Velvet ducks into the car and I let Alma yank me up the steps onto the bus.

Alma: "Remember that day in the cafeteria? This was not the field trip that I intended."

Me, wiping juice from my lips: "But you were right, Alma! You were right!"

Alma and I are sitting in the back of the bus. I get a feeling and turn and see that Velvet is trailing us. I vow to stop calling her a skank in my head. I will drop the fur by the door of the school on my way inside. It is now Velvet's. She deserves it.

BECAUSE

Conjunction. A word that connects things.
As in, "Why you do me like that?" "Because." Nuf said.

Alma goes to the main room of the library for study hall and I go to the back room for In-School Suspension. They don't even bother to call my mother anymore because she changes her number every other week. Actually she changes her boyfriend every other week, because that's how she has phones in the first place. That's also how I have a phone. (See F for Fine Print.)

ISS is in a room at the back of the library, and I can see Alma through the window. It's like that Tantalus thing again. I have a lightbulb. I know she feels me like I feel her. But she don't want to admit it yet. I got a secret weapon, though. The problem is Mr. ISS Teacher, who won't let me leave my seat. I decide he needs some convincing.

Me: (Making the sound of a ticking clock.)

Mr. ISS: "Can you stop that?"

Me: (Pulling out my eyebrow hairs.)

Mr. ISS: "Can you stop that?"

Me: (Pulling out my eyelashes.)

Mr. ISS: "Can you? Uh, that is disg—!"

Me: "You like that? I can do it all day." LONG PAUSE. "But I don't have to."

Mr. ISS: "What do you want? Gum?"

Me: "Ha. No. Yes. And also, just to go see her." I point through the window at Alma reading cookbooks. Cookbooks of food that she is never going to cook or eat.

Mr. ISS: "I can't do that. I can't have any trouble."

Me: "Nah. No trouble. I just want to give her this." I show him.

Mr. ISS: "That's it? Uh. Okay. You got five minutes."

SCORE.

I make a field trip to Alma's table and sit across from her. Alma don't look up from her book. I do a big sigh and set the apple in front of her.

My eyes say: *I only have this one left. A bonafide Honeycrisp. But I was saving it. Not for my dinner. For you.*

Alma looks over the top of her book. Her mouth don't say nothing. But her eyes say: *For real?*

My eyes say: *I didn't even take one bite. Not even a lick.*

The librarian says: "Shhhh."

Alma and I look at each other like WTF and laugh.

Alma puts her book down. She laughed so she knows I win. "Hey," she says, "today's your birthday." She takes a bite of the Honeycrisp. My stomach growls.

"I guess so." But I don't want to talk about that so I pull out my dictionary. "Check this out. I made it while you wasn't talking to me."

She flips the pages and wrinkles her perfect nose. Even her damn nostrils are pretty.

"Silly," she says. "*Always* comes after *Afraid*."

I don't drop-kick her because she's Alma. (See B for Bestie.)

"I remember when you used to think LMNOP was one letter!" She smothers a laugh. "And it started with an E!"

I don't split her lip because she's Alma. I do slam the book shut but Alma sticks her hand in the way.

"Wait," she says. She turns pages and reads me for what feels like a century. "I changed my mind. We can pretend you did the mistakes on purpose. Whatever's confusing we'll just call poetry. Symbolism. Famous writers do it all the time."

Famous writers? Alma always makes the stupit things I do seem smart. A writer? I can't even imagine myself typing in the price of a Big Mac at McDonald's. I can't even imagine tomorrow. Tomorrow is for people like Alma. I'm still somewhere between today and yesterday.

The librarian says, "No eating in the library!"

Alma passes me back the apple. "I'm regifting," she says.

"Why?"

"Just because. Now, you heard the librarian. Go! Call me tonight. Oh. And FYI: I still detest you."

I grab the apple and run away before I drool in front of her. I love you, Alma!

BESTIE

My *noun*, my verb, my adjective. Best-ee rhymes with free! Synonym: Nobody Hates Alma.

Alma don't take nothing for free. When the teacher handed out school supplies at the beginning of the year and all the kids were stuffing their pockets, their backpacks, their assholes, she wouldn't take them.

"What are you crazy?" I say.

She ignores me and says to the teacher, "What can I do to pay for them? Can I clean your boards?" When she says it, she don't whisper. Everybody hears.

After Alma ignored me like that, I didn't get mad, because—

Okay, I got mad. But I'm always mad so Alma don't really notice. Mostly what I get is jealous. Because I can never be like that.

So why don't I hate Alma? Why don't everybody hate Alma? Back to the school supplies and the flashback.

Some new girl wearing two different shoes stands up. Against her chest she holds free binders, free notebooks. Free pencils stick out of her pockets. Free egg burrito breakfast sticks to the corner of her mouth. "So what," she says to Alma, still chewing. "You think you better than us?"

Alma knows not to sweat it. She knows I have her back. But I always let her speak up for herself first. She's my bestie, not my bitch.

Alma says, "What I do has nothing to do with what you do. I don't know your life. You do what you need to do. I do what I need to do." She looks down at the girl's pants.

New girl throws down her books and all the free shit she's holding. I stand up. The class scoots back their desks to make a ring like Madison Square Garden. Teacher buzzes the office. Ding ding ding. Fight over before it begins.

Alma: "You sew that yourself?"

New Girl with Two Different Shoes: "Whatchu say? Did I what?" She's breathing hard like they really just threw down.

Alma, all calm, cool, and collected, points and says, "Your pants. I know they didn't come like that. How did you do that? I could never do that. Did you do it yourself?"

New Girl with Two Different Shoes takes a step back. Opens her mouth, closes it. Repeat. Finally says, "Uh. Yeah."

Alma says, "Could you do that for me? I have pants that are nice but not in style anymore. Do you think you could do that to them? Not for free, of course."

New Girl with Two Different Shoes gains her bearing: "Uh. Of course not. Nothing's for free."

Alma: "Right. Maybe I could help with your—" Alma looks at the girl's books spread over the floor.

New Girl with Two Different Shoes: "Uh. Maf?"

I sit, put my head down on my crossed arms so no one can see my face, and smile. Nobody's allowed to see my smile. Nobody but Alma.

Alma says, "Deal."

Then Alma does something funny. She walks right up to New Girl with Two Different Shoes, the girl who stands two heads above her and is ten times as wide, and does that thing that only Alma can do. She wiggles her finger and gets New Girl with Two Different Shoes to bend down. Alma whispers in her ear.

Nobody, including me, knows what was said. Alma wouldn't tell me. Which didn't make me mad.

Okay, it made me mad. (But mostly it made me jealous.) All I do know is a week later, just when everybody forgot about the whole thing, Girl with Two Different Shoes is wearing a matching pair of Mary Janes and Alma is wearing the cutest pants. Even Alma forgets about it. But I don't.

Not when I see Girl with Two Different Shoes getting slipped a bag of clothes from one teacher and then another. Not when I see her holding a brochure with a sewing machine on it from the vocational school. Not next quarter when I see that Girl with Two Different Shoes all sudden don't need no free school supplies no more.

BLOW

Noun and verb. Rhymes with know, like in
"You don't know my life."

Alma sings Happy Birfday to me on the phone. Alma not speaking to me was hell, but all that matters is that she is speaking to me now. I want to ask her to hang up and sing on my voicemail so I can keep her voice.

(Wait, what?—you think I'm corny? Just because you a lonely-ass motherfoe with 500 Fakebook friends and not a single real one ain't my problem. See D for Dear Reader and shut your face.)

"*Happy* fifteenth birthday," Alma says. "I would have called you no matter what, you know. I wish I'd gotten you more than a regifted apple!"

"I know you would have," I say. I think, *This apple is the best present I've ever gotten*, but I don't say it because I'm too busy crunchin on it.

"So did you get a phone for your birthday? That's what you asked for, right?"

"No. This is another one I jacked from one of my mother's guests. I—"

"Wait a minute," Alma says. "Willy is in the dishwasher again!"

Alma puts her phone down hard. Alma is always throwing her phone down to pull kids out of the dishwasher. (Her mother uses the dishwasher to keep the bread and chips fresh so the cockroaches don't get them.)

"I'm back. I—wait! Now Willy's at the—STOP! *Mijo!!!* No, *no* outlet!!! Outlet NO NO!!"

The kids over Alma's house have been electrocuted so many times they all have hair like Sideshow Bob. I think about my convo with my mother as Alma wrestles a kid off the kitchen table: "Ba aba baba!!!" One of Alma's babies accidentally hangs up on me.

I wait: 5, 4, 3, 2—Ring.

"Sorry," Alma says, out of breaf. "So what are you going to do tonight, Macy? You have to do something special on your birthday."

"I am. I'm talking to you." I curl up on the couch with the phone. "Tell me about *your* birfday. Was it the best you ever had?"

"It wasn't because you weren't there."

"Oh, yeah, you're so over it. Jesus, STOP . . . Was your dad there, Alma?"

"I think he was. The DJ. I swear he had the same nose as me."

"Shit. I would have been able to tell. I know exactly the way your nose is—"

"I know, girl! That's why I will never forgive you!"

"Let's change the subject . . . Tell me about your best birthday when you were a kid."

Alma does. It was her fifth, when she danced standing on her daddy's shoes. She saw a picture of it.

"So," I say, digging in the couch cushions for crumbs, "your best birfday is the birfday you can't actually remember?"

"Sometimes it's better that way. So I can fill in the blanks the way I want to. A picture keeps the best parts of a memory and leaves the rest out. What's yours?"

"I don't have a best—or worst. For me those two things is always mixed together. I only have the one I remember the most. It was my twelfth. Before I met you. I had the whole thing planned out. My mother said, *Seriously, a piñata, Macy? I thought last year was your last kiddie party. Don't you want to have a dance party? We can get Dance Dance Dance on the Wii. You can have a girls-guys party.* Well, I did not want to have a dance party. The school dance was enough. Guys rubbing up their sweaty junk all over you. Why, just cause Pit Bull is playing, is that all right? So anyway I said, *No, I want a fucking piñata.* My mother always chose the biggest piñata in the warehouse at Party Town. You know the place, Alma?"

"Yes," Alma says, adjusting the phone with her neck so she can change a diaper. "It's right near Lucky's Lotto behind the pregnancy testing center."

"Right! She and Daddy always strapped the piñata to the hood of the car. The neighbors clapped as we pulled into our house. They were all invited—except for 3211, of course."

Alma and I both say: "3211. They is ghetto." We laugh.

It gets quiet.

"Don't stop, Macy."

I don't. I can't. I tell Alma about the bags and bags of candies that filled up the trunk. Cherry bubblegum pops, wax candy tubes that turn your teeth blue, taffy that once stuck Zane's teeth together. My mom had to pry his teeth apart with a butter knife! Stay away from the Choco Tacos—they give everyone the runs—but there was fruit punch sugar straws that you could use to suck up your caramel soda, and don't forget the Cry Babies! Anytime I got hungry later, I'd just pick up a couch cushion. From one birfday all the way to the next, I could still find a chili-pepper chocolate buried in the seat.

And that's just what went into the piñata. Never mind the three-layer chocolate crunch cake. After it's gone, you're digging in the back of the freezer like a dog just to get a taste of one more chocolate crunchie.

"I had tiramisu this year," Alma says. "So much of it, we'll be eating it until next Christmas. And yes, I saved you a piece."

"I don't know what the hell that is, but I know I want to eat some. I love you, Alma!"

"You lie," Alma says. "Now get back to the story."

"Right. I was just telling you about the cake. As good as the cake was, it was cardboard compared to the barbecue. Daddy was the master chef."

Everybody always said he should have his own cooking show. His show would go against Hell's Kitchen sort of like Batman vs. Superman. Daddy would drop his brisket on the table like a bomb, and nobody talked until nothing was left. Cops came by in a cruiser once because it was too quiet on the block. Everybody was too busy chowing down to talk.

"Yes," Alma said, and sighed. That sigh was her trying to think back to a time when she could remember her own dad. Trying to remember a smell or a touch. A dad is maybe the only thing I have that Alma don't. The only thing she envies me for. Even though he's in prison, he's still mine. She isn't ugly about it, though. (See B for Bestie.)

"But back it up," I said. "We ain't even covered the outfit or the getting my hair done. No hand-me-downs or flea market buys or Goodwill. My mother used to take the bus and come back with the type of outfit *you'd* wear, Alma. A sweater, matching skirt, tights, new shoes, panties in a three pack, perfume samples in little foil packets. We had to *represent*. Obviously 3211 was not invited, but my mother sent me to JJs for some gum, just so they could see me and Zane walk past—him in his Mac Daddy herringbone hat and me in my patent leather shoes."

"Seriously? Zane in a fedora and you in a dress?" Alma says. "Do you have any pictures?"

"Nah, I destroyed the evidence. Anyway, my outfit was perfect that day. I mean, there was even a panty-bra set. Matching, you know? By the way, I wore panties back then, not boxers."

"Wow. When did you get your first bra? I got mine at eight."

"I got mine at eight too. These DDs were ready for combat by nine!"

"And one day you'll tell me why the big transformation to sweatpants and sneakers last year?"

"Can't tell you." *Because I can't tell myself.* (See I for I Don't Want to Talk About It and P for Pink.) "Just happened."

Anyway, so back then on my birfday I was like a Barbie with all the accessories included. No stuck zippers, no stains. I wore a towel over my dress at breakfast so I wouldn't spill eggs on it. My mother planted me on a folding chair and told me not to move a muscle. Once all the guests got here and the adults got caught up, we was going to take pictures. Then everybody showed up all decked out. Every kid that sat down next to me got a warning: *NO grass stains on tights, NO dress sleeves as napkins*, getting yelled at like they already had. Of-fucking-course, the parents turned what was supposed to be hello-qué-pasa into a century-long convo.

"Forget this," I said, pulling a thread out my sweater. "Rip that Band-Aid off, that's what." I let Zane pull a thread into a sleeve hole. My neighbor Rochelle shimmied off her slip. Headbands became boomerangs.

Macy! my mother screeched, but she couldn't beat my ass because the neighbors was watching and somebody would say something to somebody else—namely 3211—and they would call CPS. Ha!

Now I was free. I could eat barbecue with my bare hands. But the second I took my first bite, my mother was screaming at me to help her on the grill. I looked up to ask her where Daddy was, but her eyes told me I better not ask. I just pretended I was Daddy and got it done with a smile. I even cracked his jokes. I thought about how proud he would be when he got back from wherever he was at and saw that everybody got a hot plate. When he didn't show up after everybody was served, I found myself staring at my plate not able to eat a bite.

It was time for the cake. My mother brought it out crying all over the candles. *Cut it out, Mami—you're gonna jinx my wish.* To protect my wish, I picked up my whole cake and ran. I heard my mother cursing at me as I headed into the bafroom and locked me and the cake and my wish in it. *I WANT MY DADDY!!!* I screamed over the candles. *NOW!!!* But I didn't blow. Even at that moment, knew better.

Three hours later my mother pounded on the door with something hard. I cracked it open and she shoved the phone through the crack. It was Daddy singing me Happy Birfday. He told me he'd see me on parole. He said the blow the cop found on him wasn't even his. I said, *I don't care, just tell me when you're coming home.*

"Oh Macy," Alma breathes when I get done telling her all this. That's all she says, and that's all I want her to say.

"You know what I wished, sitting there on my toilet with a big-ass melting ice-cream cookie cake?"

Alma is laughing and crying. "No. But I know what you didn't wish for. For your daddy."

"Yes. That's right. That would a been stupit. I wished for that barbecue on my plate. The barbecue Daddy always set aside for me special. The best parts—with the juicy fat."

That night, I crept out to the grill on the front porch. Crispy sausage steam still stuck to the air. A piece of sausage had fell into the coals. I pulled it out, wiped it off, and swallowed it whole. My mother had left the bottles of barbecue outside. One lick of the barbecue sauce became two and so on. After I polished off the bottle, I snuck back inside.

Next I took a little taste of the oil from the pan sitting on the counter. Found some hamburger buns to dip in that oil. I just kept thinking, *By tomorrow, all that will be left is the smell.* So I ate and I ate. My mother woke up to the sound of me throwing up. I couldn't even look at barbecue for months.

Alma: "Macy, this year I want you to make a wish. A wish for you. M—"

Me: "Did you get what you wanted this year, Alma?"

Alma: "Okay. So we're changing the subject. God, Macy! . . . I wished to go away. Yes, I know it sounds spoiled—I know . . ."

Me: "If you know me and I know you then you know you don't need to explain."

Alma: "I wanted to go away. Just anywhere. To my cousins in Cali. My aunt in Washington. Anywhere. My mother told me we couldn't afford to go away with all the kids. When I told her I meant just me, she freaked out."

Me: "Just you, huh."

Alma: "Macy, I—"

Me: "No, I get it. No offense taken. I'm sorry you didn't get what you wanted."

Alma, in her soft voice: "I'm sorry you didn't get your wish either."

Me: "Actually I did. I just didn't know my wish until I knew yours."

Alma: "What? I demand you tell me."

Me: "I would, but if I told you . . ."

"Macyyyyyyyyyyyyyy!"

"If I told you, it would jinx it. But I can tell you something. For the first time, my birfday don't blow."

"Really?" I hear Alma yawn. "Then that's good enough for me."

We hang up. I grab a lighter and I burn the whole house down to a little pile of ashes.

Just kidding. Because, Dear Reader, if I was burning down anyone's house it would be yours, you nosy-ass motherfoe.

What I really do is I pull up a floorboard.

This is where my dad used to hide his drugs from Yasmin. With the glow of the lighter's flame I make sure the space is still secure. There's still a bag of powder under there so I know my mother don't know about the hiding place. I tape the hundred-dollar bill my mother threw at me to the bottom of the board. I hide it there for Alma—for her escape. It is her birfday gift. I won't give it to her right now. It will be a gift I give her when she needs it the most. When she needs to get away. I relight the lighter and sing:

Happy birfday to me . . .

Even though it's just a lighter, I can't help but press my lips together and . . .

BOOK CLUB

Noun. As in, "You can find me in da (book) club."

George and I wait in the hall for Alma. A few times a semester, regular and AP English classes combine for what Miss Black calls a meeting of the minds. This means Miss Link's AP kids peer tutor our stupit asses. The class is split in half today. I always stay with Miss Black's half because Miss Link can't handle my difficult ass.

George catches a glimpse of Alma before I do and vrooms toward her. Alma knows to stand perfectly still. I run ahead and get the door. George picks up Alma's stack of library books and her little ass. He squeezes his throttle and bursts into Miss Black's class.

Miss Black: "Jesus, let me have my coffee first!"

We sit. I fucking hate sitting. "When I'm older," I tell Alma and George, "I'm going to have a apartment kitchen with tables but no chairs, a living room with NO couch."

Alma: "They make desks like that. Where you actually

get to stand. Maybe you could talk to the principal about getting one."

Me: "Talk. Principal. Did you use those two words in the same sentence?"

Alma: "Yes. Talk. Speaking of which, I got onto the debate team."

Me: "Debates. Like the ones for president? So you get to tear people up and hang them out to dry?" I imagine winning debate after debate. My attendance trophy sitting in the shadow of my big-ass debate trophy. "Do they serve muffins?"

Alma laughing: "No, no, no, no. It's very polite. You get assigned a topic and you have to prove why you're right."

Miss Black: "Blah blah blah blah something about foreshadowing."

Me: "Assigned. That sounds like homework. I'ma pass. But I gotta topic of discussion for you. My mother said school makes everyone stupit. Is school making me stupit or am I stupit to begin with?"

Alma: "You are not stupi*D*."

Miss Black: "Blah blah blah blah blah something about irony."

Me, getting passed a book: "If I ain't stupit, then I shouldn't have to read *To Kill a Mockingbird*. Want me to summarize that shit for you? If you brown or black, you going to jail. The end." I toss the book behind me. Me getting passed another book: "And I shouldn't have to read *The Diary of Anne Frank* either. I mean, I get it! White people had fucked-up shit happen to them too. Never fucking forget! PS, black and brown people, get over that shit, you lazy-ass motherfoes." Me getting passed another book: "I do not wanteth to readeth *Romeo and Juliet* becauseth none of the wordeths make no senseth." I pass the book on.

I dance in my chair. "This book club is not da club I pictured," I say.

Alma laughs behind her fist. Like her laugh needs protecting.

"Da Club, Da Club," George sings, shaking his sumo wrestler's body. His Ninja Turtle helmet slides over his eyes. (See H for Helmet.) In his Chewbacca coat, George looks like a bear in heat.

Everyone is cracking up.

I laugh on the inside because I don't like doing what everyone else is doing. I do not want to laugh when you laugh. If I cough, why do you need to cough, motherfoe? If I yawn . . . you get the picture.

Now George is huffing and puffing. Miss Black holds up a pass without even looking up from her work.

The class takes too long to stop laughing. I pound my desk: "ALL RIGHT THEN!"

Miss Black says, "Thank you," and continues whatever she was saying that I ain't been listening to. But she must have other bones to pick because today she ain't bothering with me. As for Alma, she's so smart she always has her homework done a week ahead of time. But nobody hates Alma. (Again, see B for Bestie.)

"Is there anything you would read?" Alma asks. What she means is: Have you ever read *anything*?

I think real hard. Even with Alma I don't want to say the last thing I can remember reading cover to cover is *Runaway Bunny*. That was my brother's favorite. (See B for Burners and G for Gas.)

Finally, I say, "When I was little I really liked to read the backs of cereal boxes. I read the whole thing top to bottom. My favorite words were *fresh* and *goodness* and *sweet*. I would read those words over and over again. Now I prefer the directions on the Kraft Macaroni box. *First. Then. Next.* I like steps. I read the recipe for the Taco Bake over and over. I like the words *golden brown.* I guess you could say I haven't *progressed* much."

"My grandma read to me all the time," Alma says in her soft voice that she uses when she's afraid she might insult me. "Books from the library. When I went to kindergarten, I already knew all my letters and numbers."

Miss Black: "Shut the hell up!" (Okay, that's not what she said. It's what she meant, though.)

"So, is my mom right?" I whisper to Alma. "Does school make everyone stupit? I started off liking reading but now I hate it. Did school make me stupit or was I stupit to begin with? It's like the chicken and the egg, right? The chicken and the egg. Mmmmm."

I love to eat chicken but not the Church's Chicken kind. The kind in the cartoons that have this smell that wakes a guy up so he floats toward the oven in his sleep. I always asked Yasmin, *Could we make this?* She'd say, *With what? How we going to get a chicken?*

Alma: "Blah blah blah blah! So? Macy?"

Me: "Uh, what was the question?"

She sighs. I try her patience.

BLESSING

Noun. Bless rhymes with a big-ass mess. And Alma already told me B for Blow don't go before B for Blessing, so I don't need you to tell me. Who is you anyway? You don't know my life. This dictionary defines my ass, not yours.

Science teacher taught us about genetics today. Kids in our class talked about how their whole family had blue eyes or how their mom's side had the cancer.

Our whole family has been to prison. Even me. Don't know if it's something in our genes or not.

I was there because I was born there. My mother told me when I was in her belly, she could see my hand under her skin. She said the women in the prison would lay their hands on her belly. Press their hand to mine. I've seen it in my dreams. But am I dreaming of what my mother told me or what really happened? How far back can a person have a memory?

I want to ask someone: When those women in prison touched my mother's belly was I blessed or was I cursed?

I look at my mother and her guest on the couch. They start singing the song "Bend Over." Guest cracks a joke about my father bending over in prison. My mother titty-twists him. He atomic wedgies her, yanking her thong a foot in the air. I think more about genetics and I feel queasy.

Because this shit is the reason why people like me end up talking to abandoned buildings. I focus on a easier question: When is the CPS bitch getting here?

You remember CPS, Dear Reader? (See A for All About You.) Every time a car pulls up outside our place my chest gets tight. Is it Daddy with flowers or a shotgun? Is it CPS with Zane AND a court order to take me to foster care? My mother told me foster care might as well be prison.

Another caseworker is supposed to pick Zane up from his secret location and bring him to my house. We're all going through the Mickey D's drive-thru. Then we're all going to prison to see Daddy. I know. You're so jealous. Hater.

Yasmin: "Wait outside, Macy. I don't want the CPS bitch in my house. She got no right."

I step outside for air. There isn't none. Only the stank of dumpster and grease.

Oh shit!! I can see Zane from a mile away! I jump up and down like I'm six, got a dollar and see the ice-cream truck. My brother's shaggy head hangs outside the window like a dog's. ZANE!!!

"Woof! Woof!" Zane barks as he and the CPS worker pull up in a silver Prius.

I stick my head in the window and the stank of old French fries hits me. Probably from all the other kids CPS kidnapped.

Miss CPS flashes her badge and tries to tell me her name. I cut her off: "Got any gum?"

Zane: "Woof! Woof!"

Miss CPS: "Young lady, no need to be rude. It's—"

Me to Zane: "Good boy!" I rub his ears. He starts licking

up on my face. "Nasty!!!" I push him off by the face, but we're both laughing.

As I climb into the backseat I see Miss CPS's's's (I HATE apostrofees with the letter S) frowny face in the front mirror. Zane and I chow down. We're rolling past 3211 now. The whole family stands all up in our business folding their arms, nodding their heads, and no doubt clicking their tongues. Zane flips a paw. I flip a finger and throw a chicken McNugget.

Miss CPS: "Hey, Macy, you stop that!"

I do stop. But not because of Miss CPS. Because, I realize, I wasted a perfectly good McNugget. And because 3211 can't see us anymore and every gang member looking for a reason to start shit can.

Zane, how-fucking-ever, don't have a STOP button. He keeps flipping his paw in the back window.

"Bad dog!" I say.

"Arf! Arf!" Zane whimpers. "Wooooooo!"

"Don't be sad." I open up the window. He sticks his head out, happy.

Miss CPS: "Do you think you ought to encourage his behavior?"

Me: "I think somebody ought to encourage *something* about him."

That shuts her face up.

I stare out the window, taking in every store, every restaurant, so I can find the exact place where normal ends and prison begins. I'm feeling too many fucking feelings. I kick Miss CPS's seat. She says *stop*. That makes me mad. Being mad is what I need.

"Why does everything good go fast and everything that sucks go so slow?" I ask. "Is the prison at the ends of the earth?"

Miss CPS offers me gum to shut me the hell up. She has opened the gum floodgate. I must have it all. Then, lucky for her, Miss CPS's GPS says, *You have arrived at your destination.*

In the distance I see the words: Something Correctional Facility. I never heard of no one coming out the cooler being correcter than they used to be.

We pull up by my mother's car in the parking lot. Her latest guest is driving and she's in the passenger seat. Miss CPS hops out to meet them, but Zane stays put. It's been weeks since he's seen my mother. Ever since the court order, she's not supposed to have unsupervised contact with him. My mother says that means if he's in the hospital bleeding to death because his foster parents beat him down, she can't so much as stick her head in the room if CPS ain't there. His own mother.

She has gotten out of her car and taps on the Prius's's window hard like she's trying to get a dead fish to move. I open Zane's door. He lunges out and tries to bite her.

I grab him by the collar.

Miss CPS writes a note on her pad.

"What the fuck, Zane?" my mother says, raising her hand to hit Zane on the head. I jump up and give my mother a high-five.

Didn't fool Miss CPS. She takes another note.

My mother is about to say something to Miss CPS before Mr. Guest sticks a cigarette in her mouth, smacks her ass, and walks her to the side of our car by her ass cheek. He whispers, pointing to Miss CPS's's notes. She nods.

I grab Zane by the belt loop and lead him across the lot toward the steps of what looks like a factory. Everybody else follows. EVERYBODY.

Me to my mother: "Is Mr. Guest coming in?" I pretend to

let Zane loose on him before yanking him back. I look up at the prison windows in the distance and wonder what my daddy can see. My mother follows my stare. She gets a lightbulb. DUH.

My mother: "I—uh—m." (That awkward moment when you need your ride to wait outside.) She manages to squirm out of Mr. Guest's arms like they were getting ready to kiss good-bye the whole time. "Of course not," she says. "He's got better things to do."

Then I change my mind, and I'm sorry I warned her. I want Mr. Guest to go in so Daddy can see him.

Me: "Like what?" My scalp itches like I'm growing horns. "I mean, he drove you all this way. I think Mr. Gues—"

Guest: "Rico, damn it! My fuh—" (he looks at Miss CPS) "name is Rico."

Me: "Rico! Yes, yes. You should go in. I'm sure Daddy would want to thank Rico for taking his—" Insert a long-ass pause here. For all you ignorant motherfoes, you can fill in the blank with:

- Cheetos
- car
- bed
- couch
- TV
- wife

"*What*, Macy?!" my mother screams, stomping her stilt.

Me: "Uh . . . for taking us to see him."

Rico: "Uh. I don't—"

My mother: "—want to interrupt our family time?"

Me: "Oh, thank you, Rico, for not interfering with our time. Zane, thank him."

Zane: "Grrrrrrr! Rrrr!"

Rico: "What the fuck did he say? What the fuck is everybody saying?"

"All right!" Miss CPS interrupts all of us. "Macy. Why don't you lead Zane inside? Maybe hold him by the hand instead of the belt loop. Sir? There's a waiting room with a television."

Rico: "Television? I got me a phone. And I don't feel like going through metal detectors. I'ma cool it outside."

We push through giant doors and go through a check-in station where guards inspect our bags and our shoes. Of course, Zane refuses to take off his shoes.

Zane: "Grrrrrrr! Ruff! Ruff!"

"God damn it," my mother says. Miss CPS takes notes.

Skinny guard: "Y'all are going to have to get your shit together or y'all will have to leave."

My mother to me: "Take him to the car."

Miss CPS: "No, that would not be appropriate. Let's—"

Me to my mother: "You take him to the car. *You're* his mother."

My mother to me: "How dare you say *I'm his mother*!"

Skinny guard scratches his ear and raises his voice: "Look, y'all have thirty seconds. I don't have time for this."

Miss CPS calls her supervisor. My mother has a lightbulb. She lunges for Zane's shoes. Zane bites her. My mother is screaming. Miss CPS is trying to put Zane back on his "leash." Zane is climbing onto the conveyor belt of the X-ray machine.

As a result, we get told the visit has to be rescheduled. In addition, the SWAT team that has descended upon our asses tells CPS if Zane does not get his hyperactive self away from the X-ray machine, we gonna have a problem. A guard with a tattoo of a eye on his eyelid grips his Taser.

"No," I say real quiet like Miss Black do. She is the sensei of silence.

Everybody shuts the hell up. Whoa. DOPE.

Guard with tattoo of a eye on his eye: "What?"

Me: "No. You can't cancel the visit. I didn't do nothing. Why shouldn't I go?"

My mother: "No, no, no. She don't go if I don't go." My mother throws me the evil eye. My ears feel hot.

Miss CPS: "Actually, Yasmin—"

Skinny Guard: "A'ight. You go with"—he looks at Miss CPS's's badge—"Miss Lebowitz."

Yeah. And I might as well lock myself in a cell because it would be safer than going home with my mother tonight.

Then my mother does the worst thing she could do. She looks worried.

FUCK. "Wait!"

My brain talks to itself: With what my dad is going through, this ain't gonna work. Yeah, my dad, the man no one here seems to be thinking about. He's probably been talking about the visit to his buddies all day. He's probably covered head to toe with tattoos of my mother. My mother. The one he is needing the most.

It's happening again. Too many feelings. Like I'm carrying a tray of 10,000 dirty dishes. I'd rather just let em crash and walk on glass. FUCK. FUCK. FUCK.

Me: "Please let my mother in. I'll get my brother out of there and we'll wait here." I talk in Miss Black's soft voice.

Miss CPS: "No! The whole purpose of the visit—"

Skinny Guard: "Miss Lebowitz, only God knows the real

78

purpose of anything." He turns to my mother. "You got five minutes." And now he looks at Zane, who is sitting on the X-ray machine's conveyor belt swinging his legs. "Zane, you one lucky dog to have this girl looking out for you."

I snap my fingers. Zane hops down, runs to me, and sits. I pat him on the head.

Miss CPS to me: "You couldn't have done that in the first place?"

Me: "You got the badge. I'm not the one in charge. *She-it.*"

A scar-faced guard waves my mother forward through the metal detector.

I drag Zane up to his feet. "We have to wait with Rico now. Just remember what to do if I say sic him."

The skinny guard laughs. My mom is about to disappear behind a huge heavy metal door. I call out: "Ma, tell him I love him."

My mother don't even turn around: "I only got five minutes. Can't remember the last time you said that to me."

I mouth: *FUCK!!!!!* With Zane's neck in one hand, I fling the door open with the other. The skinny guard catches it.

"Hey girl," the skinny guard says. "It's probly best you didn't see him. He wouldn't want you to see him like this. I know him. I'll tell him. By the way, you can write him. Any time. Without permission from anyone. All you need is a stamp."

"A'ight," I say. "Thank you."

"You're welcome. It's a blessing he have you."

I don't answer the guard. I just replay in my head what he said while we wait with Miss CPS. Miss CPS is babbling into the phone to her supervisor: "At least the siblings are getting a visit with each other. Sort of . . ."

The guard said I am a blessing—something nobody's said before and nobody will probably ever say again. Something my mother has never said. Something I know is bullshit. Something I don't want to live up to.

On the way home, I replay the dream. The dream of the women laying hands on my mother's belly—on me. I can hear them whispering, but I can't hear what they're praying. I think of when I laid hands on my mother's belly when she was pregnant with Zane and what I wished for him. That he wouldn't come out like our neighbor's baby did, missing parts. (That boy didn't have a anus. Doctors gave him tubes and a bag attached to him so he could poop.)

I prayed Zane would be strong. Is he? Does he understand? What about me? If those women knew me now, what would they say? Did I come true?

BREASTS

Noun. Yes. That's what they is called. Not boobs, boobies, titties, tetas, wah wahs, chi-chis, knockers . . .

Alma and I are sitting in homeroom listening to the guys rate the girls. Dudes are undressing maybe four or five girls with their eyes but making us all feel necked. It happens every time a girl's new tetas grow in. She had headlights before, but now they are on high beams.

"Even bad pizza is kind of good and even an ugly girl with big boobs is kind of good," one dude says, nodding at a girl getting written up for wearing spaghetti straps.

"Right," another answers. "That's what the dark is for."

Fucking profound, right? Move over Socratees, Playtoh, Neecha. Yup, I know who these motherfoes are. Miss Black threw out a bunch of their Cliff Notes last week. (See D for Detention.)

"Boobs," I say to Alma. "The dudes around here act like you personally grow out this crop," I point to mine, "so they could harvest it."

"Right? But like my mom says, boys will be boys."

"If boys gonna be boys, Macy gonna be Macy. I got a plan."
Bwahahahaha.

Alma says when I say "idea" or "plan" her heart is striked with fear.

George sits down by us and nods like he's been there for the whole convo. I fist-bump him. He goes to fist-bump me back and I know to hold on so he don't knock my ass off the chair.

Alma drops a pencil and reaches for it. The boys dash to catch a peek of her boobs like they're going for a touchdown. George morphs into Peyton Manning. The long hairy shadow he casts over Alma sends all the boys scrambling for their desks. *False start!*

Another girl walks in with boobs squeezed together so tight I swear she has a monoboob. George almost crashes trying to get his big-ass self out from the desk. He rips off his coat and throws it on the girl's chest. She screams like she's been attacked by the coat.

"Alma," I whisper, "you're cold."

Alma: "Huh? Oh! Right. I'm so cold, George!"

George rips his coat off the girl, then stops. He offers her monoboob his helmet. She shakes her head so hard I swear she gets whiplash.

He comes crashing back and knocks into Alma's desk, tipping over her water bottle.

Alma: "Oh, it's okay, George. No problem. I'll just get a tissue and—"

George throws his coat on the spill and sits back in his desk. We HEART George. Alma dabs the coat dry with a tissue and drapes it back over his shoulder.

Alma: "My desk is fine, I promise. Thanks, sweetie."

He smiles and settles in for a nap. Monoboob girl rubs hand sanitizer on her shoulders where the coat touched her.

Miss Black walks in and sits at the computer to do attendance.

I yell "HERE!" before she asks.

Me to Alma: "I was watching this documentary on TV and I found out that there was chicks who fought in the Civil War. And other wars too. They had to pretend they was guys. So they wrapped their boobs to make them look flat."

"Oh my God." Alma studies my boobs. "They're wrapped right now, aren't they? . . . They are. They look like two bricks. Two enormous bricks."

"Yes," I say. "Taped. Solid. Like armor!"

"Macy!" Alma hits the desk, lowers her voice after everyone turns around, and bends her head toward my ear. "This is absurd," she hisses. "Nuclear missiles can be hidden. Whole entire planes from Malaysia can disappear. But not *our* breasts!" She looks up at the ceiling. "What type of tape did you use?"

"I don't know. The kind I found on Teacher Man's desk."

"Then it's reasonable to assume it was just—masking tape?"

"Yes, whatever you just said, and it masks my boobs very well, don't you think?"

I fan myself with the book I'm supposed to be reading and gulp down the remaining contents of Alma's water bottle.

Alma massages her temples. "Listen. I can take care of it in gym class. I can probably cut you loose after attendance. I'll use my nail clippers."

Nail clippers . . . *These must be tools to clip nails.* I look at my hands. I glance at my shoes. My teeth have always worked fine. But this nail clipper tool intrigues me. Perhaps it can also be used for other purposes. "You bring nail clippers to school?"

"And toothpaste, and a toothbrush," Alma chirps and pats her purse.

I look at my pointer finger, which has served as my toothbrush many a time. "Ain't you fancy. PS, I don't want you to cut me open."

"I'm *going* to cut you open, Macy. Otherwise you'll develop a rash. And who exactly do you expect to apply the ointment, huh? Why in the hell do you need tape anyway?" She points to my hoodie. "Aren't XXL man jerseys enough?"

"Enough is never enough," I say. "Enough is never enough?" Do I know what that means? Wait. Yes, I do. "Enough is never enough!" No. Wait. That don't—

Alma smacks me. "Macy, why?"

"Why not? Why do you want to walk around with those things"—I point at her chest—"*here*?" I point outside the window. A police car is chasing a Subaru that's chasing a Ford Pinto.

"Macy, females are supposed to have breasts. I like my breasts. I would never want to *not* have my breasts."

"Really? I'm truly fucking flabbergasted." I start saying flabbergasted over and over again. *Flabbergasted flabbergasted flabbergasted.*

"Macy! A, you are clearly spending too much time" (she drops her voice to a whisper) "with George. B, this is news to you? That I like my body? Macy—you're sweating. How much tape did you use?"

"I don't know. Teacher Man had a six-pack on his desk . . . And more in his closet . . ."

Alma stands up. "I'm going to cut you open!"

Miss Black: "Excuse me, Alma?"

The bell rings. Alma throws her axessories in her bag and I know to run.

Even in the tape my boobs are bouncing like basketballs. Damn! Alma is on the track team. She knows how to run with big boobs.

Halfway down the hall, I'm out of breaf and sweating. The tape is sliding off, I feel it! Noooo!

Alma tackles me to the bafroom floor and drags me kicking and laughing and screaming into a stall. She reaches under my hoodie but I wiggle out of her grip. We wrestle. At one point, both our heads are actually sticking out of the head hole. I'm laughing so hard I can't breathe. I also cannot breathe because my boobs are taped together.

"You're actually pretty strong," I say to Alma.

"Check out my baby-lifting arm," Alma giggles, flexing a pretty impressive bicep. "Tanya, my mini-me, is eighteen pounds now . . ."

Unfortunately for her, her baby-lifting arm is no match for my machete-wielding arm. (See C for Clang.) That is part of the problem. I know how easy it is to hurt her. I try to eject Alma from my head hole—but—

"*OW!!!*"

Shit! I let go.

Alma squirms out of my grasp and somehow pulls both me and her out of the head hole into the hoodie. We wrestle. I'm crazy ticklish all sudden, and somehow we both end up tangled inside the sleeve of my T-shirt and my bra strap.

"Just stay still!" Alma says, making her first cut with the clippers.

Teacher voice: "Just what is going on in there?"

I'm overheated. Enough is enough.

I twist out of my shirt. Exhale. I jump up and down to get the circulation in my jugs going again. The door swings open.

Teacher Lady: "Oh my God! You're topless!! And you? Alma? What on earth? I—"

Me: "Are you flabbergasted?!"

Teacher Lady: "Both of you out! I mean—I thought I had seen everything, but this? I would write this up, but I can't even imagine finding the words!"

She don't write us up. A fifty-year-old woman who's written up kids we all know for bringing their mom's cocaine to school, stabbing someone in the eye with a pencil, giving five-dollar hand jobs in the parking lot, could not write up two girls in the restroom because she thought we were lesbians. *That* was too much for her.

Teacher Lady couldn't write it up—so I did.

BRING IT

Verb.

I don't even care. I'll take you down like Chinatown.

BURNER

Noun. Burn rhymes with turn, yearn, and never learn.

The substitute assigns the class to write a narrative essay on a childhood experience. I point out, "The last I heard, this was English and not counseling."

The substitute picks up a clipboard and scans it. Her eyeballs bulge. She babbles something under her breaf about insurance and looks up at the ceiling. God is currently a large water stain. I guess the water stain answers because she says, "Maybe if this is too hard, you can go to the resource room to get some extra help?"

"What are you saying?" I say all loud. "Are you telling me that because I'm emotionally disturbed that I'm *stupit*? Maybe it's your ass that needs to get some *resources*."

Some chick says, "Should we hit the buzzer?"

A dude says, "No, no! Not yet." Same chick says, "Freddy!!"

The buzzer is hit. Two milliseconds later the Assistant Principal is standing there with a big-ass bag of Doritos.

"I see you brought me resources." I walk over and snatch at the bag the AP is now holding out of reach.

"Why don't you come work with me in my office today, Macy? I reserved you a window seat. "

"Does the seat come with those Doritos?"

"I can accommodate that."

I go. I eat chili-cheese perfection. Yesterday I ate a envelope the CPS worker left for my mom so she could pay bills. You can lead a horse to water, but in my mom's case you got to hold her head under the fucking water, you know? Now I want some water . . .

In my dictionary (because I ain't giving it to no substitute), I write my essay on a childhood experience.

Narrative Essay
By Macy Cashmere MYOFB

The TV in the bedroom was broke. My mother and daddy were firing up in the living room. I was, I don't know, maybe eleven. Zane and I smiled because we loved when they sat on the couch together. I made it real nice for them in there. I put out a bag of Hot Cheetos. I emptied the ashtrays because if not they used cups and ashed on the carpet.

We knew not to go in there. Problem was, there really wasn't too many other places me and Zane could go. The couch was our bed and they were on it. What was we gonna do in the bafroom? You could only play pirate in the tub so many times. Couldn't go outside. We was under house arrest. I got into too many fights, and Zane was a wanderer. Once when he was five he escaped and walked to my school all by hisself. You know what Zane said when he found me at the blacktop? He needed someone to open the wrapper on his Pop Tart. Damn!

"Uh!" I said to get my parents' attention. "The CPS worker said we need privacy!"

My mother flipped the finger. It was meant for CPS, not for me. Daddy stood up. My mother kicked him in the ass.

"Damn, Yasmin! She's stressed, that's all. Hold up! I got a lightbulb."

Daddy put up cardboard from the new TV between the living room and the kitchen. Problem is, Zane is not a fan of walls. I saw in his eyes what he was gonna do.

"How bout we play a game?" I begged him. I ran to the closet and grabbed some of the games the CPS worker left. I wanted to play Concentration with the cards, but we couldn't make any matches. I ran back to the closet to check but two seconds later I smelled something burning. "Who put the toaster on?" I said. I knew we didn't have no bread. I sniffed the air. "Damn it, Zane!"

Pop! Up came a queen and a jack all black and smoky.

I brought back a game called Hi Ho Cherry-O. Hi ho? Cherry-O? I thought it might be nasty, so I inspected the back and the front.

Turned out it was a game about counting fruit. I wanted to play. But dang! All the cherries was gone.

"Where's all the cherries, Zane?" I shook him, but he just laughed, and I had my answer. Ever seen a boy poop a iron? I have—from the Monopoly game the CPS worker left the last time.

Operation looked good. It had some pieces. But of course, it didn't have no batteries. Zane tried to eat the ribs. I smacked his mouth and he cried.

"Ay in there," Daddy said from the couch. "Take it easy!"

"Don't make me come in there!" my mother yelled as if *in here* and *out there* was different. I thought about starting something with Yasmin, but I didn't. I wanted Daddy to be happy.

I opened the fridge and pulled out the butter and syrup. In the cupboards was a shitload of Sudafed and I pulled out two bottles. I pulled the medicine cups off and made our favorite recipe. Inside the cups I squeezed a swirl of sugar, butter, and pancake syrup, the only things in the fridge. (What? You thought I was going to say I drank up all the Sudafed, didn't you? You stereotyping motherfoe.)

I picked Zane up and set him on the counter by the stove and we ate up. I leaned against a burner and jerked forward like I got shot out of a gun.

Damn! I mouthed, shaking my hand. Yasmin must have left a burner on. But it wasn't a burn I felt. I said to Zane, "I think I got shocked!" Zane started laughing. Even though it didn't hurt as much anymore, I kept jumping up and down and cursing to make him laugh. But Zane didn't do anything for more than thirty seconds. He yawned and started playing with the trash can pedal. *Gong! Gong! Gong!* I touched the burner with my pinky. Yup. I got shocked just like you do when you touch the sides of the patient in Operation. Only for real.

We polished off the Syrup Surprise. Zane cried when he saw the empty syrup bottle. I could hear from the living room that my mother and father did not want to be disturbed. "Shhhh!" I said, but he wouldn't. I covered his mouth, but he bit me. Damn! I eyeballed the burners and made sure they were off. Zane's attention span was about the same as his short-term memory. I touched the front right burner. *God damn it!* I mouthed. I got shocked. FOR REAL. He laughed. I didn't. That shit really hurt.

WTF? The burners were on when they said OFF?

Zane stopped laughing. He pulled up a chair to the stove. He wanted to touch them too. I tried to pick him up and put him on the floor, but Wolverine scratched me. He hopped back up to the chair and touched the burner.

Nothing.

I poked at it. I got shocked. WTF? I poked again. No shock. I poked another one and I got shocked. I poked it again, I didn't. Which burners was broke and which wasn't? I touched all four one by one. Sometimes I got shocked. Sometimes I didn't. This game was better than Operation! Being a bit distracted, our dumb asses didn't notice the shadow parting the clouds of cannabis smoke.

"What is you two doing?" My mother smacked me upside the face. "Is this how you act with your baby brother?" she yelled.

Daddy yanked my mother off me. He was wearing his underwear. I looked away from what was sticking up out of it. "What are you doing, Yasmin?"

Wiggle! my brain told my hands. *Wiggle!* But my hands didn't listen any better than I do.

"Teaching her right from wrong, that's what! You don't even know what's going on! Always siding with her!"

"Oh, c'mon, baby! Just put them in the bedroom and let them stay in there. I'm dying."

"No! That's the only place that's mine! Forget the whole thing. I'm not in the mood anymore anyway. I'm going to bed." My mother stomped off, slammed the door, and locked it.

"Oh, it's like that," I heard Daddy saying from outside the bedroom door while I dragged Zane into the bafroom.

It wasn't the first time we had slept in the

tub. Wasn't gonna be the last. "Arg, me hearties!" I said to Zane, pulling him on my lap with my right hand. The left was twitching from the shock.

"Fine, Yasmin!" Daddy stomped off to the living room. The TV blasted on. Soon smoke drifted under the bafroom door. Zane fell asleep on my belly. I drifted, thinking about my hand. What if I woke up tomorrow and found out I could twist the lids off of anything? What if I could throw a slipper from clear across the room and smack a cockroach dead on the first try? Just when my superhero dream got good I heard my mother's door open and my daddy say, "Sorry, baby."

Next thing I knew I woke up to daddy screaming. I tripped climbing out the tub and scrambled to the living room. My mother was aiming the sink nozzle at the cardboard. Flames had burnt part of the living room wall. I locked Zane out the house and got pots of water from the bafroom. Twenty minutes later the fire was out and I went outside to get Zane. And who out of all the people on the planet Earth was waiting with him? Our neighbors from 3211, holding up their cells.

That night we got a knock on the door. CPS wanted to know what happened. My mother talked about me playing with burners. "You could have burned Zane to death," my mother said. "You hear me? You hear what I said?"

I nodded. I knew I would *always* never stop hearing what she said.

After CPS left, I stood in the kitchen. I hated my own tears. I set my hand on the burner. The shock rippled through my arm to my heart. I wanted to dry it up. I wanted to dry my tears.

But I never have.

I'm sitting in the AP's office and there are still tears left. I feel them. If I turn around she will see them.

"Give me your assignment and go to your next class," the AP says.

I crumple up a piece of paper so she thinks it's my narrative essay. I make a big to-do about throwing something out in the trash can. Just as the AP turns around to tell me about how she used to be a English teacher and blah blah blah about drafts, I drop a match in the can.

I do not get far, as my AP knows kung fu.

"Dang it, Macy," she says, blocking me with one hand and aiming her fire extinguisher with the other. "That came out of left field. Sugar-honey-ice-tea, I'm pregnant. I can't be doing this right now!"

I get sent home sick. You can't suspend a emotionally disturbed girl for being emotionally disturbed even if she tries to light shit on fire. And you can't send her to class smelling like smoke.

CALL

Noun. (I don't feel like writing anything.)

My mother is talking to my dad, I know it. We go two rounds WWF-style before I wrestle the phone out of her claws. I'm outside. The snow's melting. The street looks ugly, like a cake with the icing licked off. The warmth of my mother's face on the phone warms my cheek.

I've had this convo with my dad a hundred times in my head, but this time it's real. So why can't I think of nothing to say?

"Hello? Macy? You there?"

"Hey, Daddy."

"Hey, baby girl. I miss you."

"Me too."

"You staying away from them boys?"

"Uh, yeah."

"Yeah?"

"Yes, Daddy."

"Everything okay over there?"

"Uh, I guess that depends on what okay means."

"You gonna tell me if anything's going on, right?"

"Yeah," I answer real quick. Not because I feel right about it. But because I know what will happen if Daddy hears a second of silence.

"Good. Don't worry. I got it all worked out. I'm going to come home and get Zane back and then everything will be just like it was."

"JUST like it was." I repeat it.

"Give me back to your moms."

"Ain't you gonna ask me nothing else?"

"Like what? Is there something going on?"

"No."

My mom flings open the door and sticks her hand out for the phone. I throw it hard so she almost drops it. She slams the door and locks me out. It's not like I'm even mad at her. I'm mad at my dad and I can't even explain why. The only thing I understand is that I can't let myself be mad at him. He and Alma are the only people in the world I'm not mad at and that includes myself.

Later that night I grab the phone. Do an instant replay on the convo like Daddy's really on the other line. Say all the things we should have said. Call Alma and don't say much of anything. Just to hear someone say good night.

CANADA

Noun. A flashback that should be a flashforward.

Daddy promised to take me to Canada one day. Canada is a place where they have lots of trees. If you have a lot of trees then you have birds nesting in them. I like birds. Birds like blue jays and cardinals. NOT pigeons. I stoled many books out of Miss Black's trash can (See D for Detention) about birds and nature and shit. I'll never get why she's always throwing that kind of shit out. Zane drew on all the pictures but always listened when I read to him. And never laughed at how bad I read.

If you have trees you also have squirrels. Our neighbors at 3211 used to keep squirrels in a wire cage. I'll never forget when my mother and I went stealthy one night and set them all free. In Canada they have squirrels but no one puts them in cages because what the hell do you want with a crazy-ass squirrel in a cage anyway? Seriously? What if everybody did that? Who the hell is going to bury all those nuts in the ground? You want to do it? *She-it.*

For real, it's a shame squirrels don't sting. Or butterflies. Anything that people want to get their hands on and keep. Finders keepers, that's what we all fucking are.

In Canada, if the birds shit, you don't even know it. Shit lands on the trees before it lands on you. If it ever does hit the ground, it just mixes with the soil. Birds shit out seeds. This is good for the soil, according to the science magazines Miss Black dumped in her recycle bin last week. Soil is different than dirt. If you have soil then you have worms. If you have worms you might have a flower. Here we have dirt. We also have a lot of shit but not the kind that grows anything.

You can't walk ten feet without stepping in shit. Once I even stepped into a baby diaper with shit in it. I mean really, people? Serious-fucking-ly?

In Canada it snows every day so no matter how dirty it gets it's always clean. Zane and I could eat the snow right off the ground and it wouldn't matter. You remember you got a soul every time you take a breaf.

Daddy promised to take me to this place. I was probably eleven years old. He promised we will make footsteps in the snow. But my mother said, *Canada? What the fuck is there to do in Canada? You can't wear a bikini in Canada.*

Goddamn it, I thought. When the word *bikini* was mentioned Daddy had trouble with his attention span. You would too if you saw my mother in a bikini. Anyway, here's the flashback:

My mother says to Daddy while he's distracted from Canada, "Remember my business?"

I say, "What business?" And think, Can you run it from the couch?

My mother says, "I'm calling it Arts from Crap."

I like this but I don't tell her this. I know she wants me to like her idea. But she does not want me to tell her I like her idea because I better not think that she needs my damn approval. That's disrespectful.

My mother: "Remember, I'm going to sell tin-foil bikinis. Wait up. Let me show you my latest creations."

She runs to the bedroom and changes. After a long time she walks out the bedroom kind of how you would expect someone to walk when they're wearing tin foil. But I have to admit, she looks good.

Looking at my mom in tin foil makes my dad look—more distracted.

Looking at tin foil makes me think about baked potatoes. At school the baked potatoes have tin foil on them. I say, "Don't they put the tin foil on the potato so the insides get hot?"

My mother: "Shut up."

But she knows we're now thinking about all these ladies' breasts baking on the beach like hot potatoes, which is not a sexy thought. I laugh. I can't help it.

Laughing at my mother generally gets me a smack but I'm used to that. She can't smack me that hard anyway wearing tin foil. It's when my dad laughs at my mom standing there in that tin-foil bikini that all hell breaks loose.

Tin-foil bikinis are not made to stand up against all hell breaking loose. My mother starts screaming and waving her arms around: "I want to go to California! What the fuck is in Canada?"

Zane starts copycatting my mother, windmilling his arms around—then stops. "Your titty," Zane says.

There it is: my mother's boOb hanging out.

My dad says, "Hey now, save that for later," and he hugs her and squeezes her ass. But she only gets madder and I know why. It's not just because his hug broke her other breast out. It's because deep down she didn't really want him to think she was just sexy in that tin-foil bikini. She wanted him to think she was smart.

I can't say any of this, though. What do I know about what she thinks? my mother would say.

She stomps off into the kitchen and rattles around in a cabinet. She throws tin foil everywhere like it's a parade and Daddy follows her trail and her tail into the bedroom.

I pick up the foil. It could come in handy at a later date. I follow the trail of it into the kitchen. Out of a cabinet spill dozens of tin-foil bikinis. All different kinds. I wonder two things.

One: has anyone been checking tin foil inventory at the Super S? (See S for Super.) And two: how did my mother manage to make these things without anybody noticing? I look around for the black hole she had obviously disappeared herself into.

The thing was, the beauty of 'em was that they weren't meant to be worn. They looked like those statue-things you see in a museum. But not one for old people with paintings in it of people from a long time ago. I always think those people look hot and itchy and then I want to scratch. Once at a school trip to a museum in fifth grade, I took off everything but my panties I got so itchy.

So I imagine a really cool museum. A cool museum that has things in it like my mom's tin-foil bikinis. Tin-foil bikinis. Now mass produced at a Walmart near you. Even your couch-sitting ass could afford one. The bikinis keep in the heat where you need it most. You could even go to the beach in winter. In Canada.

CIRCLE

Noun. Synonyms: my space—my zone—leave me alone.

I stand in the bafroom and draw a imaginary circle around myself. I learned to do this in middle school. I remember the counselor's words:

"You are the center," he says, walking around me. "You are in control."

He draws a circle around himself. "This is my circle. This is my space. That is yours. Think of yourself as a planet. Think of me as a planet. What would happen if our circles collided?"

Some little kids walk into the bafroom and start playing in the sink, but I tell them to get out. I stand there in my circle. But I'm not just a planet. I'm a star. I'm the sun and I burn like hell. Everybody needs me to shine, but I don't need them for nothing. I can look down on them but they can't look me in the eye. I burn. I burn because I'm mad. I'm mad enough to shine for the next zillion years. And you need me too. Love don't make this world go round. I do.

I stand in my circle thinking of everybody revolving around me. My mother, Daddy, Alma, Zane, everyone. Daddy leaves, but somehow, I always know he's coming back no matter how long it takes.

I see Alma. Forget Saturn's rings. She makes them look like cheap dollar-store bracelets. She's the perfect beauty. The kind you can see but not get your sticky little fingers on.

My mother sweet-times it slower than Neptune. You'd think that would give us more time to talk but it don't. No matter how hard I try to talk to her, she's always moving away from me. She don't want to get burned.

My brother Zane is Pluto. The planet that's not even a planet—that looks dead to everyone except that one crazy-ass motherfoe who never stops believing there's life out there. That crazy-ass motherfoe is me.

I think of what would happen if gravity pulled us together for once. I see us all becoming one big-ass star. A supernova—

Somebody flushes a toilet and I blink. It's a little kid from the Child Development class. I'm not in outer space. This fucks up my intergalactic vision. I toss the girl out and the next two kids trying to use the potty.

The door flings open.

Teacher: "What is going on in here?"

Me: "Has any kid since the beginning of fucking time ever answered that question?"

Teacher: "What? Get out of here."

Me: "Apparently, you have not read my Behavior Intervention Plan. Ain't no one telling me to get out of NOWHERE. Don't make me step out of my circle. You not even a planet. You an assteroid."

The teacher: "What? What did you call me?"

I can't understand what the teacher says next because of all the screaming in the hall. Outside the bafroom kids in wet shoes sit in puddles of pee, pulling off their pants. Other kids are jumping in the puddles. What makes it even more epic is the teacher slip-and-sliding in pee trying to round them up.

This gives me an instant flashback of my mother trying to hit Zane:

Like a Tom and Jerry episode, my mom chases him under tables, over couches, and back again. Of course, I join in just for shits and giggles. This makes him laugh. This makes my mother mad. He's bad so he's not supposed to be laughing.

Yasmin stops chasing him and goes after me. Her chancla whacks me in the neck before she catches up with me. It hurts a lot but it is also funny.

If you look in our house you can see our circle—the exact place Zane's foot went into the couch—the place where my mother's chancla went through the window.

Sometimes I run that circle chasing our shadows. If I run fast enough the screaming goes away and I can just hear the laughter.

CLANG

Noun. Rhymes with BANG! you're dead.

Miss Black found out our ignorant asses ain't never heard of this dude named Hans Christian Anderson. So today she brings in a fat book with pictures and reads out loud to us like we little kids. One story she reads is about a dude who packs a bag and seeks his fortune. Just like that. Like there's no question that anyone who looks for a fortune is gonna find it.

I make a decision. After I get home, I'm lacing up my sneaks. I'ma go for a walk. Being that a girl walking to JJs last week got raped and set on fire, I also decide to take protection.

We have this machete that my great-grandmother used in the sugarcane fields. Daddy said it got passed down to him, and one day he was going to pass it on to me. One day happens in books—but in the real world? I decide today is that one day, bitches.

After I get home from school, I make sure the coast is clear. I lift the mattress (COOTIE ALERT: CODE RED) and pull the machete out. I spray myself and the machete with Fabuloso (See F for Fabuloso) and do a cleansing dance I make up on the spot. I'm cootie-free and IT IS MINE!

It is heavy, with a light wood handle darkened by sweat in the middle where your hand goes. The sweat stain is narrow, like an abuelita's hand. I fit my hand there, and it is a perfect match. The blade is long and silver and sharp and has little chips in it, like she was in a duel or something. Little spots of gold rust the blade. My abuelita kicked ass. I wish I could of known her. It kind of feels like I'm taking her with me. I pack my backpack with the machete and off we go!!!!!!!

The sun is shining just like in them books. Theme music pops in my head. Some of my mother's old-school music. I'm hearing Ice Cube's "It Was a Good Day."

It don't take long before I get hungry. Damn, if I had a dollar for every time I've walked past the Dollar General with only 99 cents. Or better yet, if I had a penny for every dude's nasty thoughts as I've walked past the General . . .

"Why don't you smile?"

"Oh, I could make you smile . . ." Insert obscene gestures.

Dudes been saying this since ancient times. Picture Mary Mother of God walking down the street. "Oh baby, let me see that ankle . . ."

All sudden "Mi Machete" is playing in my head. I take my abuelita's secret weapon out my backpack. Check out what I look like in the reflection of the blade. Freshly shaved head. New eyebrow piercing. Million-dollar smile. That's right. I'm still Be-oo-tee-full Bitches!

"How do you like me now?"

Nasty dudes ain't smiling no more. One spits on the sidewalk. Another calls me a slut.

I decide not to scalp their asses. But I picture doin it and hanging their skins on my backpack. I'm a warrior.

I cross the street. Three dudes is playing football in the field. I pull my hat over my eyes and hunker down. I'm one of them. I make the winning touchdown. I'm MVP, man. I do a victory dance. Hold up my Heisman to the sky—WTF? Ash rains down like I'm under a damn volcano. I look up at the fire escapes. Whoever ashed disappears like the smoke from their nasty cigarettes.

I dust off my head. It's all good. I'm taking a walk.

On to the junkyard. Dude comes out a abandoned limousine. Hangs off the inside of the fence, puffing clouds through chain-link diamonds.

Shaking his head, he says to me, "Tetas like that ain't meant to be in a sweatshirt."

I'm about to tell this motherfoe he should write for Cosmo. But I don't speak. I let Abuelita speak for me. I raise up my machete like Agüeybaná II held up his macana in battle against Ponce de León. (What, your ignorant ass never heard of Agüeybaná? It ain't my job to educate you.) Dude climbs into the limo like if he just wishes hard enough it'll fill up with gas and GO!

I walk off with my machete raised high to the sky and enjoy the silence . . . For about one milli-fucking-second.

Till I see the cop car roll up.

I freeze like a cockroach. No cops showed up for that girl who got set on fire until after she was burnt to a crisp. But apparently I am like Magneto when it comes to attracting the law.

The cop car stops in front of me. One cop's white, the other cop's brown, but all that matters to me is both is blue. Cop in the passenger side squints at my face. Takes inventory. His eyes light up when he sees my chest. "Oh, it's just a girl."

Just? Well *she-it*. For once in my life having big boobs has benefits.

White cop on the passenger side steps out. "Young . . . lady," Officer Po Po says, hands hooked on his belt, "you can put your hands down. Slow."

Whaat? So they can say I was trying to cut them? Hell to the no. If I'ma die today, I'ma do it right so Zane gets a paycheck tomorrow.

"I thought you supposed to put your hands up. That's what I'm doin."

The officer in the driver's seat talks shit into his radio and steps out the car.

Officer Brown nods at Officer White, then looks at me. "What do you need with a machete?"

"Don't know how I been living without it so far."

Officer Brown folds his arms on his belly. "Well, this is a problem."

Shit. I'm gonna be joining my great-grandmother. Names start flashing across my brain one after the other.

RIP DeAunta Terrell Farrow, Trayvon Martin, Andy Lopez, Eric Garner, Michael Brown, Ezell Ford, Akai Gurley. Tamir Rice, Dontre Hamilton, Terence Crutcher, Rekia Boyd, Samuel DuBose, Philando Castile, Alton Sterling, Alfred Olango . . .

Several things I got in common with the above:

I ain't white.

I got issues.

I exist.

"Yeah." That's all my big fat mouth can say. If this was Yasmin, I'd have something to say. If this was the principal, I'd have something to say. If this was the president of the United States of America, I'd have something to say.

"Lay it on the ground."

Lay it on the ground so he can take it. The only piece of my great-grandmother. The only piece of un-fucked-up history I got.

"No."

Zoom away from us and out to Dollar General. Ladies and their bags of hair products and plastic Santas crowd the parking lot. Empty chain-link fence now has bunches of dudes hanging on it like dirty underfed tigers waiting for a scrap. What was only a handful of kids playing touch football is now enough to fill the field. Cop White's got one eye planted on me, one on the yard.

"Why don't you leave that . . . girl . . . alone?" comes from a crowd of men at the Liquor Barn. They set their full bottles down and pick up empty bottles from the ground.

"I'm only going to ask you one more time, young lady."

Even if I wanted to, I couldn't move. I'm a statue. I got so many do's and don'ts shooting off in my brain, I'm gonna get myself shot. Will my mother cry for me at my funeral? Will they let Daddy out to pay his respects? I could just see my coffin getting lowered into the ground, and Zane jumping in after it. My hand is sweating. My arm's shaking with the strain of holding up this machete that my abuelita held up for a lifetime. I'm gonna drop it.

Plastic bags flutter all over the ground of the Dollar General parking lot. Ladies drop their shopping bags and hold up their phones. The ghosts from the fire escapes have reappeared. Can't see their faces. Just the smoke and their hands holding out phones. Football players are filing off the fields and onto the street. Some aiming phones from behind cars. Some from on top.

Now, you're thinking my walk was a one-way trip. You're using your prior knowledge to assess that I won a instant vacation to the afterlife. You're thinking this incident got hashtagged on Twitter, a million hits on YouTube.

Or maybe you're thinking all those phones finally made a difference. That instead of filming my death, they saved my life. Forget about all those other homies that died on candid camera, I was the lucky one.

You'd be dead wrong. What saved me wasn't all the brown and black sistas and brothers risking life and limb to bear witness.

What saved me was the white ho.

"You leave her alone! I'm live."

Velvet's standing there in her knee-length pleather boots, furry short-shorts, and my sweatshirt, holding up her phone.

Officer Brown lays his hand on his gun. "Lady, you need to back up."

"Hey, I know you." Officer White mentally frisks her. "You're dressed like you're on the clock."

"Yeah." Officer Brown nods at his partner. "Maybe it's you we ought to be questioning."

Both officers turns their back on me and target Velvet.

My cowardly self flees the scene. Other than the herd of dogs, there is no high-speed chase. Me, my hoodie, and my machete do end up on the news for five minutes before a shooting in our neighborhood bumps it off the agenda. A baby girl in her stroller killed by a stray bullet. In broad daylight. No suspects. May she rest in peace.

CLASS

Noun. What people think you got if you got money.
What people think you don't got if you poor.

It's five o'clock, and I know it's time for my mother to be at her parenting class. The door busts open.

Dude with the sunglasses says to the bald dude: "Put her on the couch!"

My mother is giggling. She's wearing a huge white boot over her left foot.

I hop up. "Ma, what happened?"

My mother: "I was at the hotel. Applying for a job. There was no Slippery When Wet sign."

Dude with the shiny head: "Should sue their asses."

Dude with the sunglasses: "Yeah. You could get some big money. My cousin is suing Apple. A selfie he took blinded him and he fell down the stairs."

Me: "Thank you for input. Get the fuck out."

Dude with sunglasses: "*Damn!*"

Dude with shiny head: "Rude."

They leave.

Me: "Ma, you got to get up. Your class."

My mother: "Like this?" She points at her foot. "I got a doctor's note."

Me: "Ma. I read the paperwork. If you miss two you get kicked out. Doctor's excuse or not. You lose Zane for good."

My mother: "What? That is bullshit."

Me: "Yeah, but that's the rules, Ma. I can't change them and neither can you. Ma, *please*. I will carry you there."

My mother: "I could have gotten a ride if you wasn't so rude."

Me: "Oh shit. Ma, what do I do?"

My mother reaches in her purse. "Give them this. Hurry up."

I run out the door with two joints. The dudes are about to pull out onto the street. "Hey! *Hey!!!*"

Dude with the shiny head rolls down the window.

"Please. Could you please help us?"

He eyeballs the joints. "Oh, now she wants to be friends! Whatchu need, honey?"

Me: "A ride."

Dude with the sunglasses: "I would've given Yasmin a ride for free, but if you offering . . ."

I hold up the joints and lead them back to the house. Soon they're carrying my mother to their car. I watch as they pull away. There's no guarantee that my mother's going to get where she's supposed to go. But she's headed in the right direction, and that's more than I can normally say about her.

I tried, Zane.

COURT

Noun. Where even a kid can get a life sentence.

Court looks just like it does on TV. There's a American flag to make it all look official. A judge in a shiny robe sits on a throne above everybody else. I would like to sit in that chair. "Silence!" "Overruled!" I imagine myself in a Judge Macy TV show.

Beside the judge there is a box where the witness gets to talk. Like the penalty box in hockey. A guard stands by it, so serious I want to tickle him.

The audience is full of suits, ties, and stockings mixed in with T-shirts that say things like *Ghetto Word of the Day: Cologne. Hey bro do you think you cologne me fitty bucks?*

My mother is not in the audience. She had a visit with Daddy and what with her foot in a boot still, she could only hobble to one place and not two.

I'm the witness. I will be sitting in the box. I will be speaking into the microphone. Witness to what? Robbery? Murder?

Yes, but that's not why I'm here today. The crime today is being me.

I'm sitting down with my lawyer. Having a lawyer made me feel fancy at first. Zane has a lawyer too. His lawyer argued to take him away. Mine is arguing to keep me home.

I met my lawyer when she came to pick me up:

"They're not allowed to yell at me, right? Cuz I yell back."

"No. No one will yell. Mr. Katz will just ask you questions."

"He's CPS's lawyer. They want to take me away."

"Well, that's one way to look at it. The other way to look at it is you'll be with your brother."

I hated her for saying that. I mean what did she have to choose today? Her lipstick? Her fucking shoes? Soon I'm asked to go up to the box. To swear on the Bible to tell the truth, just like on TV.

Me: "Uh. 'xcse me. But what if I don't believe in the Bible?"

Mr. Katz: "Do you believe in truth?"

Me: "Uh. Yeah."

Mr. Katz: "Can you swear on that Bible to tell it now? Pretend the Bible is whatever you like."

What would I swear on to tell the truth? I take a minute and think. What truth do I have in my life? Who haven't I lied to? Alma. She is the only thing about my world that is TRUE. I pretend to hold her hand and I repeat the oath.

Mr. Katz asks a bunch of questions about my age and my school and my friends. He thinks I don't know what he's doing. Warming me up. Making me comfortable. Making me think he's on my side. (See A for All About You.) Then he gets down to business.

Mr. Katz: "Does your mother go out a lot?"

Me: "She's old enough to go out. I'm old enough to stay at home."

Mr. Katz: "Unless you correct me, I will assume that is a yes."

Tricky motherfoe.

Mr. Katz: "Tell me about family time."

Me: "Oh. We're together a lot."

Mr. Katz: "Would you say you fight a lot?"

Me: "You never fight with your mom?"

Mr. Katz chuckles. "All right. Tell me about your bedroom. Do you have privacy? Wouldn't you *like* privacy?"

Me: "You can't take me away because we're poor."

Mr. Katz: "No, of course not. What about Zane? Do you think he would like to live with his sister?"

Mr. Katz is the devil in a navy suit.

Me to Me Myself & I: Yeah. What about Zane. I overheard my lawyer talking on the phone. She said Zane was living in a big-ass house. With his own room and bafroom. Would I like to be with Zane? Shit, I taught him how to tie his shoes. I know his favorite everything. Yes I want to be with him. But then what happens to my mother? What would she have to come home to? Who would hold her back? And if I gave up my mother, would I have to give up my daddy too?

Me to Katz: "You all told me yourself Zane is better off. You made him go, but you'll never ever make me do nothin, so go fu—"

Judge Lady: "*Young lady!*"

I get to stay with my mother. My lawyer says I'm old enough to have a voice and that Mr. Katz knows that and that he was trying to get me to volunteer to go with Zane. CPS will be checking up on me, she says. Same old same old.

On the ride home I picture my mother waiting. Is she smoking and nail-biting? Or just smoking and doing her nails? We pull up to the house. Her bedroom light is on.

My lawyer: "All right, young lady. I will be seeing you soon. Here's my card. Keep in touch."

Me: "Yeah. I'll be sure to do that." I walk in and throw the card on the floor.

My mother, coming out of her bedroom: "You're home."

"Good observation, Ma."

"Your dad is okay. He said if they took you he'd bust out of jail. Crack skulls."

"And what about you, Mom?"

"What about me what?"

Me: "Yeah. What?"

My mother: "Okay. Be like that."

She stomps to her bedroom and slams the door. I punch it. She punches it back. We keep going like that that until my hands are bloody and I can't breathe. I lean against the wall and close my eyes. Catch my breaf. And the door opens. Nobody is there. I feel a breeze coming from the bedroom window. How long has my mother been gone? I start to wonder if she was ever really there. If I am. If any one of us is.

CUTE

Adjective. AKA Dawg Daze.

Miss Black gave us *Hatchet*. *Hatchet* is a book. I sit on my couch and open my assignment notebook mainly because I can't find the remote to the TV. So—I got to find one unexpected use for a object just like the main character does in the book. AND write about it. I have a lightbulb. I will use *Hatchet* to turn on the TV and kill two birds with one stone. I aim the book at the power button.

The TV don't turn on. But the book lands face up and me and the main character, Brian Robinson, face off. "You think you have it bad because of some wolves?" I ask his loozah face. "I mean, at least you *had* a damn hatchet." After my walk, I put the machete back under the mattress exactly where I thought I found it—but my mother's spidey sense must have told her something was up. When I went back for the machete, it was gone.

Let me tell you something, okay? I don't want to hear about Brian Robinson whining about a pack of wolves. I'll be impressed when there's a book about a kid using a box of pencils against a pack of chihuahuas.

A chihuahua may be cute when it's a puppy, but not so much when it's missing a eyeball and thirteen of its half-breed cousins are surrounding you to get at your peanut butter and jelly sangwich.

Just call me Agüeybaná. *Fuácata!*

So hello. The next time you see that *cute* little puppy and you're holding it in your arms, and you're thinking he's so warm, think of this: so is pee. The next time you're thinking of how fun it would be to feed it, think of the day you're so broke from buying dog food you're checking ingredients on the back of FiFi's food can and saying to yourself, *That don't sound so bad.* (This is Macy Cashmere, and I approve this message.)

And think of this:

I'm home. I'm sitting on the floor. My mother is preoccupied with some shit in her room. A nice warm breeze is coming from a hole in the floor. A commercial for I don't know what comes on. There's a lot of sexy people in it and I'm supposed to buy I'm not sure what but whatever it is it will make me sexier.

Pitbull pokes its head through the hole.

And I don't mean a bald-headed, blue-eyed Cuban dude telling me to get my ass on da flo. Mr. Worldwide got nothing to do with the mangy body trying to follow its head into my space.

I jump three feet in the air.

Pitbull's chomping on the wood of the floorboard. I run, jump, and grab the *Hatchet* book and start beating it on the head. It eats the book. Whole. WTF?! I beat it with the remote control. The battery cover comes off and it eats the batteries. Noooooo! Them things are expensive!

Now I'm mad. So is the dog. Maybe he prefers triple As? I don't know but he looks like one of those Hungry Hungry Hippos lunging forward for marbles and every time he does, more of his scabby body pulls through.

"Ma!" I scream, booking for her bedroom. I fling open the door, but she's not in there, even though she was a minute ago. I hate it when she slips past me like the ninja.

I run to the kitchen. All I can find is a plastic butter knife. I stop. Is the dog laughing? No. That is God.

Damn it! What would Brian Robinson do? If only I had read more than the back cover!

He'd get the machete, stupit ass.

I step into my mother's bedroom. What could be scarier than her mattress? A chill shimmies up my spine because I know the answer.

Her panty drawer. That's where my mother must have stuck the machete after she suspected I took it from under the mattress.

Attention: This is a broadcast of the Emergency Cootie Alert System.

If my great-grandma could spend ten hours a day seven days a week cutting down cane, I can do this, man! I close my eyes. 1-2-3! I feel all sort of things that ain't panties!!! Ahhh!!! But I pull it out, improv a speedy cleansing dance to counteract the cooties, and head back to THE HOLE.

This is going to be messy.

Pitbull's gums look like moldy ham. Teeth stand right up to my machete. I don't want to die. But I don't want to swing this knife.

His torso is through the hole. I could count his ribs he's so close.

I raise the machete. But I can't bring myself to do it. Not because I'm a pus—ball? (See A for Afraid.) I mean, the idea of steel slicing through skin and bone does turn my stomach. That's not even it, though.

It's that I get him. I don't blame him. But . . . it's him or me.

Chah! Chah! Chah! Splat! Splat!

Dog sinks down. I drop the machete and sink into the couch. Another warm breeze comes through the hole. And a whisper . . . *It's yours now.*

Abuelita? Is that you? What's mine? The dog? That's nasty!

No, stupit ass. The machete.

Oh yeah! The machete.

I grab the Fabuloso and some rags. Shine up the machete. Do another cleansing ritual complete with my best moves. I have found my weapon. I have danced. I have killed. I have survived.

I hold my machete up to the sky. And yes, in our living room, you can actually see sky after that time Daddy accidentally shot a hole through the ceiling trying to get that woodpecker. Did Brian Robinson watch the sun glint off his blade and say *How do you like me now, bitch?* I don't know but 195 pages is too much to find out. Plus, this whole situation brings new meaning to that shit: the dog ate my homework.

I spray some Fabuloso down the hole, stick a cushion on it, and sit down on what's left of the couch. (The rats will take care of the rest.) For a minute, I consider using the machete to change the channel, but think better of it. I stash the machete in my backpack and actually turn on the tube with my *bare hands*. A commercial with a dog riding a vacuum comes on.

It's cute.

DADDY

Preposition, which is time, location, direction.
(Wherever I am, he's with me.)

Today is a school fundraiser. You can buy barbecue plates at lunch. Your family can come, assuming your family ain't too busy smoking joints on the couch.

I'm waiting for Alma. She is buying barbecue that she isn't going to eat. I have to keep myself from drooling on the table. A teacher's kid is standing across from me. If I used the word *cute*, that's what he is, with his shiny parted black hair and clean nose, but I don't use the word *cute* and neither should you, you ignorant-ass motherfoe. (See C for Cute.) The less attention I pay to him, the more he keeps paying to me.

His coleslaw slides off the side of his plate, that's how little attention he's paying, his hot dog falling sideways, the ketchup all mixing together with the mustard. So I turn to him and say: "Don't you got something better to do, Daddy?"

He laughs, and if I was to use the word *cute*—which I wouldn't, you ignorant-ass motherfoe—I would say his laugh

121

was the cutest thing I ever heard. He picks up a French fry and says, "I'm not your daddy, silly! Want one?"

"Want one what?"

"Come here, sweetheart," Teacher Lady says, smiling so hard I think she chips a damn tooth. She leads him to another table.

Sweetheart.

"Macy, I got you pickles." Alma sits down.

Me: "My parents used to call my brother Zane daddy."

She pushes her tray toward me. Crunches on some celery sticks and leaves the rest. "My mother calls my brothers daddy. She always called me mami when I was little. Till the boys started calling me that. Now she calls me Alma."

Me: "Damn! My daddy still calls me mami."

Alma: "Your daddy. You had a visit with him, right?"

Me: "Yeah. No. But I saw Zane. Sort of."

Alma: "Okay . . . Well, when I was real little I had visits with my dad. My mother would put ribbons in my hair. I'd wait and wait until my braids were loose. I'd chew the ribbons to shreds."

Me: "I'm starting to forget what he smells like. What his cheek feels like."

Alma: "Macy! You can't let that happen. It happened to me. Get your dictionary out. Write it down."

So I do. Alma reads over my shoulder as I go.

We were at the Super S (See S for Super). Zane was staring at a blonde on the cover of a *Hustler.* She wore a belt, but she didn't have no pants to be holding up—or anything else either. Some fool had framed the magazine between a box of Captain Crunch and Fruity Pebbles. I snatched it from Zane's sticky fingers and smacked him with it on the back of the neck.

My mother came up behind me like she do and smacked *me* on the back on the neck. I smacked Zane again because I couldn't smack her. She smacked me again and pushed me face first into the popcorn.

"Come here, Daddy," my mother said in the baby voice Zane and my daddy liked. (ICK.) Then she opened her arms and pushed him against her ginormous breastices. (Double ICK.)

"Can anyone say cooties?" I said to Zane. He flipped me the finger, then went back to sucking his thumb.

"What's going on?" Daddy said.

"Look, Daddy." I waved the nudie mag at him. I did a double take. "I didn't even know private parts had all those parts. I mean, what is that?" I was going to have to investigate. I pulled out my pants at the elastic waistband to take a peek.

Daddy was not down with my compare-contrast. "Don't be doing that!" he said. He snatched the magazine away like I was touching the lid of a toilet seat and smacked my hand away from my pants.

"Why not, Daddy?" I pointed to Monsterbaby buried in my mom's chest. "Zane had it first anyway!"

"You had this, Daddy?" Daddy said. He held up the magazine, flipped a few pages, and cracked a smile.

"He's a bad boy," my mom cooed, rubbing his hair.

"Hey," Daddy said to my mother, "whatchu think of this page, baby?" I tried to look and Daddy waved me off.

I rolled my eyes and walked to the chip aisle to look at all the flavors of Doritos that I couldn't have. I smashed pork rinds to dust inside their bags. Then I heard my dad say to my mother, "What, you want him to be a faggot?" To my brother: "You like that, Daddy? Yeah? But you gotta wait, okay? She's too old for you anyway. I'll save it for you."

"Stupit," my mother said, and then there was a clunk. From under the aisle, I could see Zane's poopy butt on the floor.

"What?" Daddy said to my mother. "I only look at her because she reminds me of you."

I peeked over to the other aisle. Daddy was kissing my mother. My mother's eyes were angry and open at first, but as soon as they shut, Daddy shoved *Hustler* under his shirt.

Thirty seconds later . . .

"Put THAT back," my mother barked, yanking Zane out of the candy aisle. "I don't have enough for it!"

THAT was a pack of Bubble Yum. My mother looked at me and nodded her head in the direction of the gum. *Take it,* she mouthed. I looked away like I didn't know what she meant. But I knew.

Cursing under her breaf, she turned away and dragged Zane, kicking and biting, to the counter. "Marlboros, please," she said with Zane in a headlock.

"That'll be six seventy nine."

(Alma: "Seven bucks with tax? Do you know what you can get with that? Two gallons of milk, a bag of rice and beans . . ." I know!)

"*Six seventy nine?*" I shrieked. "FU—"

Daddy slapped his hand over my *CK* and we all walked to the car. Not that we had anywhere to go. We'd been parked outside the Super S for weeks. I sat in the backseat with the hole. It was like sitting with your ass sinking in a toilet. Zane was next to me hugging his knees and rocking.

My mother looked in the rear-view mirror and said to Zane, "Come here, Daddy. You know Mommy got your back."

Zane climbed over the seat of the car and sat on her lap. She handed him the gum she managed to take when she pretended to put it back.

In a split second Zane proclaimed: "THIS AIN'T BUB-BLE YUM! AND YOU ATE SOME OF IT ALREADY!"

My mother shot me the evil eye— (Alma: "Because you didn't steal the gum." Me: "Yup.")

Zane started kicking like a donkey. In national taste tests, blindfolded, Zane preferred Bubble Yum to Big Red ten to none.

After he kicked out the windshield we all slept together in a park tunnel. For a while after everybody fell asleep, I was awake. Listening to everybody breathe at the same time. We was a heartbeat family.

But not anymore.

When I'm done writing, Alma looks at me. "God. This is going to sound totally messed up." She twirls her hair. "But I wish I could remember things like you do. No matter how bad the memory."

I know she's trying to picture her dad. Long pause, then she frowns and blinks. "So, hold up. Did you say you saw Zane at the prison visit or not? I'm confused."

Me: "Uh. Yeah. I saw him. But not *my* him. Somebody else's him. CPS says he's better off now. Meaning he has a better family. That's some bullshit. I'd rather have my fucked-up family than someone else's. Zane didn't have a choice because he's so little, but I do."

Silence. Alma is twirling her hair again. Alma has left the building.

I wave my hand in front of her face. "Here's where you're supposed to say you feel me."

"Yeah. Imagine having a choice."

"That's not what I meant."

Alma don't say anything.

DEAR READER

Noun. Dear rhymes with FEAR.

You are the person that I'm going to hunt down and assassinate when I find out you took my dictionary. I will hit your head so hard against the sink you won't remember anything I wrote, so put it back, you bitch. Yes, the sink. That way I can wash your blood off my hands so I don't ruin my sweatshirt.

DETENTION

Noun. Rhymes with pointless, time-wasting,
most uncreativist shit. Cuz if a kid messes up,
boring the shit out of them might help.

While we work on the writing prompt of the day, Miss Black walks the room and checks homework. She checks on me every day without rolling her eyes. She even frowns when she puts a X by my name as if I ever get anything else. "That's three, Macy," she says this morning. The rule is, whenever I get three Xs in a row, I get detention. Only the detention she gives me is during lunch.

Flash back to the first time this happened, beginning of last year:

"Lunchtime detention? You're kidding me, right, Miss B?"

"No joke, Macy. Or it's in-school suspension with the AP." The AP don't even let you sleep during ISS. *"And if you don't show up—"*

"She will get in her car and track my ass down. She-it. It's a violation of my civil rights."

I eat my burnt shriveled-up hot dog on the way from the cafeteria to Miss Black's classroom. She motions for me to sit down in the front row where she can watch my every move. Damn!

Then she sets a twelve-inch hero cut down the middle on her desk. Imagine slabs of shiny salami, maple ham, provolone cheese, slices of pickle, spicy mustard that clears your sinuses. My jaw drops big enough to fit the whole dang sangwich in all at once. I bury my face in my hands, which I chew on so I don't leap up on her desk and chew on her sangwich.

"Eyes are bigger than my stomach," Miss Black mumbles to herself, taking a bag of jalapeño chips out her lunch box. I'm watching her through my hands like a serial killer watches through the blinds. "Always order too much. Even got a cookie."

I moan. One drop of drool spills out my mouth and onto my jeans so I cover it real fast with my hair. (Yes. This was what Alma calls my pre-bald, pre-sweatshirt period.)

"You know what," Miss Black says, putting down her sangwich without having tooken one bite. "I can't be eating all this. A girl has to watch her figure!" (This was when Fiancé was just her "significant other." Significant—yeah, I'd say. Ain't no man ever gonna come between me and a sangwich like that.)

I wipe the drool off my face before I lower my hands.

"Maybe you could get caught up on some homework, Macy. Then, if you got the time, split some of this with me?"

I proofread. Imagine if life was like one of these paragraphs where you could insert or delete shit at will. Delete Daddy being at the wrong place at the wrong time. Insert a mom for Yasmin, so she learned how to be a mom and I could have a grandma.

Miss Black ain't eating. She's cleaning and organizing closets. She's recycling perfectly good paper, a binder, spirals, and a pile of books.

I'm done. But I don't say anything for a minute. I wish I could *just stick the sangwich in my pocket. I don't want to be the monkey rewarded for doing my tricks.*

"Well?" Miss B says.

I push the paper to the top of my desk. "Done."

"Help yourself to lunch. I got to do some copying." She grabs the cookie and takes a bite. Picks up a stack of papers and leaves me in the room. Alone. Miss Black is cray-cray.

I look to the right. I look to the left. Nobody yet. Only a matter of time though before some teacher sticks her head in, sees me, and accuses me of sneaking in here. I launch myself at the salami like I got shot out a cannon. Devour the sangwich in chunks and layer by layer. Realize while I'm licking my fingers that I didn't leave Miss Black her half of the chips.

Oops.

I wipe my hands on my pants. Pace. Pull out tonight's homework. More grammar and a essay. In five minutes I do what I generally can't do in five hours. I finish Part 1. Stick it on Miss Black's desk with a IOU: PART 2, TOMORROW. I PROMISE.

I look at the clock. I got five minutes. Miss Black is still not back. I start backing out the room. Detour to the recycling bin. I mean, reduce, reuse, recycle, right?

Can't explain it. I may not read any of it but I want it all.

I close the door a little. Shove as much "trash" as I can into my backpack until I'ma tip over. I wonder, could I get detention again tomorrow?

DISTURBED

Adjective. Synonym: Me.

It's no secret that I'm disturbed. I hate all people and the promises they make. I hate the shit they say when you know what they're really gonna do. Everybody got their fingers crossed behind their back including me. I hate kids because one day they just gonna be a people too. I hate everyone. I hate me. I hate you. Fuck you. (And PS, Alma ain't a people. She's a person.)

Fuck you for sitting there. Fuck anyone for sitting anywhere. Fuck you for reading this. Don't you have better things to do?

DEEPEST

Adjective. AKA: Secret. AKA: Truth.
AKA: The hole you didn't know was there.

George and I dance in our seats. Alma's AP class files in behind Miss Link to mix and mingle with our degenerate asses.

Alma's teacher, Miss Link, argues with Miss Black like she do every time we combine. Miss Black ignores her like always and does whatever she planned to do in the first place.

Miss Black passes out little slips of paper. She sets a big bowl on her desk. She holds up a long lighter.

She has our attention.

Gum stops being popped. Heads look up from phones. George stops combing his coat.

Alma's teacher pays attention too. Her inner monologue is written all over the wrinkles on her forehead.

Miss Black: "Today you'll write down your darkest fear." She flicks a lighter. "When you're done, toss it in this bowl."

Miss Black scribbles on the board. *Narrative Writing: Dig Deep!*

Alma arranges her pencil on her desk next to two erasers and a teeny tiny stapler. But nobody hates Alma. (See B for Bestie.)

Kid with the crunchy mohawk: "Man, when I was a kid, I made sure every part of me was covered with a blanket at night. Like the blanket was axe-murderer proof."

Me to Alma: "At night I got on every light in the house including the closets. If your house is dark, people don't think you're home. So they get to thinking—maybe they'll stop by. Help themselves to your TV, your bling . . . Then they help themselves to you." (See K for Kitty.)

Alma: "Dang, Macy. That's dark. If I wasn't afraid before—"

Me: "You should be. I am. Because it don't matter how many times I lock the door at night—Yasmin is just going to let in the exact kind of asshole I was trying to lock out."

Alma: "Oh, sweetie."

Sweetie. Alma is the only person on the planet earth who would ever dare to call me that.

Alma pats my hand and turns to her blank slip of paper. Curtains her desk with her hair so no one can see. Not even me.

I sit up and crane my neck. "What's yours?"

Alma shrugs but still won't let me see. WTF???

"What? You once ate without a napkin? You only combed your hairs 99 times?"

Alma turns around so fast, her hair whips my face: "Yes, Macy. That's it." She turns around again, but this time I duck her hair.

For real? She really isn't going to show me? I'm confused. I do what my counselor does to me. I lean in and whisper into her hair: "You are tapping your foot, Alma. I think you are angry. Am I right that you are angry?"

"Shhhh!" Alma. The only person who could shoosh me and not have her neck under my shoe.

Alma leans on her elbow. I tap it. "Uh, could I borrow a—"

She slams the pencil on my desk. Yup. She's pissed. She flips her hair so I can't see her face. Obese Kid: "Rats!"

Like ten kids jumping on their chairs: "AHHHHH!"

Obese Kid: "No!! I mean, like I'm. You know. Afraid of them—don't even play like you're not!"

Me to no one because Alma isn't listening: "Rats? One time, at home, a rat came swimming up through my toilet. Straight from a squat I launched up three feet in the air. I'm thinking of a career as a stuntman." She don't laugh.

Pretty Girl: "Cockroach!"

Like ten kids: "AHHHHH!"

Miss Black: "No no no no no. If you can say it out loud, it isn't your deepest darkest fear. It has to be something you cannot speak, but can write."

Pretty Girl: "NO, FOR REAL! A cockroach!! It's crawling out of Mina's backpack!!"

Me: "Aw. It's leaving home. Probly for the first time." I flip off a sneaker and *FUÁCATA!* Score. There should be a category for my talents in the Olympics. The GettOlympics.

Obese Kid whispers and points to me: "*She* scares me."

"Hey!" I tell Big Boy. "Write it! Don't say it!"

Miss Black flips off the lights. It actually gets quiet. I look around the room. George is carving his deepest fear into his desk. V-A-N. V-A-N.

Poor George. That's how his little sister died. She thought a white van was a ice cream truck. Whoever was in it pulled her in and drove off with everybody screaming and running behind it. George tried to jump on the back and got hurt real bad. By the time they found the van, his sister had been tortured to death. Every year people throw roses all along the street where the van turned the corner and got away.

Miss Black flips on somebody called Baytoven. I get serious. My deepest fear. Not darkness. Not rats—not even after the toilet incident.

Let me explain first. I'ma do a compare-contrast: Here at school and at home.

Okay, at school the bafrooms ain't pretty. But, if somebody vomits it's like the bat signal goes up and Pepe comes running. There's a rat? Pepe will do everything short of swimming through the toilet to catch its flea-bitten ass. Some kids call him grandpa.

Could be rain, snow, sleet, hail. I still get here at 7:30 every day because as long as you get through those front doors, it's gonna be dry and warm. Pepe opens them up for me and I can feel the blast of heat—feel it—not imagine it.

At home? Last night, the temp dropped twenty degrees. My mother offered for me to sleep in her bed to keep warm like Zane used to do. Like I used to do waaaay back in the day. But waaaay back in the day my mother's bed did not have cooties. Me, rathering to die of hypnothermia than Ebola, chose to sleep under the couch cushions.

At school if there's a arch criminal on the premises we go on lockdown. We do not wear spandex for them and ask if they have a cigarette.

At school, there are different rooms for different things. Ain't one room for everything. I swear one night after one of Yasmin's dates I threw out the table. Woman brought it back in, though. Zane and I had to do a anti-cootie ritual. At school, there is a room for eating. I can smell whatever is on the menu around nine. When I eat, all anyone wants from me is to throw out my tray when I'm done. NOTHING else.

At school you celebrate things All The Time.

At home, time stops.

It stops on Fridays at 3:15. The last day I know where the food's coming from. You're fucked if it's a three-day weekend.

So my deepest fear . . . is that someone will find out . . .

I scribble it down real tiny.

I HEART school

Even Alma don't know. And if she don't know, no one ever will.

I look at Alma. She making a tent with her arms to cover up her desk. Like always, she folds her paper like origami. This time a swan. (Which will make it easier to find.) She tosses it into the bowl.

I have a lightbulb. My new greatest fear. It makes me more afraid than anyone finding out my secret. What is it that I don't know about Alma?

She's still writing.

Don't have much time to think about it, though. George is done carving V-A-N into his desk and is standing up. Somebody has to stop him from throwing the desk at Miss Black's bowl and setting it all on fire.

DIDN'T

Contraction. A verb and a adverb crunched together
till they both break. As in: I didn't do it. Why didn't
you tell me? You didn't ansuh the question.

George ends up throwing all the shit on Miss Black's desk on
the floor. After I chill him out, the counselor and the AP escort
him and his coat to the office. Kids raise their hands to help her
clean it up. I get a lightbulb.

Me: "No. Stop. I'll clean it up."

Kids no longer volunteer. I get up and spic-and-span
her desk. Oh, look. One piece of paper got kicked under it.
I reach under and grab it. I can't help it if the swan flew up
my sleeve.

Alma and I part ways, her to the world of advanced
placement and honors and me to the Planet of the Apes—AKA
regular and remedial. A lifetime later we come back together at
the cafeteria.

Me: "So. English. It was . . . uh . . . interesting."

Alma stops sipping her water bottle. "Yes. Miss Link thought
the fire was very inappropriate—a violation of fire code."

"But the activity was thought provocating, no?"

"Thought provoking? The—wait. Wait! You didn't?!"

"No. I didn't. Prove it."

Alma slams the table. "Where's my swan, Macy?"

"Swan? What you mean talking about a swan?"

"Don't make me search that sweatshirt."

I'm in no mood to have anybody touch me, even her. "Nah. I can't fight. I got my period. I'm sorry." I pull out the swan and flap it. "Actually, no, I'm not sorry."

Alma snatches it. "I trusted you!"

"You trusted Miss Black. I didn't make no promises. What's all this about you being afraid of—*you*?"

Alma puts her head down. Buries herself in hair. I part some of it.

Me: "If you don't tell me what you mean by being afraid of yourself, I will tell everyone"—I drop my voice and cover my mouth—"you listen to country music."

Alma pops her head out of her arm tent. "You wouldn't. How is that fair? How does that even make sense? If I don't tell you my secret, you'll tell one of my secrets?"

"Not fair, but genius, I think."

Alma looks away. "I'm afraid of *me*, okay, because . . . last night my mother was working. So it was just me with the kids. Normally this is no big thing. But two of the kids had the stomach flu. And when that happens it spreads like the plague. I cannot afford to get sick right now. So I'm trying to take care of them without contaminating myself."

"Cooties."

"Yes. I'm cleaning up throw-up and spraying with Lysol. I'm trying to keep my other brothers from stepping in it. I'm trying to cook dinner, but I can't leave the flame on the stove when I'm running to take care of my sick babies. Because Wally uses anything—blocks, his truck—to climb up to the cabinets and the fridge. So I have to keep turning off the burner and I get ang—frustrated. I take all of Wally's trucks away and he screams. I check on the rice and it's mush. I turn up the heat and run to clean up the sick bucket. William's eating crayons. Gisselle's drawing in vomit. I lost it."

Me: "What did you do?"

Alma: "I locked all the kids out so I could clean up. By then they were all contaminated. I had to run showers for them. The rice burnt to a crisp. My mom was pissed."

Me: "Lost it, huh? Did you even yell? Break anything? *This* is your darkest secret?"

"No! Of course not." She whispers, "This time I didn't lose it for real—just on the inside. But I felt like I was losing it on the outside."

"Seriously. You're scared because of a feeling? And you can't share that with nobody? I'd be scared if you *didn't* feel that way. Be checking your ass for wires and a battery. And PS, Alma, they're not *your* babies."

Alma: "Really? So Zane's not your baby?"

Me: "A'ight. Back up. Point taken. What I mean is, feeling angry at something like that is normal. Feeling angry about nothing—or about everything—ain't."

Alma flaps her swan. "I feel angry all the time."

"Really? You're like the Hulk, aren't you?" I pretend to bust out of my sweatshirt.

Alma's on the verge of tears and laughing at the same time. "I don't show it. I can't. I'm not like you."

Me: "Where does it all go?"

Alma: "Nowhere."

The first bell dings. Alma gets up and tosses her swan onto her tray like trash. I grab it. And her pizza. The only thing she ate was the crust.

We kiss good-bye and go our separate ways till after school.

DOLPHIN

Noun. When a dolphin has a baby, other dolphins
will circle the one giving birf to protect it.
And *we* the ones higher up on the food chain?

A bunch of kids are crowded around the art teacher's desk. On the wall behind it is a giant wall calendar with a picture of a dolphin on top and a giant X marking next Tuesday underneath. Art Lady says she loves the way a dolphin smiles. She points to the X and tells us that every year, kids get her dolphins for her birfday. She shows off her dolphin earrings from last year's valedictorian.

I look up from my desk. "Hint, hint," I say to all the kids. "Personally, I like to think just my presence is a gift."

The art teacher glares toward me but not at me.

A left-handed kid takes out a planner and writes down *dolphins.*

"Shit, is that how you get extra credit around here?"

"That's enough, Macy."

"You know how much of that dolphin shit I see at the junkyard I pass every day? Maybe for your birfday you should get less dolphin shit and do more for actual dolphins."

"Office! Now!"

Thank you, Art Lady. I was craving something from the candy bowl anyway.

Principal: "I really don't have time for this today, Macy. I'm short on staff in the office as it is. What is the beef between you and the art teacher?"

Me: "She just hates me."

Principal: "Do you think if you actually did any of her assignments she would hate you less?"

Me: "I do her assignments. Some of them." (A couple.) "I just do them in my way. Why does everything have to be only one way at this school?"

Principal: "Macy! In the adult world we don't always get our way. You have to grow up—"

Me: "Grow up? I been grown up forever. When can I just be a fucking kid?"

Principal: "Language!" (Sigh.) "You're coming with me on my rounds. Move."

I zip my backpack. Check to see if the pockets are closed right. Scratch my temple because of a deep thought. La Jefe's foot starts to tap. I count to three—THEN I move. Like I'm wearing lead sneakers.

La Jefe takes me on her morning route to the Child Development room. This is one of Alma's electives! In middle school, Alma got a award for volunteering to read to the kindergartners during her recess. She would sing and us kids would stick our heads into the library just to listen.

Principal: "Find a seat in the back, young lady."

I find a desk that creaks every time I move—which is A Whole Lot. I see Alma in the front of the class. She is sitting in a rocking chair. She looks up at me and nods. A big-ass book is spread on her lap. Kids are at her feet. I cozy up in my sweatshirt to listen to her read. But it's hard because none of the little kids are listening. They're squirmy and loud.

Something's wrong with Alma. She's reading all the words, but she's not doing any voices. She's talking where she should sing. Is she sick? I lean forward. She's not coughing or sneezing. She's smiling. Sort of. At least her face is in the upright position. For some reason I get to thinking about that dolphin poster again. And its smile. And whether it's really smiling at all.

Then Somebody is touching me. Somebody vertically impaired. That Somebody throws a book at my desk.

Somebody, AKA the Pre-K Kid, says, "Read this to me. You have to do what I say."

"Me?" I squint my eyes. Grit my teeth. Crack my knuckles. "Ain't you afraid of me?"

Pre-K Kid: "Why? I had a aunt who had chemo. Don't worry. You could get a wig."

Before I burst into hysterical laughter, I feel it. I don't have to look up to know the principal and the teacher are ready to tackle me. And that's one reason why I get up, go sit in a beanie chair with the kid, and open up the book, *Green Eggs and Ham*.

Me: "You know, these is the only kinds of eggs and ham in my house."

Pre-K Kid, tilting her head: "My mom makes me pancakes. I like pancakes. Sometimes she makes them with chocolate chips. But not green. You should come to my house for breakfast."

For a minute, I contemplate it. Mmm. Pancakes. Then I contemplate the look on the mother's face when she opens the door.

Me: "Hello, your kid invited me—"
Mom: "Ahhhhhhhhhhhhhh!!!!!"

I look at the kid for the first time and flinch. This little girl has curly hair like my baby sister did. If my baby sister had lived, she could be this girl.

I do what I've figured out Alma is doing. I read to the little girl with one side of my brain and think about something else with the other side.

My baby sister was born a preemie like me. I had to stay at home with Zane so my parents could look after her at the hospital. While they were gone, I was on the phone with Alma 24/7. She schooled me on how to make baby formula. She told me to quit trying to make milk out of my tit-breasts because only Mary Mother of God could do that. As you might imagine, I tried anyway. I had to give up after Zane was getting too interested in audience participation. I stole formula. (See I for I Don't Want to Talk About It.) I learned how to boil the water but cool it right so the baby's mouth wouldn't get burned.

When my parents brought my baby sister home, they looked like the living dead. My mom had to have a C-section. She got fired from her job at the diner because she missed so much work. They put Baby Girl in her crib and collapsed in their bedroom. In the middle of the night she cried, but neither of them moved. I wheeled her crib by my couch. Stared inside. My little girl was so tiny, I knew it wasn't right. Zane kept staring through the bars. He kept shoving stuffed animals in.

I hissed, "Stop shoving shit in there!"

I cleared the crib and kissed Baby Girl's head. She had a whole crop of hair. I checked her chest to make sure she was breathing. I felt bad for her. I wondered how long before we all wiped that smile off her tiny face. I took pictures of that smile with my mother's phone.

The next day my mom wheeled Baby Girl back into her room all pissed off. But the next night, I was up making formula. After that, the crib was permanently parked next to my couch at night.

A week later my mother came out of her coma. I remember her trying to dress Baby Girl in a itchy pink tutu outfit that was way too big, saying, "She's a perfect little girl."

I asked, "Isn't there something more comfortable you could dress her in?"

"Shut up, Macy. What, you think you know everything now?"

The baby started to whimper. I reached out to pick her up.

"I got this," my mom said, glaring, grabbing her and rocking her too fast. Baby Girl cried louder.

"Hey, Yasmin, let her do it," my daddy said, walking into the room. "You need your rest." He picked Baby Girl up and handed her to me. He planted a kiss on the baby's forehead and started walking Yasmin out the room massaging her shoulders. "Yeah," my daddy said, "she's going to make it. She knows it."

And I did do it. Rock her. Change her. Even maybe sing a little. What I didn't do was sleep. At all. Three days later, I blacked out. Literally. It was light when I last remembered being awake and dark when I woke up. I jumped up. What day was it? Oh my God! Did Baby Girl wake up and I not hear it? Shit! But the house was completely quiet. Nobody was up but me.

I peeked into the crib. At some point Zane had stuck in all these stuffed animals again. I threw them out. Fuck! How many times did I tell him? A stuffed horse hit the wall right on its plastic eyeballs. But Baby Girl didn't move. I looked in the crib to fix her blanket. Baby Girl still had that smile. I reached in to touch her face. She was stone cold.

Baby Girl was dead.

What happened next? My mother said things to me she tried to take back later. (See I for I Don't Want to Talk About It.) I said things to Zane about those stuffed animals I shouldn't have said.

My dad just broke shit.

Pre-K Kid tugs on my sleeve. She has another book in her hand. I blink.

Pre-K Kid: "Stop talking to yourself. Read this."

But now the teacher clears her throat. The class and that little girl, my baby girl, race to their seats. Alma piles up all the books she read to them this period. A little kid reaches his hands up to Alma to be picked up. She leans down and pats him on the head and shoos him away.

Dolphins don't smile because they're happy. They don't smile at all. We see what we want to see.

Like my parents wanted to see in my baby sister's face.

My sister didn't smile because she knew she was gonna make it. She smiled because she knew she wasn't.

DO NOT DISTURB

Verb. No vacancy.

If you stay at a fancy hotel, you eat at a restaurant every night. Food is not served in old potato chip bags. Food is served on plates. At a fancy hotel, they clean the room every day, not just if CPS is coming. They make the bed with crisp sheets, not sheets with crispy things on them. If you want privacy, you put a sign on your door. This tells the maid to stay the hell out. She'll have to come back to get you those fresh towels. Fresh does not mean you stick them in the dryer at Mr. Bubbles Laundromat because you can't afford the washer and at least the heat will kill the bugs. I learned about all these things from movies like the one I'm watching now.

The floor starts shaking. My mother is moaning about Papi, and she don't mean her daddy or mine. Mr. Guest snorts like a pig. I turn the movie volume high. This tells them that I'm awake. This tells Mr. Guest to come out the bedroom with his clothes on. This tells them Do Not Disturb.

He comes out the room smoking a cigarette. He walks to the fridge for a beer. I worry that besides his socks, the only thing he is wearing is the refrigerator door. I turn the TV up. It's my force field.

Mr. Guest comes over and stands by the couch in his underwear. He burps and takes a swig of beer. "So you like that new TV I got you, ah?" He's standing so close I can smell his sweat and her sweat all mixed up. His thing is like a foot away from me. I move over. He sits down.

"Manny!" my mother calls. "Where you at?"

He don't move. I turn the TV louder and louder. He grabs my hand on the remote and lowers the volume. "What is this shit you're watching?"

He yawns and scratches his balls. "Maybe one of these days you want to say thank you." He puts his hand on mine.

I rip my hand away, throw the remote at the TV, and run toward the front door. "You're gonna pay for that if you broke it!" Mr. Guest yells.

"Pay for what?" my mother yells, coming out the bedroom in a sheet. She sees me unlatch the door and go out. "Macy!"

In fancy hotels, the doorman holds the door for you. Your mother don't come screaming out the door half necked in a sheet. I run down the steps and lock myself in the car. I hot-wire it so I can listen to the radio. I'm in that hotel. Setting my baggage down for someone else to deal with. I breathe on the car window then write with my finger:

DO NOT DISTURB

EVEN YOU

Noun. These things happen.

It could happen to you. It could happen to anyone.

FABULOSO

Noun. Forget Lysol, Pledge, Mr. Clean,
this is a all-purpose product.

My mother cleans the house. Which means she hides all
her pot.

Me: "CPS is coming?"

My mother: "Tomorrow. They never say the time." She
actually hands me a phone. "Here."

Me: "Really?"

My mother: "Don't get too excited. I give it a couple days
tops before Steve shuts it off."

Steve? I don't recollect no Steve. A car horn honks outside.

Me: "Not Steve, right?"

My mother: "Later!"

The door shuts behind her. After surfing the web for a few
minutes on Steve's data plan, I call.

Me to Alma: "They're coming."

Alma: "Who's coming?"

Me: "THEM."

Alma: "CPS? Again?"

Me: "They come every month. With board games. But I know the real game now. And how to beat them at it."

Alma: "What are you going to do?"

Me: "An exorcism, that's what."

Alma to herself: *I'm not going to ask. No. I can't stand it.*

Alma to me: "Macy? Why an exorcism?"

"Because that's the only thing that's gonna get this house clean. I went to the dollar store. I'm going to use Fabuloso, a all-purpose cleaning product. Better than holy water. Let's say you have a lot of guests. And a lot of stains. Fabuloso cleans that shit right up. I wish I could make all the guests dip their hands in it before they come in."

Alma: "Right. I get it. I use it too. Peas, carrots. Poop, pee. It works. Sorry, baby's crying. Good luck! If anyone can do it you can!"

After I tie a bandanna around my mouth, I grab my trusty bottle of Fabuloso. A archaeologist would have a easier time excavating a fucking pyramid than cleaning our floors. Or walls. The ceiling too? Damn it. Where to start?

First thing I spray is the door handle. It's deadly, man. If there's ever another Black Plague scientists will trace that shit to us.

With old socks, I scrub down the kitchen floor. I swear if the world ended right now I could survive forty days with all the Kraft Macaroni and Cheese caked on it.

On to the couch. I'm going to need a ancient spell to clean this motherfoe. I scroll Steve's playlist. I turn on LL Kool J's "Mama Said Knock You Out." That will do. I need a sacred drink, something to put me in the right frame of mind. Kool-Aid ain't gonna do it. But Fabuloso? It's the next best thing.

I'm not stupit, though. I'm just gonna take one gulp. One, two, three . . . It burns . . . I'm ready.

I scrape and scrub and start to realize the color of the couch now is not the color it started with. Nasty. I hear something and turn down the bass. Is that screaming? I press my ear to the cushions. Sprinkle more Fabuloso. "I command you in the name of—"

For the first time, I realize I'm smelling something new. I inhale deeply. Normally my brain smells of fire and smoke: cigarette and pot smoke. But for right now—it smells of lavender. I swear a weight has been taken off me because I feel lighter. I rub some on my hands. Every bad thing I have ever done is clear! I head toward the mattress. This will be my biggest challenge yet. I may have to take another swig.

Ring!

Me to Alma: "I sip a took."

Alma: "You what a what?"

Me: "TOOK. A. PISS. SIP!"

Alma: "Of what?"

Me: "You know."

Alma: "Oh my God—you didn't. You drank Fabuloso? Call Poison Control!"

Me: "On. One. On. I mean no! I fnk my fun is numb."

Alma: "I'm calling."

Me: "Neth you have ot hang pu on me. You reven do that way-two call ginth right."

Alma: "Okay—okay. But don't drink anymore! Just talk to me, Macy. Can you tell me why?"

Me: "Be to I want Fabuloso!"

Alma: "You *are* Fabuloso!"

Me: "No, no on! I want to be Fabuloso in my soulllll."

Alma: "Macy, get up. You need fresh air."

Me: "Nah. I'ma nap."

Alma: "Get up, bitch."

Me: "Ut id foo all me?"

Alma: "Get up and open the damn door, bitch. Your neighbors at 3211 said they're gonna kick your ass."

Me: "Ait. hTaw did ouy say? I gonna ick er ass?"

I hang up. I get up. I open the door. Whoever it was must've started running. I run to catch them. After about two blocks, I stop running. I begin to think, Alma *tricked me*. I also begin to think, *I do not feel Fabuloso*. I throw up. I half-crawl, half-walk back.

Make it through the door and trip on a screaming phone. "Macy blah blah blah this instant!" I tell it I'm going to nap on the porch because some idiot sprayed the whole house with Fabuloso.

FINE PRINT

Noun. Rhymes with squint.

Miss CPS sneezes as she walks through the door and my mother walks out of it. My mother can't be present when me and Miss CPS have one of our little convos.

Me: "Smells Fabuloso, don't it?"

Miss CPS: "Achoo!" She tilts her head. "Is this a new couch?"

Me: "Heh heh heh."

Miss CPS: "Okay. Well, I already talked to your mom. She did quite a job cleaning up in here!"

Me: "Yes! She worked till she dropped. Ain't you going to take a note about that? Snap a pic?"

Miss CPS: "Um, yes. Of course. Absolutely! Maybe you can open a window while I do that?"

I do. "Okay. Well." I walk to the door and open it. "Bye!"

Miss CPS: "You're funny! So I thought we might hang out and play Spit."

Me: "S-p-i-t? I must admit I'm intrigued." I wave her to the new table.

Miss CPS running her hands over it: "Nice."

And now a word from our sponsors: Did your last table have cigarette burns in it because your mom and her guests kept using Cheeto bags for ashtrays? Duck tape on the legs? Did it have knife stabs from playing Five Finger Fillet? Blood stains from a guest trying to get fancy? Razor cuts in from the coke? No problemo! If you do it with Manny you get a brand new(ish) one. No money down. Just you.

I like the card game. It does not actually involve spit, but it does involve speed. Each person gets half the deck. You each lay down a card so there are two piles. You each say *Spit!*

I like saying *Spit* loud. Each player slaps down a card on either pile. If, like, you see a card that has a jack, you pound down a queen or a ten. If you see a ten, you could put down a jack. You have to go in order but not in one certain order. I like choices. The object is to get rid of as many cards as possible as fast as possible. When you have no more cards you slap the lowest pile.

Maybe sometimes I slap the CPS worker instead of the pile. Hee hee hee.

I win the first round. "No one can outslap me."

Miss CPS shakes out her hand. "I feel that!" She checks a text. My stomach has been growling the whole time, but now Miss CPS can hear it.

Miss CPS: "We'll pause the game so you can fix yourself a snack."

THIS IS A TEST. Fail and get a one-way ticket to foster care!!! PLEASE STAND BY.

I walk to the fridge like I'm walking the plank. Sweet-timin it, I open the fridge. A full fridge.

Kool-Aid winks at me from a pitcher. Kool-Aid, the nectar of the gods. Twinkies, Ho Hos, and Little Debbie cakes stick out the cabinet. There is milk without chunks in it. Fruity Pebbles. Yabba-dabba delicious! Thank you again, Mr. Guest.

I fix myself a bowl. I stare at it. The milk is turning blue.

Miss CPS: "Don't let me stop you."

She isn't stopping me from nothing. But Daddy's words are. *You let me know if anything's going on, okay?* I can't eat it.

Until Miss CPS gets on the *do you want to talk about it* eyes. "Is anything wrong?"

I shake my head. I eat. Miss CPS plays with her phone until I'm done.

Miss CPS: "So Macy, how is school?"

Me: "I don't know. Why don't you ask it yourself?"

Miss CPS: "Ha. All right. Anything new in your life?"

Me: "I thought I found God. But then, shit, I lost him."

Miss CPS: "You always keep it interesting."

Me: "That's me. Here for your entertainment."

Miss CPS: "Well, I'm here for you if you need me."

Me: "If I need you to take me away from my mother? Uh, I'm good. But thanks."

She leaves. I hurl all the food in a Hefty bag and launch it out the door. I stick my finger down my throat and throw up blue and red and yellow—the only rainbow I have ever seen.

FIELD TRIP

Verb. Emphasis on the word trip, as in tripping out.

My mother comes into the house holding a giant Hefty bag of groceries. The bag is slit on the side, and she's struggling to hold everything in.

"What the fuck, Macy? I found this outside. A milk gallon exploded! Why did you throw the groceries out on the lawn?"

"Give me a minute to make something up."

"Fuck you. You know how much money Manny—"

"Yeah, yeah, Manny spent all his crack money on us. Maybe if you'd get a job—"

"Shut up, bitch, I been applying all over the place!" She tried to get a job at WalMars, she tells me. The leader of the WalMartians called her, she says, and left a voicemail.

She forgets all about the groceries and pulls out her phone. Puts the message on speaker so I can hear. It's a manager. He says *Thank you for applying. We have had over one thousand applications. We are sorry to say we cannot offer you a position at this time, but we encourage you to apply again and wish you good luck on all your future endeavors.*

"What the fuck?" she says.

What the fuck, I think. Over a thousand applications to be a cashier? "Don't sweat it, Ma. Probly easier to get into Harvard."

"It don't matter," she says. "I interviewed for a job at the Taco Garage." The Taco Garage is called that because you can get tacos on the inside and get your car washed on the outside.

When my mother gets the call from the manager of Taco Garage three days later, it's like we've won the lottery.

She says to me and everybody she can get on the phone that we are going to buy our own washing machine *and* a dryer. We could get a new stove in the kitchen (See B for Burners) so we can cook without being electrocuted. I say, "How about some toilet paper?"

She says, "How about just a sock?" This means I should stuff it. In my pie hole.

I say, "I need socks too." She throws a shoe at me. "Shoes too!" I say, ducking a flying Big Red. *Kaboom.* "And Fabuloso!!!" (See F for Fabuloso.)

On my mother's first day of work, she says George and I can stop by for some free chips. George and I head over after school to see this momentous shit take place. Somebody is going to be a boss of my mother. Somebody is going to tell my mother where, when, how, and how much.

George and I watch my mother work. She carries around a pad and pencil and asks people what they want, very official-like. She says words I have never heard her say like: *What can I get for you?* This is different from her usual: *What, are your damn legs broken? Get it yourself.* But like the immortal Tupac said, I Ain't Mad. I like watching her write down orders. When

I peek over her shoulder I can see the fancy swoop of her letters. I've never really seen her write anything before. I mean, I'm the one who writes all the school notes, except for her signature.

"You know, George," I say, licking salsa off my thumb, "maybe things are looking up. I bet Yasmin gets to take home free food, too!"

George sings, "A T-bone steak, cheese, egg, Welch's grape!"

"Maybe she can be a manager someday. Maybe I can work for the Taco Garage and then take over the business one day," I tell George, passing him a lime.

My mother's boss overhears me. Chuey says, "Forget about one day. How old are you? Eighteen?"

"Fifteen."

"Um. Maybe you can bus tables. Make a few bucks in the back, doing dishes. You come talk to me later, okay?"

"Okay!"

For the first time in a long time, my crystal ball ain't as black as a bowling ball.

FEED

Verb. You are what you eat. (And yes I know feed comes before field, you obsessive motherfoe.)

I'm on the phone with Alma. I'm on hold. Alma is feeding a baby. Alma is always feeding someone or something. They got three dogs too. Feeds everyone except herself.

Alma: "I'm back. So, anyway, our latest project in Tomorrow's Leaders is to collaborate with local artists for the multicultural fair next week. My partner and I are working on making an African shield."

Me: "What part of Africa?"

Alma: "What do you mean, what part?"

"I mean, you go up one block in my neighborhood and the gang signs change. So how does the whole continent of Africa got one kind of shield?"

"I don't know." I can hear her thinking about my question. "Anyway, we're carving them out of real wood and they'll be on display at the Cultural Arts Center."

"Cool. Do they work?"

"What do you mean, do they work?"

"I mean, can they really shield you against anything?" I'm picturing walking to school with my machete (See C for Clang) and a shield.

Alma: "No, Macy. They are art."

Me: "Art sounds useless, no offense."

"None taken. Why are you breathing like that? You sound like a prank caller."

"I'm climbing the gutter on the side of my house."

"You're what? How are you talking to me if you're scaling the side of your house?"

"I taped the phone to the side of my face."

"Macy! What's with you and tape? Are you crazy?"

Me: "You already know the answer to that."

Alma: "Why are you climbing the side of your house?"

Me: "Hey! I'm waving at you. If you climbed on your roof with a pair of binoclu-binoclulars—thingamahjigs, you could probly see me!"

"Macy, you get down, right this instant!"

"You said right this instant. You are so adorable."

"MACY."

"Okay. Okay. In five minutes. I have a plan." I figure I have five minutes total to get away with it. "I'm getting out my wire cutters."

Alma to me: "Why? Whyyyyyyyyyyyyyyyyyyyyyy?!!!"

Me: "Because nobody bought this cable anyway. Half the block is stealing cable with this line."

Alma to God: "WHYYYYYYY?!!!"

Me: "Because I want to see what is going to happen."

Alma: "You can't do this, Macy." She says it like I'm about to give the codes to nuclear silos to North Korea.

Me: "It's done. I only have four minutes to get the other box cut."

Alma: "Macy, you are going to electrocute yourself!"

Me: "Probly. It wouldn't be the first time." (See B for Burner.)

Alma: "Blah blah blah blah blah blah." She talks too fast for me to understand what she is getting all yelly about and also she uses very big words. I think I heard the word *incorrigible*. "And who is gonna cut that tape off the side of your bald head? Not me, okay—"

"Yes you will. Love you. Shhhh."

Seriously, I now have three minutes. Even Spider Man would be stressed. I scale a telephone pole and let my wire cutters do their work.

Back on my roof, as I'm balancing on the gutter, I imagine the scene taking place on my block. People are aiming their remotes at their TVs like Dwayne Johnson pointing a M4A1 Carbine. People press down on the power button so hard they suffer thumb disfigurement. (*Have you suffered permanent thumb disfigurement? Call Lawyer Charlie Ton. He'll fight for YOU!*) Just like a banging of drums before the Super Bowl, there will be a banging of remotes against end tables. I swear that I can actually hear it all now.

I mean, people are about to get up from the couch.

Children's toys are violated, their batteries yanked and reinserted into dented remotes. I get out my binocs. I made them myself.

Phone: "BLAHBLAHBLAHBLAH!"

Shit! I almost fall off the roof. (The gutter actually does fall off.) I forgot the phone was still taped to my head. The phone shifts, pulling on my little tiny hairs and skin. "Ow. Ow! Ow!!"

Alma: "Blah blah blah. It's stuck to your scalp, isn't it? Isn't it, Macy?!"

Me: "You think peanut butter would work?"

"That's for gum in your hair! *Hair*—which you haven't grown overnight, I suspect! Do you even have peanut butter?"

"No. Manny's allergic to peanuts."

"Macy! I'm watching the kids, so I can't help! You're going to have to sleep with it on your head."

I aim my binocs over the neighborhood. "Oh, shit. They're coming out!" I tell Alma everything I see.

A man in a Dallas Cowboys cap comes out the door checking the terrain. I can't see his face. He grabs his crotch. He spits. The man with the Dallas Cowboys cap is holding a knife. He may have to cut whatever it is that broke his television. (I stop, drop, and lay as flat as a girl with DDs can.)

Three barefoot girls follow behind him. They are zombies. They definitely have not eaten any brains lately so they are hungry. They don't step off the porch. They watch to see who the lead zombie will kill so the television will turn back on. There are other girl zombies too. I can see them pressed against the windows watching.

A grandmother steps out the house next door. She looks up at the sky. Could *this* have been caused by God? I laugh because—I am GOD.

She looks at her front door in horror. She knows in five seconds the kids will realize the TV don't work.

It is unleashed.

Kids between two and ten pour from doors, out of windows, and off the rooftop, spilling out onto the street. They blink in the sunlight. Boy in a Pokémon shirt: "What do we do now, Uncle?"

Uncle, a boy in a SpongeBob shirt, about three years older than his nephew: "I don't know. I ain't never been past JJs. Let's cross to the other side." And with a wave of Uncle's hand, all the kids fan out and head on to many adventures.

Me: "It is done."

Alma: "And how are you going to get down?"

Me: "I'm gonna—" I look at the gutter crashed to the ground. "Oh shit."

FLY

Noun. As in, a fly in my soup.

Next time George and I stop by the Taco Garage, about a week after my mother's first day, I see a customer with a pointy mustache sit at one of my mother's tables. Mustached dude needs two chairs, one for each ass cheek. George shakes his head and goes to the restroom.

Yasmin steps back and knocks over mustache man's water. She says she is so sorry. He says he would forgive her if she got some of that spilled water on her T-shirt. I expect her to dump that water on his head.

But Chuey swoops in behind her and says, "Well, sir, that depends on how much you're going to tip, right, Yasmin? Go get the man's food, okay? I'll clean up here."

I stand up ready to rip off that man's mustache with my bare hands. George comes back from the restroom. I get him up to speed. He's ready to crack skulls, he's just waiting for me to tell him which one. My mother sees us and shakes her head.

Mouths, *No, please. I need this.* We sit down.

My mother shakes it all off and delivers food to her tables like she is in a competition: World's Top Waitress. Meanwhile George and I count our change to get a pack of baloney down at the corner bodega. If we flip a few of those on mustached man's hood and let those sit, his paint job will be fucked up beyond recognition.

Two seconds later it's like everybody finds a fly in their soup. Everybody at my mother's tables.

First mustached man starts yelling at her. He told her three times that he wanted the Special Number Three, not what she brought him. He says she's no good and he ain't paying.

Chuey says the meal is on the Garage. He gives my mom the eye. Another customer complains. Yasmin gave her the wrong drink. Turns out she gave everybody the wrong everything. I'm thinking mustached man upset her so much, she couldn't concentrate—until my mother throws her notepad down. She locks herself in the bafroom.

I pick up her notepad. I read it. Or try to. WTF? There are fancy loopy letters everywhere. But they are not cooperating. They are not making words.

Chuey goes into the women's room. I stand outside it and crack the door. "Poor baby," he says, "maybe you ain't no good at this. Don't feel bad. But I have an idea. Got it from looking at you."

My mother stops sniffling. "What idea?"

"We just got a liquor license. Gonna set up a margarita bar out back. It's real simple. You and maybe some of your girl-friends can work out there, won't even need a notepad. Less you could find one that's waterproof! You just need a sponge—and a little string."

Turns out Chuey wants my mother and her girlfriends to serve drinks and wash windshields at his car wash. In string bikinis no less. When George and I walk in there a couple days later, there is my mother scrubbing that mustached man's car. There is his hairy finger sticking a five in her bikini string. I guess it's all right if he's giving her a five. Chuey's words echo in my mind: *Maybe you could work here one day.*

"We better be leaving," I say, elbowing George and marching our asses straight out of that Taco Garage.

We go back to my place. Apparently my mother has gotten her first paycheck because there's food. There's Big Red and Oreos and Cap'n Crunch and Chef Boyardee and even milk to put in the bowl.

George plops down on the couch next to me. He sings, spraying chip crumbs, "Doctor doctor I'm so sick. Call the doctor quick quick quick."

Me too. I don't even think I can eat. But the sickness don't last long. The soul is willing but the flesh likes chili cheese. I can't resist a Dorito.

"Hear that?" George asks.

Whatever it is is scratching on the bafroom door. George is my backup. He shadows me. I grab Manny's baseball bat leaning in the corner and tiptoe to the bafroom door. Holding the bat in one hand and the doorknob in the other, I crack the door and swing. I stop myself and hit the door—before I hit the itty bitty puppy dog that trip-traps out. Apparently my mother bought something else with her cash. I decide to name it Washing Machine.

George shrugs and goes back to the television. *Sesame Street* is on and it's doing the letter S, and not even the sudden appearance of a puppy is going to mess with the word *Shizam*.

I pick the dog up by the scruff of the neck and cradle her. Her body is so warm in my arms. I get all the feels. Till I feel her pissing on me.

Maybe Washing Machine's name should be Of Course.

FIRELIGHT

Noun. All light brings is shadows.

That night, my mother comes home super late.

"You quit yet?" I ask.

"Quit? Have you seen these tips?"

"Have I seen your *what*?" I throw her shade. "Nasty."

"These *tips*," my mother enunciates, "got you those Oreos. And a puppy."

"Yeah, I named it Washing Machine." I spit the Oreo I'm chewing onto the rug.

Mr. Guest stops by. "Cute dog."

Fuck you, says Washing Machine.

My mom dumps frozen hot dogs into boiling water. Mr. Guest opens up cabinets. "Got any beans to go with that?"

"Beans? You can't give a dog beans."

"Wait," Mr. Guest says, "ain't you gonna make me none?"

Guess the honeymoon is over, dude.

My mother blows on a hot dog and carries it to the couch. Flips on the TV and hand feeds Washing Machine.

Mr. Guest whines worse than the dog.

"Okay!" My moms sucks her teeth, then gets up and makes another pot of dogs from what's left of the pack. I already ate two raw. The hot dogs don't sit right in Washing Machine's stomach. She poos all over the place. My mother don't get mad, though. (She don't clean it either, damn it.) Mr. Guest just steps right over it. I wrap my hands in plastic bags and get the rags and Fabuloso. I'm the one gotta sleep out here on the couch, motherfoes!

Washing Machine hops on my mother's lap. She talks to the dog in this high-pitched voice like you'd use for a baby and kisses her all over her face.

"Can I get some of that sugar?" Mr. Guests leans toward my mother's face. Until—"Fuck! It tried to bite me!"

"You scared her. She's just a baby."

"Time to put Baby to bed." Mr. Guest stomps toward the bedroom. Washing Machine is kissed and tucked into her bed by the TV.

"If you sing that dog a lullaby, I swear I'ma—"

"Hater!" My mother laughs and follows Mr. Guest to the bedroom. So does Washing Machine.

"Yasmin! Get this fucking dog out of here!"

The dog screeches as it's launched from the bedroom to the hall.

"Welcome to my world." I kick off my sneaks and hop on the couch.

But the dog boomerangs back and starts whining and scratching at the door. After a minute my mother opens the door. "C'mon in, baby," she says, scooping up the dog, "you can sleep with mama."

"What?" yells Mr. Guest. "I wasn't planning on sleeping!"

Washing Machine bolts into the living room with Mr. Guest on her tail. He reaches for her collar. "Fuck. It's biting me! For real!"

He tries to shake her off his sleeve, but she ain't letting go.

"Macy!" my mother shrieks. "Do something! Grab the broom."

"We have a broom?"

"Shut up! It's in the kitchen."

Thirty seconds later: "Grab on this, Washing Machine. It tastes better." Mr. Guest is released. I lead Washing Machine to the couch and toss the broom. I hold her by her collar and scratch her ears.

"Prolly got rabies!" Mr. Guest says, looking at the nip like it's a gaping wound. "Fuck this, Yasmin." He flings the door open and storms out.

My mom squats down in front of the couch. "It's okay, he's gone. Come here, baby."

Washing Machine growls.

"Macy!" My mother backs up. "Let her go!"

"Okay." I throw a hot dog at the half-open door. "Now's your chance, girl. Run!"

"Bitch, I meant to me!"

But the dog don't run. She curls up by me, yawns, and stretches out.

I rub her back. "I'd say you crazy, but who am I to talk?" I grab the remote and make a blanket cave for us. "This is as good as it gets around here."

My mother looks at me funny but don't say nothing. After a minute she disappears into her bedroom.

Something fuzzy tickles the back of my brain, but I keep it out of focus. Hit my head with the remote and the TV turns on. I'm in a cave. I'm in front of the firelight. I can't talk. I think but not in words. All I see is cold hard stars. All I have is a dog to chase away the wolves.

BURY

Verb. What, you thought it was gonna be "funeral"?
Bite me. Because. I'm tired of the letter F.

On Sunday afternoon Mr. Guest pulls up. Asks if we want to go for a ride. "We could go to the park. I got take-out." ("And some party favors," he whispers to my mom like I'm deaf.) "Bring the dog." He shakes a bag of dog treats. "Let's bury the hatchet," he says to Washing Machine.

Fuck you, says Washing Machine.

"Macy!" my mother barks. "I need you to get Washing Machine in the car."

Me: Hysterical laughter.

My mother: "Okay, what do you want?"

"World domination. To be beamed up into a fucking space shi—"

I rub my arm where she smacks it. "Fine. I want to skip the pep rally Friday."

"Macy, last thing I need right now is CPS banging down the door—"

"If I'm there by ten they can't count me absent, so CPS won't get called."

Big sigh. "Deal."

Five minutes later I'm in the back of Mr. Guest's car, holding the dog. Mr. Guest holds my mother's hand. Now I'm mad. All that nasty stuff is one thing, but holding hands is worse. I let the dog go. Oops.

Washing Machine snaps at Mr. Guest. My mother tries to grab her, but the dog's all teeth and spit. Mr. Guest is driving out of his lane.

"That's fucking it!" Mr. Guest cries. "Take the wheel."

My mom guides the car back into the lane.

Mr. Guest punches the dog. Clamps one hand around its jaws and uses his other hand to roll down the window.

"Stop it, Manny! What are you—!"

He chucks Washing Machine out the window.

"Oh my God!" My mother pummels Mr. Guest with punches. But he shoves her away and gets both his hands back on the wheel. Lets the car roll to a stop.

"Both of you! Get out."

We scramble out and he drives off. We backtrack along the side of the road till we reach Washing Machine's crumpled little body. My mother crouches down by her. We hear a whimper.

"We got to find a vet!"

"Ma. I'm not sure we could even move her without her insides spilling out." Not to mention that we don't know where to find a vet and can't afford to pay one. But I don't say that because my mother starts bawling.

"I had a dog when I was little. Don't know what happened to her after my mom dumped me at the group home."

Is this for real? The woman is actually crying. "Take off

your hoodie, Ma. We'll wrap Washing Machine in it." She's still warm. Maybe . . . ?

We walk through the park, thinking maybe we can ask one of the ladies walking their dogs where to go.

"Ay Dios mío," a little old lady says, "poor thing! Did you find him by the road?"

We nod.

"I tell you where to go. The doctor there has a heart. She'll help."

Fast-forward to the vet's reception room. A nurse carries Washing Machine into a exam room. The receptionist gets Kleenex for my mother. The doctor asks to speak to me. "So here's the deal. The dog is holding on, but she's not gonna make it. The most humane thing we can do is to put her down now."

I relay this to my mom.

She bites her lip. "Okay."

We stand by the table where Washing Machine is laid out. In the quiet of this room, you can hear her breathe. I swear she looks like she's smiling, and I get real sick—like dolphins are swimming in my stomach. Like my baby sister is swimming in my brain. I want her to be on this table so I can hold her hand, instead of her dying alone behind the bars of a crib. My mother strokes Washing Machine's head and I wonder, is she thinking the same thing? I've see the dead, but never the dying. I'm scared.

I'm stroking Washing Machine's fur, but I feel my sister's curls.

My mother and I carry the dog in a box to our backyard and bury her.

Next day, I get to school, wave to Alma and George, and lay my head down.

From behind me: "What's that on her pant leg?"

Some dude: "Oh, shit. It looks like dried blood!"

"Fuck," I say and run off to the bafroom. Because it *is* dried blood. I lock myself in a stall. I'm laughing. Not sure where the laughing stops and the screaming starts.

Alma: "Macy! Macy, talk to me."

The stall door flies open. I scream again.

Alma screams back.

We scream together.

Till a teacher is standing outside the door screaming, and I'm laughing again. Every cell in my body is vibrating. Every hair is standing up.

For once I yelled into the dark and it wasn't just my voice that answered back. I want to cover my ears and listen to it all the way home.

FUÁCATA!

Noun. Synonyms: In your face!

You put everything out of reach.
Errday of my life is Friday 13th.
You take one look at me,
Want to throw away the key.
But I'm the gingerbread man, bitches.
You can't catch me.

FUNHOUSE

Noun. Like the kind with warped mirrors
and scary clowns

Manny stands in the doorway kicking snow off his boots: "Qué pasa?! Miss me?"

I grab a pan from the stove.

My mother grabs my arm tight and says to the Dog Killer, "Manny! You're back."

Manny: "Never left. I just had to see a man about a horse, remember?"

My mother: "I must have missed that."

I catch the look in her eyes. Hate.

Manny: "Here. I brought you flowers. And candy, baby. Let's have some fun!"

Me, gripping the pan: "Yeah. Fun never stops with you."

Manny throws the flowers on the table. "Hey. What's your problem?"

My mother pulls the pan out my hand. And actually holds it—my hand. Squeezes it. I'm frozen. When was the last time we held hands? Memories are shuffling like a deck of cards.

"Nothing," Yasmin says to him. "Let's go to my bedroom."

Manny leaves behind him the smell of somebody who's bathed in cologne but hasn't showered in a couple of days. My mother, one step behind him, turns around and holds up her hand.

She mouths, *Wait.*

FUN AND GAMES

Nouns. Our house, our rules.

There are two rules to the game.

Police can't be called.

CPS can't be alerted.

Instructions:

Put empty beer bottles under couch cushions. Smash that shit. Sprinkle over floor from bedroom to door.

Text Mom to wear shoes and hide Manny's.

Call George in the middle of the night. He shows up in pajamas. Like real ones that match and shit. Even slippers. He sits on the couch in the dark. All he's got to do is stand up when the time's right.

(Me in a whisper: "Thank you." George whisper-singing: "I'll be there! Just call my name . . .")

I HEART George.

I'm feeling pretty Gifted and Talented by the time my mother creeps out the bedroom door. She flinches, squints into the dark: "Who dat?"

"Our stunt double. You got the shoes?"

"Yeah. Manny didn't even notice."

"No, for real?" (Insert sarcasm.) I open the front door. "Now on my count. Run back in the bedroom. Tell Manny your husband's home, oh shit, blah blah blah."

My mother nods.

5, 4, 3, 2 . . .

"Oh my God, Manny, Augustine's home!"

"What the—when—what—?"

Manny bum rushes out the bedroom. Crunch, crack. "Ahhh! My feet! What's happ—ahhhh!"

George stands up in the dark. Makes like he's cocking a shotgun.

Manny crashes through the doorway, leaving a trail of bloody footsteps all the way down the street.

A neighbor is standing on her porch.

I shout: "Burglar!"

Neighbor: "Serves him right, S.O.B.!"

Things settle down. I grab the broom and make a path for George.

George: "I'll be there for you! When the rain starts to pour!"

Winner takes all.

FUNERAL

Noun. Yeah, motherfoe, I was saving it.
Why fun is in that word, I'll never figure out.

The sky's a dirty sponge. With all the cracked ice, the ground looks like it's covered with broken glass. Alma and I are sitting on a park bench eating Doritos. Well, I am at least. For these five minutes I'm feeling full. For these five minutes the sun is in front of us, the shadows at our backs. It's cold, but the cold is on the outside, not in my bones. A prostitute is wobbling through the rubber chips toward the slide in the tot lot.

Alma watches. "I don't get how that happens. When did she start? When did she decide?"

"Probably just happened to her."

"No. Life does not just happen."

"That phrase *shit happens* exists for a reason, Alma." I squint. "Damn. She fancy. That's some—fur coat." I stand up. "Hey! Hey, girl!"

Alma: "Macy! What are you doing?"

What I'm doing is chasing a prostitute through a tunnel.

Up a ladder. Down a slide. I trap her in the play dome. She is throwing rubber chips at me.

Prostitute: "What the fuck do you want?!"

Me: "That is not your coat. Where did you get it?"

Prostitute: "It's my coat!"

Me: "You are wearing my mother's purple fur coat. And if you don't tell me where you got it I'm going to suffocate you with it."

Prostitute: "Your mother? *This* was Velvet's coat. This was—Oh shit! You're the girl she told me about. The girl with the muffins. Oh shit. Oh shit. You don't know."

Alma finally catches up to us. "Macy! Let's not know! Let's go."

Me: "Where is Velvet?"

Prostitute: "She's dead. Our pimp found her at the junk-yard. In a fucking tub."

Me: "What the? What?"

Alma covers her ears with her big furry mittens. "Oh God. Now we know. We'll always know!"

Me: "WHY DO YOU HAVE HER FUCKING FUR COAT?"

Prostitute: "We were taking turns with it. She was my bestie."

Me: "Take me. Take me to where—you found her."

Alma: "No, Macy! This has nothing to do with us."

I turn to Alma. "Go home if you want."

"No! If you're going, so am I."

The prostitute takes us past the titty bar called Hole in the Wall. Under the gutters there's patches of gray grass like the scruff of a wet beard. We move on past potholes of snowy soup. Rag weeds blow around the Super S like old lopsided weaves. (See S for Super.) Spiderwebs like a ripped stocking stick on a bush. Finally, we find one skinny tree.

We're standing in front of the junkyard now.

Prostitute: "Stand on the tire hill. Look past the strollers. You'll see it."

Alma: "Macy. You can't go in there. What about the dogs?"

Prostitute: "Animal control took them away. Because of the police. And everything."

Seconds later, we're tripping up the tire hill. The sun is gonna set and I know we have to make it quick. Alma has babies to put to bed.

Me: "I see the tub."

Nancy (Alma asked her her name, damn it) says, "I can't. Not again." Nancy throws the coat in the air and books it. It lands on a stroller and Alma pushes it toward me.

Me: "God, no matter what you're always pushing a stroller."

Alma: "Shut up. Are we really going through with this?"

Me: "We have to. If not us, then who?"

Out of nowhere, *bam*, the baftub is there. I think about my baftub at home and how many times Zane and I slept in it pretending it was a pirate ship or some shit to get Zane to fall asleep. For once, couldn't a baftub just be a baftub?

"Nobody should die like this." I kick a broken bicycle.

Alma hugs me hard. I don't let go till she do.

"Alma, get me fire."

Alma disappears and comes back with a coffee can filled with gasoline. "You do it."

I lay the coat inside the tub. Pour gasoline all over it.

We write our names on the side of the tub. Alma *was here—Macy was here—Velvet was here*. Damn it.

We light that motherfoe up. Baftub looks like a Viking funeral boat, smoke sailing out the junkyard into the sky.

GAS

Noun. Rhymes with never last. Yes it does.
Miss Black says that's a near-rhyme, you ig . . .

"Ain't you supposed to be at work?" I say to my mom when I get home.

"No. I don't like it no more. It's cold now so Chuey moved us inside. Now he wants us to dance. Anyway, Jaime says he don't want me working for Chuey no more. He's got things lined up. Gonna give me money to stay home, if you can believe that?!"

Me: "Well, shit, I can tell you really thought this through!"

I stomp into the bafroom and stare at the mirror, just like I used to stare out the window with Zane. Flashback time: you knew I'd get to it eventually.

I'm staring out the window with Zane.

My mother says, "STOP, you're going to see something."

By "seeing something," she means be a witness. I already am, but I ain't going to say nothing about nobody.

"Get away from there," my mother says.

Zane says, "I'ma wait. I'ma wait." What he means is he's going to wait at the window until Daddy gets home from prison.

My mother tells us to shut up and get in the car. I ask her does she have enough gas.

She says, "NOW."

We both get in the back. She turns the radio up.

If the car music is turned way up you don't think about running out of gas. You don't think about how you have nowhere to go. You just drive.

"If we run out of gas," I say to Zane, "we can just up and move. It would be a adventure. Wherever the car dies is where we live. If it dies at a pizza shop, we live by the pizza shop."

"Pepperoni!" Zane claps. "Pepperoni!"

"Oh shit," I say. "It would be fate. Our mother could get a job. AT THE PIZZA SHOP."

If Zane had a tail, it would be wagging. He opens a window. Sticks out his head and lets his tongue hang out. (See B for Blessing.)

Sometimes at night Zane and I would stick our heads out our bedroom window and howl at the moon. I still do sometimes, thinking maybe somewhere he's howling back.

I start to relax. I keep checking the gas gauge and making wishes. Let it die at the Chinese restaurant. At the skate rink. At the bowling alley.

But then I start thinking. It would still be us. Same shit, different bowling alley.

I want it to be like a shipwreck. A plane crash. When the car dies I want to end up in the middle of nowhere. Where the food is nothing we've ever eaten, the language nothing we ever speaked. Maybe if we could just start fresh knowing nothing and no one, then we would figure everything out. I start thinking about Canada again. I start to relax. To tune out.

So does my mother. She's jamming to the radio up front and hits the window button by accident. The window closes on Zane's neck. And then the car runs out of gas.

Me: "Ma!"

Zane: "Gwrft . . ."

God: "Did you not say you wanted—?"

My mother steers us to the curb. Hammerfists the button. Jams the key in the ignition: "It won't open! Oh my God!! OH MY GOD!!!"

Me: "You're gonna break the key!"

My mother: "What do we do? Oh my God!"

Zane turns white, then beet red.

Me: "I don't know. Get in the back and hold him so he stops moving around so much."

My mother: "Okay! Shit!"

We switch places, her in the back, me in the front.

I know breaking the window won't work. Daddy showed me how to mess with the wires a bunch of times, but I've never done it alone. I move the seat back so I have room to work.

The car turns on. The window goes up. Zane throws up. I channel the Force, jackhammer the button. The window goes down.

Zane slumps over. We have to get to a hospital.

What my mother says to the doctor is we kids were probably messing around with the buttons. That she's going to sue the car company. Maybe we could sue—if the car wasn't a 1982 model repossessed from seven generations of migrant workers and abandoned at a 7-Eleven before my dad got it.

The doctor asks why Zane's head was sticking out the window in the first place. "If he was in a seatbelt, and a booster seat . . . as required by law," he adds.

"He's never been right in the head," my mother answers. "He

must have . . . wiggled out of his seatbelt—and thrown the booster seat out the—no . . . Wait—"

I put my head in my hands. The doctor calls CPS. My mother says it's discrimination. Really LOUD. The doctor says he's going to call security. She starts pulling me out the door.

Me: "Ma? We can't just leave Zane here!"

"He's not going anywhere, Macy. We gotta bounce. We'll go home, get his things, come back."

I keep stopping as she drags me out Zane's room. Out the hospital.

My mother: "Would you hurry up? We might need a jump."

I look up at the building where Zane is sleeping in a bed with a neck brace. Where Zane will wake up and not know where he is.

My mother sweet-talks a guy for a jump. She talks to herself all the way home. But not to me. She knows better.

She tries to turn on the radio. I punch it off. Literally.

The next morning Sleeping Booty actually wakes up when it's barely light out. She throws a bunch of clothes into a Hefty bag.

I grab a Sharpie so I can sign Zane's neck.

We run out of gas and have to hitch a ride home. The driver wants to kill us but that's only because me and mother won't stop fighting. He tells us to get out a block away from home. My mother heads off to a "friend's" house. I walk home alone. That's when the neighbors tell me CPS has been knocking on doors looking for me. They took Zane from the hospital. (See *A for All About You.*) I tell my neighbor to tell my mother I'm at George's.

I run to George's house. He answers the door. It's the first time I've seen him without his helmet and coat on. His hair is black and thick and sweaty except in one spot where a scar runs across his scalp.

I can see George's mom sitting in front of the television. "Is Valentina here?"

Valentina. George's dead sister.

187

George: "No, no, no. Macy."

His mom takes a long time to stand up. She blinks like her brain is erasing whatever it had drawn over me. I think maybe she only stands up when she has to go to the bafroom.

George: "Mommy, you can sit down." That's the first time I've ever heard George speak in a complete sentence.

Me: "Uh. George. Uh. I need . . . Can I . . ." God, am I really asking him what I'm asking? "St—st—"

George: "Steak?"

Me again: "St— St— Steak? Yes. I need steak."

George makes me a steak.

Don't take long before CPS gets to me. The neighbors told my mother and everyone else—including 3211—where I was.

George tells his mom, "Tell CPS, Mommy. Okay? Macy stay. Macy, mom, okay?" And she tells the CPS worker: She can stay.

The house is clean. No cockroaches. Food in the fridge. Steak and rice on the table. The worker lets me stay.

I stay two weeks. George keeps a clean floor. It's cleaner than my kitchen table.

I HEART George.

As soon as CPS is out the picture, I go back home. Daddy's out on probation. But there's no barbecue, no cake as I had always imagined it. "How could you let this happen?" he keeps asking Yasmin, and as mad as I've been at my mom, I know that's bullshit.

Losing Zane was a group effort.

He punches holes in the wall that I have to plaster. He breaks a window I have to replace with one from the junkyard. It's the first time I'm madder at him than my mother. Shit, he had heat in prison. He didn't have to worry about freezing to death. We do.

When the lights come flashing down our block, we know they're for him.

"I'm sorry, Yasmin. I'm supposed to be the man of the house! Why am I like this? Macy, I'm sorry!" He falls to his knees and cries.

I don't think I ever saw him cry before. Not even when Baby Girl died. Daddy had finally run out of gas.

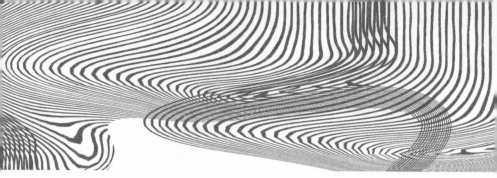

GIVE UP

Verb.

When I get home, I see my mother has been here but left. I flip through the mail on the table. *Somebody's* got to look through more than the Victoria's Secret ads. I find it torn open. Paperwork from CPS.

It's like finding a book about you in the library. I turn the pages. Some things about life are forgettable. Like no one remembers how many times they've read STOP on a stop sign. Some things are so real they are a part of you. They aren't just a thought. They're like a organ. A part of your brain. You want to cut it out, but if you do you know it will kill you.

Yasmin MYOFB has given up her rights to Zane . . . Zane will be adopted by—My mother walks through the doors screaming into her phone.

Me: "Zane's going to be adopted? *What the fuck, Ma!*"

My mother into the phone: "Just sign the papers, Daddy. What? And you're gonna do for Zane what needs to be done?

We never have but we're gonna get our shit together now?"

Me: "Give me the phone!"

My mother pushes past me, runs into her room and locks the door.

Me with the papers in my hand: "*I will set these on fire, Ma!*"

My mother behind her door: "Shut up, Macy! You don't have a say! Do what's right, Augustine! Let him go!"

I body-slam the door but it don't budge. "I don't have a say? He's my brother!" Oh fuck, *is* he my brother? Will he still *be* my brother?

My mother: "He's your brother but remember you're not and never was his mother! He don't belong to you. It's not your decision!"

Me: "He don't belong to me? He don't belong to *you!*"

My mother: "That's right, he don't belong to me. Anymore. He belongs where he's at."

Me: "Give me the phone, Ma. I want to talk to Daddy! Give it to me now or—"

My mother: "Or what, Macy? Nothing you're gonna break is going to change anything."

I fly into the living room. Fling couch cushions at the TV and the windows. Stomp into the kitchen and throw all the bills on the floor. Knock over the table. No brain is made to think what I'm thinking. No heart to feel what I'm feeling. But there's nothing left to break that hasn't been broken. Nothing except me.

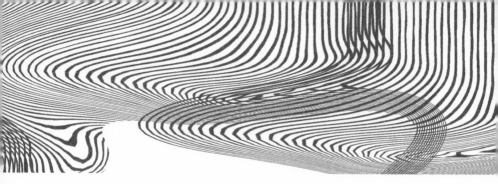

GIFTED AND TALENTED

Adjectives. Synonym: Alma.

The next week I'm not eating.

Alma comes back from the snack line and dumps chip bags all over my uneaten lunch. "Please, Macy."

She's not just saying please because she wants me to eat. She's saying it because she wants me to do the good-bye visit. I get to see Zane one more time. If I want to.

Me: "NO."

Alma opens a bag of chips and shoves one in my mouth. Moves my cheeks to start me chewing. "I can't imagine not seeing one of my siblings ever again. You can't even do phone calls? Facebook?"

"Once he's adopted his new *parents* own him. They could move to South America, and I would never know it."

I can tell her brain is running several diagnostic checks to see why she can't figure out a solution. Gifted and talented people like to think they can figure anything out. Ever since middle school she's been the person the teachers call on in class when the computers freeze.

"Slip him your handle. Since when has anybody been able to stop Zane from doing what he wants?"

"Okay." My voice is flat.

Alma sighs. "I'm not going to sugarcoat it and tell you everything's going to be okay because you'd hate me and you know that it isn't."

Me: "And it won't be ever again. And there's nothing I can do about it."

Alma force-feeds me fruit salad like I'm one of her kids in a high chair. "That's where you're wrong. This visit. This is the something you can do. The only thing. Don't take that away from Zane." She stands up and picks up her tray. "I gotta go. Getting out of school early today. Family stuff."

GOOD-BYE

Future perfect verb. Hello and Good-bye: A perfect circle I will follow back to you, Zane.

I meet up with Miss CPS a block away from the house. I told her my visit and my mom's had to be separate things. My relationship with Zane is gonna be in suspended animation. But her relationship with him is *over*. She tried to talk to one of her girlfriends about it, all weepy and shit. I took her phone and hung up. She don't get to tell that story. Backspace. Delete. She's written her ass out.

I bring Zane's favorite dog biscuits. But when I climb into the car, Zane isn't a dog. He don't bark or jump up or lick my face.

I look at Miss CPS. "What's wrong with him?"

Miss CPS: "He's sitting with both feet on the floor, buckled in a seat belt. Ask what is right! Good job, Zane."

Zane don't wag his tail and pant. Zane, or whoever the hell is inhabiting his body—which has grown three inches and at least two shoe sizes—just sits and lifts up his lips. Can't quite

194

call what's happening to his face a smile. My mind is not absorbing reality. Is it Zane?

We go to Chez McDonald's. Zane does not crash into the ball cage, hold his breaf until everybody thinks he's dead, run up the slide and over little kids. He just sits there putting Legos together.

I get up and start digging through his hair. He don't bite me. I dig harder.

Miss CPS: "Macy! What are you doing?"

Me: "I'm looking for his birfmark."

And there it is. Yeah. This is Zane. Which means this is real.

Miss CPS: "Macy, can you let me explain? You know, Zane is doing so much better now. The Zimm—"

"Don't say their name."

"He is really blossoming with his adoptive family—"

"Blossoming. Never thought I'd hear that shit in the same sentence as Zane."

Miss CPS laughs. "Yes, well—"

"Don't laugh. Ain't none of this funny."

"Sorry. I just want you to know that his life now is—"

"Don't go there. Don't say *better*." I hold Zane's face in my hands. "ZANE!!!"

The boy in front of me looks in my eyes, but it ain't Zane looking back.

I pass him the sweaty dog biscuits. "Tell Zane I love him, okay? Tell him he'll always be my brother. *I* didn't sign no papers."

I stand up. Look out the windows and think about how long it's going to take me to get home on foot.

Then out the corner of my eye I see him. Zane. Swipe the dog biscuits off the table.

195

I ignore Miss CPS and leave.

But not before I see Zane stuffing the dog biscuits into his pocket. That's what I want to remember.

HYDRA

Noun. It's like in cartoons when you want to
get rid of the mouse so you get a cat, then you
want to get rid of the cat, so you get a dog.
Then you get a elephant.

George is walking me home. Us, mid-convo:

"Why can't we ever hear shit like, cockroaches are going extinct? Or like, there's only 100 mosquitoes left in the world."

George: "Aweemah way aweemah way. In the jungle. The mighty jungle. The lion sleeps tonight!"

"We're here." I kick a flattened soda can. "And he's here. Manny's replacement."

George cracks his knuckles.

"Nah. Nah. But thanks. Again."

George rests his forehead against my forehead. We stand there like that for a minute. Then he walks off, singing.

HAVE

Verb. What's all this bullshit about have your cake AND eat it too? What's the point of cake if you ain't eating it? Everyone should want cake. Everyone should eat it!

Nobody else would have noticed it. But I did, the second she sat: Alma eyeballed my French fry.

I shove the crispy salted perfection at her. "You can have it."

Alma: "It's your last one." She swats me away. "You have it. I don't want it."

Me wagging the French fry in her face: "You know you want it."

Alma: "No. I. Don't. Want. IT!"

Me standing up: "Then what do you want?"

Alma standing up: "I don't know! What do *you* want?"

Me: "For you to have this French fry. For you to eat it!" I launch the French fry at her tray.

She tosses it back.

This shit causes a chain reaction all across our lunch table that involves French fries and ketchup packets. I get detention. The kind that don't involve sub sangwiches.

HELMET

Noun. Buckle up, Buttercup.
If you're with me, it's Ride or Die.

I do not know why George wears a helmet. Though it probably makes less sense that everybody around here *ain't* wearing a helmet. I do not know why George wears a hairy Chewbacca coat. The kids around here think he's retarded. I know he isn't any more retarded than Zane. It's not even that they are "misunderstood." It's more like they don't want you to understand. Because YOU CAN'T.

I think sometimes that George's coat wears him and not the other way around. That coat probably has more shit living in it than my mother's bed. He wears that thing winter spring summer fall. But I picture the things in that coat like friendly little purple creatures that keep George company when he is sad.

I also know that I don't want to know.

I don't want to know everything about everybody. Ever sung a song for like ever and then found out you were singing it all wrong? And the real words sucked compared to what you thought they were?

You can't know everything about a person anyway. You can't even know everything about yourself. I don't want to know what you want me to know—what you want me to believe. You imagine me and I'll imagine you. It'll be better than anything we could come up with for ourselves.

ISLAND

Noun. In Canada there is snow islands. You can see grizzly bears and spawning salmon. You can see tulips blossom in February. You can ski down a mountain. Only *you* is not invited.

I'm supposed to be reading *The Life of Pi*. Miss Black keeps making us read books about islands. I tell her you do not have to be surrounded by water to be on a island. She says, "This is a profound idea." She asks me to explain. I say hell no. She takes a deep breaf so she does not choke me and lose her teacher license.

Miss Black tells me that I have a lot of ideas, so I should enjoy reading these types of books. She says, in fact, that I have more ideas than most people. This is supposed to be a moment when she REACHES me.

I say, "If I have more ideas than most people then what do I need more ideas for? It would almost be greedy."

Miss Black sighs. I sigh.

I tell Miss Black this is called a impasse. She taught me this word, so she should be proud. And leave me the hell alone.

Miss Black does not EVER leave me the hell alone, though.

Every damn day she keeps asking me questions about the books even when I don't raise my hand, which shrinks my circle so it's a little knot.

"Did you see me raise my hand?" I say. "I don't think so."

"In my class, everybody counts so everybody gets called on," Miss Black says. "Whether they raise their hand or not."

You can't hide in her class. I thought I'd be slick. A student's best weapon is to ask to use the restroom. The teacher may hate you, but it is a violation of my rights (See A for Always/Never) if they don't let me go. But Miss Black turned around and told me that I may go *after* I answer a few questions. All sudden I REALLY have to go. It is a EMERGENCY. My pee-pee dance could have been on *Dancing with the Stars*.

Miss Black says okay I can go if I attempt the homework tonight. I say, doing the pee-pee dance, that it depends on the homework. She writes it out on the board. Reeeeeeally slowly and in her best handwriting. I read and agree and run before I make a puddle on the floor.

As I've said, Miss Black is hardcore.

I like her homework, though. We have to watch a episode of *Survivor*. On *Survivor* all the contestants are marooned on a island and have to survive.

When I get home, I watch a episode. The contestants are marooned and they have to find food, water, and shelter. I want to tell Alma I want to be marooned with her on a island. Mr. Guest's phone is on the couch. I call her and she don't answer.

Mr. Guest walks right in front of the damn TV with his mouth hanging open. He is a permanent fixture here now, like the tires on the front lawn. He's paying for cable, and with my mother that earns you frequent flyer miles. (See F for Fine Print.) I tell Mr. Guest, "Uh. You ain't made of glass."

I don't tell him: *You're made of Funions.*

Mr. Guest walks over and picks up his cell. "Neither is you." He eyeballs me and I draw my hood. Nasty.

He sweet-times it to the kitchen. I turn away and try to block him out and watch my show. But I can tell just from listening that he's spilling the Coke he's pouring and leaving it out with the damn cap loose. I turn my head. The refrigerator door is open. So is the silverware drawer.

My mother's at the stove, stirring noodles with a fork, scratching against the non-stick pan. She uses too much oil and it spatters everywhere. Once she forgot the bottle of oil on the stove and burned a hole in it. She turns the flame on too high to light up a cigarette and almost burns her eyebrows off. AGAIN.

"Ma!" I say. "You gonna set yourself on fire!" I go over and grab the smoke and light it up for her. "Let me cook," I tell her. "Go sit." At least with them confined to the couch I can watch my show in peace.

My mother plunks down. She flips the channel. Damn it.

My mother: "Yo! The Kardashians is on!"

Me: "Ma! Flip it back! I got to do my homework." She rolls her eyes, but her cell rings so she lets me win this one.

I do eenie meenie miney moe to decide which burner to use. (See B for Burner.) The third burner still works good and if you wear a mitt you don't get electrocuted when you adjust the knobs. I saute the lo mein just right so the noodles are crisp and the broccoli not overcooked.

Guest: "Damn, that smells good. When's that shit gonna be ready?"

I flip him the finger but he just laughs and flips one back. Lets it hang in the air too long. And wiggles it.

I look away.

I turn off the stove. Mr. Guest comes over smelling the air around me and I back the hell up. He sticks his finger in the pan and bitches because it's hot. Genius.

Guest: "Damn, that's good, girl. Taste! He holds out his finger."

"I think I lost my appetite." (For the rest of my life.)

He shrugs and takes the pan to the couch. Sits and passes my mother the pan. She passes him a bong. He starts telling her how he wants to take her away to a island. He sticks his slimy fingers under her bra strap so it slides down her shoulder. Oil stains the couch. DAMN IT DAMN IT DAMN IT. He's shotgunning smoke into my mother's mouth. "You want a hit?" he says to me.

"Stop it," my mother says to him, giggling. He looks at me when he takes another hit and breathes in long and hard. I look away toward the TV.

On *Survivor*, they're recapping about who they voted off the island and who stays. I'd like to see some of those mother-foes survive in this place.

I DON'T WANT TO TALK ABOUT IT

Concrete noun.

What did I say, motherfoe?

I HAVE A DREAM

Quote.

I'm supposed to "choose two texts and juxtapose them" for English class. It can be a poem and a play. It can be a story and nonfiction. Take this, Miss Black:

I'm sleeping in the baftub again. But it's weird to sleep in it alone. Zane used to fluff up all my hair (when I still had it) and sleep on it like a pillow. He used to chew on it too. I'd wake up with spit in it. I would run the sink water. It would wash away all the sounds from my mother's bedroom. Black noise. (Yes, black. Why white people got to get credit for everything good?) But my mother would come in here half-necked and tell me to turn the damn water off unless I was going to pay the damn bill.

I close the tub drain and spread out a bunch of sweatshirts. I don't have Zane anymore—or my hair—to keep me warm. Why sweatshirts? Because the only cooties on them is from me. And Daddy. My ear presses against the cold porcelain.

I don't move though. I like the way it sounds like a ocean. I can hear my breathing. I can hear my blood in my ears. NOTHING else.

Falling asleep for me is usually like Wile E. Coyote accidentally walking off a cliff. You know how he kind of stands there mid-air and plummets to the rocks below? But this time, I don't fall, I float.

I have a dream.

Holy shit.

In the dream, I'm still in the baftub. The water is running but my mother don't hear it. The whole room is filling up but none of the water is leaking under the door. The tub starts to float. I look up. There is no ceiling. I don't know why. It's a dream, stupit. I see the moon. The baftub bobs with the current. It bobs against the wall. The wall begins to crumble.

"Open the door!"

Dream deferred.

What?

"Open the door!"

"Why?" I pop the lock.

My mother barges in. She starts rifling through the medicine cabinet. Digging through drawers, yanking them out.

"Seriously, Ma, you got the rest of the house. Can't you just let me sleep?"

"What?" she says all groggy as if she's seeing me through a mist. "Fuck, Macy. Why do you have to sleep in here? Why can't you just sleep on the goddamned couch?"

"You know why." I lay back down. "Just leave me alone."

Tampons hit me in the head. "What," my mother says, "so you could tell CPS you sleep in a baftub?"

"I don't tell them nothing, Ma!" I throw the tampons back.

From the bedroom: "Hey girl, where you at? You got the pills?"

Me: "Get out!"

She turns the shower on and high-tails it.

This time I go to get a chair from the kitchen. My mother's phone is on the counter. I call Alma. She don't answer. I drag the chair into the bafroom and push it against the door handle. I press my ear against the tub. I'm scared the ocean sound will be gone but it is still there. I breathe in and out because that is good. I can have the ocean anytime now. Macy is cold because she is dripping wet. Yes, *Macy*. Her. She is cold. *I'm* not. She's shivering in a baftub. *I'm* in a boat. I'm moon-bathing, bitches.

I have a dream.

Block by block the bafroom wall comes down. There is a big-ass tunnel. A current is pulling me forward through the hole. Ahead there are lights. My boat gets pulled toward them. I'm moving faster and faster but I'm not scared. The boat almost turns over but I hold on. Up ahead I see shore. There is a little boy standing there waiting for me.

BANG! BANG! BANG!

Dream deferred.

WTF? Are my mother and her friend doing it against the bafroom door?

Does it dry up like a raisin in the sun?
Or fester like a sore?
Then run?

Him: "Whore. You're a whore! Say it!"

BANG! BANG! BANG!

So yeah it stinks like rotten meat
Against the door it makes a beat
And yeah her sugar it crusts
her syrup it thrusts thrusts thrusts
and I will sag with every load
UNTIL I **EXPLODE**

KITTY

Noun. Synonyms: see below.

Setting: Hallway by Alma's locker.

Me: "Where you been?" I look at her knotty hair, her bleary eyes. "Never thought I'd say this, but you look like shit."

Alma: "I've been pulling all-nighters to get caught up in trig."

Me: "You need a break, girl. Come hang out with me."

Alma: "I can't. I don't have the time. I'm still behind in—"

I grab her backpack. "If you don't come with me, I will throw your backpack into a incinerator. Then you will have tons more shit to make up."

Alma skips all the way to the park. Like I didn't just take the weight of her bag off her back but the whole world. She sings. I'm the only one who gets to hear her sing like this because I don't ask her to sing. At home, anything she does well everybody wants her to do over and over and over. She once sang a lullaby and then her mom made her sing lullabies to all the kids every night and to the babies all night because that was the only way they would shut the hell up.

Right now Alma sings for herself.

We start talking about our favorite songs when we were little kids. "Remember Chitty Chitty Bang Bang?" Alma says.

We face each other, clap, and sing:

Chitty Chitty Bang Bang
Sitting on a fence
Try to make a dollar
out of fitty cents.

She missed! (We jump into a little split.) *She missed!* (We split wider.) *She missed like this!* Whoever splits the widest wins. Alma does, of course. Alma and I are having fun.

Then along comes some dude who thinks *he* is funny. You know the dude. You know what he's wearing. He has on enough cologne to destroy the entire ozone layer. You tell him to fuck off, but in his defense he is absolutely deaf from blasting his iPod into his ears 24/7.

"Titty titty bang bang," he sings, eyeballing Alma.

I kick him into a permanent split, confident that I have saved the world from his procreation of future generations.

"Ah!" he screams. "Bitch?!!!"

I pick up a rock.

He limps away as fast as his droopy pants can carry him.

Alma: "Macy! You wouldn't have . . ."

Me: "Wouldn't have shed a tear. Alma. Remember this one?
Left left left right left
My body aches
my pants too tight
my booty shakes from left to right!"

Alma laughs and marches with me.

Then we hear it from a car driving by real slow: "Here kitty, kitty, kitty."

I hold up that rock and look over. The dudes see me and shut their window.

"Come on," I say, pulling my hoodie over my baseball cap. I grab her hand and we run to the jungle gym where we can talk in private.

We walk up a twisty slide that's still wet from yesterday's rain. We laugh because we're getting all wet and it's hard to climb and we want to laugh. Need to. We sit at the top of a red and blue plastic tower. I feel the pile of rocks I've gathered in my pocket.

They are for intruders.

I lean back against a scratched-up faded plastic tic-tac-toe game and look at Alma. She is sitting criss-cross legged across from me. She is wearing pink shorts underneath her skirt.

"Unbelievable. That"—I point at her pink shorts—"is all that stands between you and them fools back there. Think about it."

"I don't want to."

I say, "Don't matter what you want when you got something everybody wants. Pussy is always in high demand."

"You call it that?"

"What do *you* call it? Your pocketbook? No? Your snatch? Your pootie? Your private place." *The parts under your bathing suit*, the counselor used to tell me. *Those parts are private.* Tell that to the boys. Tell that to the men.

She mimes a phone call. "I don't *call* it. And," she says, "it's odd that you of all people call it a pussy."

"The odd thing is a pussycat has got more to it than a pussy. Pussycat's got teeth. Pussycat's got claws. Pussycat can pounce. What's our pussy got? Lips that don't even speak."

"Lips? Thank you for that, Macy. Now I'm going to picture my vajayjay talking. Cracking jokes."

We crack up. Then we crack jokes.

"But seriously." I stop laughing. "It's slippery, not spiky. It just sits there. Can't move. Can't hide. And all that stands between us and a man who wants it is—what? A pair of underwear? It ought to spit fire. Shoot spears like Agüeybaná." I show Alma some moves. The slide and the monkey bars are involved.

"Macy!" She puts her fist to her mouth and looks around to see if anyone is watching. She is scolding but still cracking up.

"It ought to have teeth," I shout, out of breaf. "It ought to close, at least!" I sit back down. "I mean"—I lie back—"God gave animals venom. Armored plates. But the pussy he just gives *hairs*?"

"Shut up, Macy," Alma says, looking up at the sky and signing the cross.

Alma is a big believer in God striking people like me with lightning. I haven't been striked yet. But maybe, I think, looking up where Alma is looking, maybe my life is the lightning.

LANGSTON HUGHES

Noun.

Miss Black is making us choose a poem to rewrite. I chose "Mother to Son."

Daughter to Mother

Well, Ma
I know for you
Life's been a bitch.
You got the worst of it.
But what did you learn from it?
Whaat?
Life done you wrong?
But it's the same old song.
You was a child of the street
But, personally,
If I was you and you me
I wouldn't
Have carried me.
You was a child of the streets
But you didn't lace up ya sneaks
Didn't hit the road
Light was green but ya didn't go
It's easier to stick with what ya got
Then what you don't know
Now I'm standing in your shoes
And I got to choose.
Got everything to lose.

LIPS

Noun. Can you read mine?

Today the AP and regular classes have class together. George beat-boxes and I do a happy dance. We're in the awditorium. Miss Black and Miss Link set up a chair on the drama stage. Miss Black writes on a easel:

I sound my barbaric yawp against the rooftops of the world.

We're supposed to *write and reflect* about our yawp. We're invited to stand on the chair on the stage and shout it out.

I tell Alma, "I do like the word *barbaric*. I do like to stand on furniture. I may cooperate. However comma I do not understand what a yawp is."

Alma says to think about what I would shout if I were standing on the rooftop of my own house. What would I want to tell the world?

"I would tell the world to pick that shit up! Now!"

Alma says, "No, no, no. The assignment is not about yelling at *people*."

"Okay, okay!" I stand up and pace. I want to think of something smart to say to Alma. Alma is sad when she can't get me to understand something. Actually, she don't look sad. Just tired. Of my shit?

My lightbulb turns on. I shout: "YOU!!"

Alma: "No."

Me: "No?"

Alma: "I'm not your yawp. You had a yawp well before you met me. I think you *are* a yawp, actually."

Me: "Don't tell me what my yawp is."

George: "Yawp. Yawp. Ribbut. Neigh!"

I look at George galloping like a horse. "Yo, Miss Black, that better be a industrial strength chair. My boy here is—healthy."

Miss Black sighs.

Some dude walks over and says to Alma, looking her up and down, "So everybody knows your yawp, right?"

Alma: "What do you mean?"

Me cracking my knuckles: "Yeah, homie. What do you mean?"

Homie says 1st: "Please stop doing that!" 2nd: "Uh. I don't know what I mean. Nobody ever does." Homie sits down.

Alma to me: "You know, I didn't make myself look like this. I could have looked like anything. Beauty isn't art if you don't make it with your own hands. So it can't be a yawp."

Me: "Right. I'm stupit. Brains!"

Alma: "Brains? Knowing math is my yawp?"

Me: "Isn't it?"

"It is, I guess."

"You guess?"

"I don't know, Macy!"

Alma saying *I don't know* shakes me up. Shouldn't Alma be creating a PowerPoint about her yawp? How can Alma not know what her yawp is?

George is out of his seat and galloping toward us. He gets down on all fours, looks at Alma and pats his back.

"George, not now!"

George curls in the fetal position.

"Alma!!" I sit down and pet George. I know what to do. There really isn't any other way. "Giddy up, George!"

I get on. This event makes cause and effect happen. Kids all over the awditorium are riding other kids. The effect: I get sent to cool out in the office. I really reeeeeally want to sound my barbaric yawp, so I promise pretty please I will cut the shit if they let me back.

I slide back into the awditorium. The chair is gone and George is standing on what really looks like a roof. Apparently the school did *Fiddler on the Roof* this year.

The class quiets down. Miss Black aims the spotlight.

George: "Crisco!"

The class is cracking up.

Miss Black on the microphone: "George—"

Me: "He means he likes pie. He bakes pies. They are so delicious." (He sent me home with one after I stayed at his house. The world would be a better place if everyone ate George's pie.) Everyone is staring at me. "*CLAP*," I command. They clap.

George claps. He is the champion of the afterclap. He cheers. He cheers himself into a cough fit. George just had the bronchitus.

Miss Black: "Okay, George." She motions to Julio to take him to the nurse. "Macy, you're up."

I stand on the fake roof. The class starts clapping. "Shut up!"

The class shuts up.

Me: "I DISLIKE EVERYONE!!!" (The counselor would be so proud I did not say hate.) "Now clap!" Everybody claps but Alma.

Alma isn't there. I'm mad. I get down. Class ends. I go the restroom but no one's in there. I go to our conference room. At the door to Pepe's closet, I check if the coast is clear, open the door, slip in, and flip on the light.

Alma sits up from lying on the floor, blinks.

Me: "Were you sleeping?"

Alma: "No."

"You have a crease in your face. What happened? You missed my yawp! And you missed saying yours."

"I don't have a yawp!"

Me: "What about track? The debate team . . ."

Alma: "I don't feel barbaric about those things. I feel—tired."

Me: "I feel barbaric about everything."

Alma: "I don't know how I feel about anything." She lowers her voice. "Anymore."

I reach out my hand. She grabs it and stands up. Inspects me. Takes out her nail clipper.

"I got a lightbulb!" I say. "Your yawp is helping people! You should be proud and shit."

Alma does a kind of half smile. "Yes. I'm good at that. But I don't feel proud. I feel—tired." She yawns.

"That yawn was pretty barbaric."

"Shut up. I gotta go."

"A'ight, see you in class."

She kisses me on the cheek and goes back to class. I rub my cheek without thinking. Ick. A gob of lipstick.

Lipstick? When did Alma start wearing that shit?

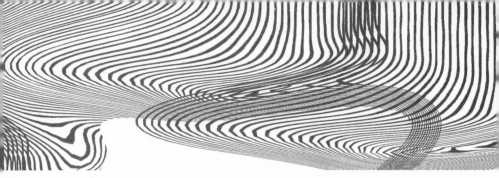

LIFE

Noun. It's a open book.

Miss Black has moved all the desks. "Today we are going to sit on picnic blankets for class."

Me: "Will picnic food be involved?"

Miss Black whips out a basket. She pulls out a book. Damn it. She says we have a open-book question at the end of class. Double damn it. But she also pulls out fruits: EXCLAMATION POINT.

This is when the counselor shows up at the door, of course. I shake my head so hard my whole brain moves to the left hemisphere.

The counselor waves to Miss Black and she steps outside.

Miss Black steps back in and asks me to start passing out the grapes.

I'm confused—why was the counselor here if it wasn't for me?—but I don't ask questions. I get up and go get the grapes and when I turn back around, Alma is gone. I don't see her again until next period.

Me: "What the fuck, Alma? Why would you go to the counselor?"

"You mean, why not talk to you instead?"

"Yes."

Alma sighs. "Look, I missed a few practices. Coaches wanted me to talk to them. Anyway, what's the big deal? You talk to the counselor and I don't ask about it."

Me: "Wait. Coach*ES*?"

Alma: "Yes. Plural. I've been super busy. My mom's been sick. Don't make a big deal. I'm already mortified. Look—my uncle is coming to help my mom out for a few weeks, so things will level out."

"All right. I wish I could help you."

"You can't. How about I help you with math?" She points to problems 2, 3, 4 . . .

I let her help me, but in the end she's almost doing it all for me and I still don't know what's going on.

LOVE SUPREME

Noun. Love rhymes with above. Supreme with dream.

It's Valentine's Day. Alma's got like a hundred secret admirers, six stalkers, and more sorry suckers sweatin her than I can count.

"You like Helen of Troy. The face that launched a thousand throw-downs." Only instead of Paris, she'd be running off with me. Even the gods couldn't stop me. We like two hands of the same clock. Always connected. Sometimes in our own space, but we always meet. Nothing without each other. At least I'm nothing without her.

"Just load me up." I'm her pack mule carting around piles of carnations, nasty giant solid milk chocolate hearts even I wouldn't eat, crappy stuffed animals holding crappier balloons.

"I wish it were that romantic," Alma says. "Helen and all that. I mean—you know what I mean. It's just—they're gonna get mad."

By "they" she means her devoted following. "Beautiful" turns to "bitch" in a hot second. (See C for Clang.)

We take a different bus route home to throw the stalkers off her scent. Alma is about to unlock her door, but her mom jerks it open.

"Hey! Happy—" Her mom's smile breaks like a dropped dish. "Hi, Macy. I'll take those."

"I guess that means I better be on my way."

Alma motions for me to call her.

When I get home my mother and a new guest are sitting on the couch eating a Supreme Meat pizza. (See H for Hydra.) The two lovebirds are going to eat sausage, ground beef, and bacon, and then bust open that box of Crunch and Munch sitting between my mother's legs.

"Oh my God," my mother says between mouthfuls of cheese, "this is so good."

Mr. Guest: "Yeah, I knew you'd like extra meat. You like meat, Macy?"

My mother: "Shut up, Nero."

Watching them, I understand why Alma does not eat meat. That's what Mr. Guest looks like sitting in the TV light. A slab of sweaty pork. I wait for my mother to go to the bafroom and set her phone on the toilet tank like always. And as always, she's so high she forgets it.

In the bafroom with the door locked, I give Alma a ring.

Me: "It's me."

Alma: "Hey you. I was just saving you a boat load of chocolate. But I'm not going to give it to you all at once."

"Okay, Mami." Sweet Tarts suck. They taste like sidewalk chalk. I hate roses. The only time I want to be handed dead flowers is when I'm actually dead. Pink makes me want to puke. I do have to admit, though, I'm a sucker for chocolate.

Alma: "I gave all the stuffed animals to my babies. Gave my mom the flowers. So what's—oh hey, hold on."

She hangs up on me. I call her back.

Alma: "Sorry about that! Listen, can I call you later?"

Me: "I guess."

Alma's mom in the background: "Whisper whisper whisper NOW!"

Me: "You gotta go."

Alma: "I love you."

Me: "I love you too."

I hang up, unlock and open the door. My mother is standing outside the door chewing Supreme Meat, sauce spilling out the corner of her mouth.

Me: "Nice, Ma. Classy."

Time-Lapse/Speed Version of what happened next:

My mother: "Who was that?" Me: "You know, who is it ever?" My mother: "You LOVE Alma? You fucking *LOVE* Alma? You never say you love me. Blah blah blah."

In con-fucking-clusion: I HATE Valentine's Day.

Next day, I see Alma in the hall.

Me: "You didn't call me back."

Alma huffs, "Sorry. My mom took away my phone."

"Why?"

"She wanted to know who I was talking to last night, and when I said it was you . . ."

"She hates me."

Alma: "She hates not controlling me. She heard me say I love you. She wanted me to be talking to one of the guys who gave me chocolates."

Me: "Like you have time for that shit."

Alma: "How do you tell someone who works three jobs that there aren't enough hours in the day? But she's always wanted me to be the show pony and the race horse. One minute it's keep the blinders on, stay focused, I'm our ticket out. The next it's all the other neighbor girls are talking to someone . . ."

"How long she keeping your phone?"

"It could be a couple of days. She's pissed. But even when she gives it back—"

"You can't talk to me? Is she for real?"

"It'll blow over. She's gone too much to keep track of what I do. Here." She gives me the bag of chocolate and splits. Just like that.

I drop my backpack at my desk and right then and there gobble chocolates like the fucking Cookie Monster. Miss Black looks at her clipboard like she isn't looking at me and walks to my table.

If this were Mr. This or Mrs. That, I would have heard: *Now, Miss MYOFB, you know it is school policy that blahblahblahblah.*

This is Miss Black, though.

She says: "Mmm, those look good, girl. My man is into those gluten-free sugar-free candies." She reaches down and says, "May I?"

I contemplate. I tap my finger against my chin. "You may." She sticks her hand in the bag and takes out a peanut butter cup. It's fine. I don't like peanuts anydamnway. Then she sets three other pieces of candy on my desk. Ties a knot in the bag. Says: "Put those away before I eat them all, girlfriend."

I get it. "A'ight. I'm good." I cut the shit and put the bag in my backpack.

In first period, Miss Black dims the lights. Says: "I was going to end class with a record today, but it seems it might be better to start with one."

Miss Black only plays records. She always says, "CDs are too clean. I want gravy on the knife."

Random Kid 1: "Oh, no. She's gonna play opera again."

Random Kid 2: "Is this gonna be on the test? Because—"

Me to Random Kid 2: "This is a test. Multiple choice. If you don't shut the hell up, then: A, will I—"

Miss Black: "All right now. We get it. Heads down."

I put my head down after launching a chocolate at R2's head. The solid ones are nasty anyway. Random Kid 2 says, "*Ow!*" George scoops up the chocolate before it hits the floor. He starts making a card for his mom and tapes the chocolate to the cover. I HEART George.

Some kids joke that we're going to play 7-Up and stick out their thumbs, but it settles down. Miss Black drops it like it's hot. The needle hits the first track.

It's quiet.

First comes the static. Enter some kind of horn. The horn makes me think of Alma yesterday . . . When she was thinking about who knows what—even I couldn't tell. But for a minute I even forget about Alma. No shit.

I'm going under. My leg jerks a little like the ground's gone and I'm falling.

I grab and grab but there's nothing to hold onto. WTF? I don't get it. I don't know all of the instruments. Funny but whenever I don't get something it's math or reading or science. Never thought it could be *music*. I try. I try harder. I've been listening to music every minute of my life, so how the hell do I not know anything about it? I don't know what to do with my body.

I close my eyes. Would my body do some kind of ballet? Imagine my stupit ass doing that. I do.

The horn fades out. In comes the bass.

Bah Bum Bah Bum Bah Bum Bah Bum

That's all.

Bah Bum Bah Bum

When the beat is damn good and ready, the words:

A Love Supreme . . . A Love Supreme

That's all.

It don't say nothing about a girl and a guy. Don't even say who loves who. It don't say love what, love when, or why.

And guess what: It has not a damn thing to do with meat pizza.

Bah Bum Bah Bum Bah Bum Bah Bum

A Love Supreme . . . A Love Supreme

Fade out to lunch . . .

Alma can't sit with me today because she's catching up on assignments in the library. It's all good though. I hear that beat in my head all day.

Bah Bum Bah Bum Bah Bum Bah Bum

Fade to after school . . .

Alma is waiting for me by my locker. I can tell she is all stressed out. She's doing that fist over her mouth thing and shifting from one foot to the other, tucking her hairs behind her ears.

She starts: "You know I do lo—"

I cover her mouth. I say: "A Love Supreme . . . A Love Supreme Bah Bum Bah Bum Bah Bum Bah Bum."

I keep doing it. I uncover her mouth. Cover it again when she tries to make excuses. I beat it on a locker. I sing it until Alma smiles and her fist unrolls. Until she says, "Macy, you can sing."

Then I smack my hand on her mouth again, hum it. Kiss my hand when it's still against her mouth. Give her the peace-out sign. She flashes it back, looking at me with a smile I don't recognize. I stare after her like the smile still hangs in the air.

Grounding all done, she calls me two days later. We talk about nothing. Just when we're about to hang up, Alma starts it up.

Bah Bum Bah Bum Bah . . .

I pick it up:

Bum Bah Bum . . .

We hang up.

A Love Supreme . . . A Love Supreme . . .

LIKE THE RIVER

Transitive verb. Sam Cooke: "I keep running . . ."

Miss Black says she ain't going to teach no more. Her husband got a job upstate that starts in a couple weeks, so they're moving and she's going into another field. I have many emotions. Okay, I have one emotion. I'm mad as hell. DUH.

Everybody kind of is. Some of us, like me, have had her twice. Now she's leaving in the middle of the semester. She makes a lesson out of it. Plays a record by the Beetles called "Let It Be." David Bowie's "Changes." Sam Cooke's "A Change Is Gonna Come." All I see is another tombstone in the graveyard of people I've known in my life. All the social workers, the counselors, and their new fields stretch far past where the eye can see. (See I for I Don't Want to Talk About It.)

MONSTERS

Noun. Sorry, Wally.

I'm watching Alma fall asleep on the wall outside maf class. She actually snores a little. I mean the girl is standing there comatose.

I tap her on the shoulder, soft so she don't have a heart attack. "Alma!"

"I'm coming, Wally! I checked. No monsters!"

"Alma!" I whisper-yell.

"Willy, did you drop Lambie?"

"Girl, wake up!"

Kids are walking past all up in our business. The bell rings.

Alma gasps. "Oh my God, I'm late for school." Her eyes pop open.

"Alma!" I shake her. "You are in school. How long since you've slep?" Her eyes are bloodshot. Skin looks like cigarette ash.

"Five days," she says, her eyes closing again. "I've been eating coffee straight out of the can. Last night I sleepwalked. Just like you see in the movies. I walked with the baby for hours. Back and forth. Back and forth." Alma shows me how she carried the baby back and forth. She drags her feet like a zombie.

Teacher opens the door and gives Alma the kind of stink eye usually reserved for me. I pull Alma off the wall and point her in the direction of her class. "Shit," I say. "I don't want to leave you!"

She makes a Grand Canyon–sized yawn. "Meet me in the restroom in five."

I'm waiting in the bafroom so long, I'm about to bust in Alma's class and cause a ruckus.

The door finally creaks open. "Hey! Sorry it took so long. The teacher had me—"

"How you holding up? You okay?"

"No. But I have something that might help." She digs in her backpack and pulls out a bottle of pills. "My uncle gave me some of these." She leans against the sink. "I looked them up on the Internet and a lot of people say they help. I need help, Macy."

I open my mouth but I don't know what to say. Who am I to say anything? I picture her walking back and forth across the room hour after hour—her feet like matches, striking up flames. I mean, I had plenty of all-nighters with Zane, but there's a big difference between one kid and seven. And I would just catch up on sleep in class.

Then I picture Alma popping pills day after day. Who am I to tell her anything? I answer myself back: Her friend. You're her friend, you asshole.

I grab the bottle from her, then hold her back while I step into the bafroom stall. She fights me, hits me on the back. Cries into the toilet as the pills are flushed.

We go back to our classes. Meet up at lunch. Don't talk about what happened. I got some change so we take the bus after school. But the thing is, no matter how much time we spend together, we both go home alone.

MAYBE

Adverb. It's what your teacher tells you not to use. It isn't a verb, and it knows it never will be. But it also knows it can mess with any verb. Imagine someone saying do you love me and imagine what a adverb like maybe can do.

Maybe is one of my mom's favorite words. I do not feel like writing a whole story about it. So Miss Black said I can write a poem:

> I should,
> but I won't.
> I can,
> but I don't.
> I would
> But it won't do no good.
> Understood?

PINK

Adjective. The color of roses.

Miss Black is gone and we have a new teacher. New Teacher Lady says we can all write Miss Black a letter. I'm not going to write her no letter. How's Miss Black going to write twenty-nine letters back? The answer is she isn't. She is going to write one letter for the class. I hate that shit. I voice my concern. New Teacher Lady says maybe I will need to write the letter in the office. I say, *"Maybe?"* I get up. I hit the buzzer myself and tell the office I'm coming. The office says: Uh, okay.

This is what I wrote. It's about my first year with her. Maybe I'll mail it to Miss Black one day before I die:

> She always smelled like roses. They were in the perfume she wore. She wore pink lipstick. Her cheeks turned pink when she was embarrassed. Once I went home and tried to make my cheeks pink like that. I pinched them super hard.

My mother saw me and smacked me super hard. "What you trying to do? Get the social worker to take you away?"

"You do it like this," my mother said, dragging me to the bafroom. I watched my mother put her makeup on in the mirror. She always wore red blush and lipstick. (See L for Lips.) She turned her music as loud as her lipstick and started singing about a guy in love with a pole dancer. I swear there are more songs about pole dancers than Shakesbeer has odes. (What? You don't think I know what a ode is, you stereotyping motherfoe?)

My mother started gluing on fake eyelashes, which was scarier than the eyeball scene in *Clockwork Orange*. (Don't Google it. No one should.) Thank God she forgot I was there. I left for the front window and pinched my cheeks in peace. Then, looking out at the gray skies, I had a lightbulb.

Canada was super cold so if I moved there I would always have a blush. Miss Black said she went to a jazz festival at Toronto once. Miss Black always played jazz. She played Coltrane while we did work. (See L for Love Supreme.)

One time when I had lunchtime detention, Miss Black left the room and I started digging through her trash looking for books. Instead I found her grocery list. At home, she ate mint M&M's. Her purse was wide open. Eyes pinned to the door, my feet inched closer and closer to it. My hand slid next to it. To close it. Her perfume bottle was just sticking out.

I sprinkled a few drops of her perfume on my sleeve. When I heard the class coming, I ran to my desk. Got out all my things. Miss Black started teaching her lesson. I listened real hard. But oh, every time I leaned on my hand, I could smell it.

That day after school I felt different because I could smell different. My eyes saw a dumpster. My nose smelled roses. My eyes saw a dead dog. My nose smelled roses. My outer eyes saw a old lady puking in a trash can. My inner eye saw roses. I pressed my nose to my wrist and breathed in deep before I walked into my house. My brain knew the month-old laundry stink, but my nose smelled roses.

I just had to get Miss Black M&M's.

Check it: When kids brought things in for Miss Black, she always handwrote them neat little notes on pink paper. Alma has some. The paper always smelled like roses too, right where her wrist rubbed against the page. I had to have one of those notes. People come and you count the days until they're gonna go. People right near you are a million miles away. But a special note somebody takes the time to write just for you means you were in their head. That kind of shit you keep forever.

The problem was the Super S, no matter how unsuper it was, cost money. And I didn't have any. But I stood in front of the mirror and had a Lifetime Channel moment. Took a deep breaf. Whatever the cost, I was willing to pay it.

I opened the door to the Super S and even the roses couldn't combat the smell. The manager had a fan on but all it was doing was blowing the stank from one side of the store to the other. My skirt almost blew up but I caught it in time. The manager looked up from his magazine and then looked me up and down. I stepped over one of the many things in the store responsible for the stank and made my way to the candy aisle.

I pretended like I reeeeeaaaaally couldn't decide between Skittles and M&M's. Like if I had to decide whether to stay on the Titanic or jump, that would have been a easier decision. I ran my hands across the shelves. The manager closed his magazine. He was getting suspicious.

I grabbed the M&M's, started toward the register to throw him off, then darted toward the door.

"Hey! Hey, bitch! You pay for that! You pay!"

I slipped on the nasty floor and caught myself. I held onto the M&M's but not my dress. It blew up completely. And no, Marilyn Munroe never ever had a moment like this.

The manager stopped yelling. I turned around and grabbed my dress. He looked at me and motioned at my legs.

What happened next? (See I for I Don't Want to Talk About It.)

Afterward, I ducked into a alley, tore off my panties, bunched them up and threw them into a dumpster. Even in all that trash, they looked like a pink rose.

And what was that underneath the egg carton? It couldn't be another pair of panties, could it? How many pairs of panties was in that dumpster? I stood there staring into the dumpster, the wind blowing between my legs. I started imagining that dumpster filling up with every pair of panties every girl had ever thrown into the trash, overflowing onto the sidewalk. I clutched the M&M's to my heart and ran home.

I crashed into a guest as he was throwing sheets out. "Why?" I asked.

"Because a man wants to know he's the only one who been between his woman's sheets."

Puhlease. "In that case, you better get us a new couch, a new rug, a new sink, and a new toilet," I told him.

I ran to my mother's room and started pulling open drawers. It felt like the fan from the Super S was still blowing on me. I felt cold and necked. Damn! My mother came after me screaming, but I put on the mute button. I flang drawers over until I finally found it. My daddy's clothes. His sweatshirts.

My mother: "Damn it, Macy! I could have told you where they was!"

Me: "Yeah right. Could have, but wouldn't have BECAUSE I asked." I ducked my mother's smacks and stocking-egg grenades as I ran from her bedroom.

I locked myself in the bafroom and took off the last dress I was ever going to wear. I slipped Daddy's sweatshirt on. The cold thawed. I felt clothed, covered, ready for my body to hibernate.

I hid the M&M's in the back of the fridge so they didn't melt. That night I dreamed of little pink notes that smelled like roses. They folded themselves up into origami birds and let me fly on them.

I woke up the next morning real early and went to the kitchen. No one else was up and the house was silent. I reached my hands up behind the old milk carton that had morphed into cottage cheese. I couldn't feel anything! My throat tightened into a knot. Damn! Somebody just pushed the M&M's behind the old ketchup. I grasped them but not too tight so I wouldn't wrinkle the bag. Only something was wrong. The package was open. Somebody with midnight munchies had stuck their fingers in and ate all but two.

I had another Lifetime Channel moment and dropped to my knees. *Ahhhhhhhhhh!* I banged my head against the floor. My mother burst out her bedroom and kicked me in the head.

"Stop banging your head on the floor!"

This gave me a lightbulb.

My mother: "Wait. What? You're just going to get up, just like that?"

Me: "Yup."

In movies, if you sleep at a fancy hotel they leave a chocolate on your pillow. (See D for

Do Not Disturb.) Not a whole bag. Just one. I grabbed a knife and held it up.

Guest, walking in scratching his crack: "Uh. Yasmin?"

My mother: "Macy?"

Me: "Hee hee hee hee."

I flang open the refrigerator. We may not have had food in it, but containers we had a-fucking-plenty. Even though we hadn't had eggs since ever, I found a egg carton. I cut off two cups and threw the rest in the trash, AKA on the floor of the kitchen. With markers from school I decorated each cup. Then stuck a M&M in each one and carried it to school.

Out the corner of my eye I watched Miss Black's face when she sat down at her desk. I would remember the face of the Super S manager every day for the rest of my life. But I would remember Miss Black's face too. The way she unwrapped the tissue paper very slow so she didn't rip it. The way she smiled like when you did something right on your test. The way she ate one M&M like it was something she might order at her favorite restaurant. She saved the second M&M for later.

Later that day, there was a little pink note pinned to the bulletin board. All period I kept glancing at it out the corner of my eye so she couldn't tell I was interested. At the end of class I had my chance. I snatched the note from the board and tucked it in my pocket. A girl saw me but she knew better than to open her mouth.

I waited until I got home to open it, to read the words that was written just for me. I didn't want my mother to see it. She was with Mr. Guest in the bedroom. I could hear her laughing through the walls. Always through the walls or into the phone. I knew her lips, her mouth, the sound of her laugh, but not her smile. Can a person laugh but never smile?

I closed the bafroom door. It was the only place I could be alone. I popped a squat and sniffed the envelope. This note was my botanical gardens. I closed my eyes.

Opened them when I felt a breeze. Popped up, then back down again, almost falling into the toilet.

Guest: "Hey, whatchu doing in here? What's that? A love note?"

"Get out of here!" I screamed, pulling Daddy's sweatshirt over my bare crotch.

My mother from the bedroom: "What's going on?"

Mr. Guest and I wrestled over the note. I ripped it away and stuffed it in my mouth. He wasn't staring at my mouth, though. He was staring between my legs. I backed up and almost fell into the tub. I was getting a queasy feeling in my stomach, the taste of that hamburger from lunch coming back up in my throat.

My mother: "What the fuck, Esteban?" She pushed him, but he didn't move until he was good and ready to.

"She got a boyfriend," he told her, not looking at her but still looking at me. I swallowed the rest of the note like it was the last Dorito on earth and pulled up my pants.

Mr. Guest walked back into the bedroom.

My mother popped her head in. I could smell the weed on her. "What was you two doing in here?" she asked. Her robe was open. I could see the hickies on her boob.

Me: "Don't you want to ask Mr. Guest what he was doing in here?"

My mother: "Trying to pee, Macy. Don't flatter yourself."

Me: "Shut up."

My mother: "You shut up."

Mr. Guest: "Woman!" He banged on the bedroom wall. "Get your ass in here."

My mother and me: "Shut up!"

My mother turned around to go into the bedroom. I wrinkled my nose at the thought. At the thought of what Mr. Guest might be thinking when he was with my mom. That he might be thinking of . . . A little bit of hamburger came up.

But I didn't let it. If I let the hamburger up, I let Miss Black's note come up. I thought real hard. About jazz and book trash and heroes and pink roses. Now forever inside me. A shield to keep everything else out.

Peace,
Macy Cashmere

POCKET

Noun. If you could make any three people in the whole world dump out their pockets, who would they be?

Alma and me are waiting for the bus. I can't see my breaf anymore and I push air in and out my lungs for a reminder. Alma raises a eyebrow and I cut it out. I kick melting icicles off the bench. A little kid's jacket is sitting on it soaking. Today jackets, coats, and sweaters clutter the school yard fence. Hats and scarves hang off the monkey bars.

"I'm so cold," I tell her.

"Cold? On the warmest day of the year? It's fifty degrees. Here," Alma volunteers, "take my coat." It's hanging through her backpack straps.

"The cold's in my bones. I have winter in my spine."

"Tell me how you are going to move to Canada again?"

"Here, the winter's in me. There, the winter will leave my body. Also, I will wear pelts. A bear will attack me. I'll kill the bear and take its spirit into my body."

"Sounds like you have it all worked out." Alma turns away

and shakes the coat in front of my face. I stop talking and take the coat. I nod.

The nod means *Thank you*. Thank you for the coat. Thank you for the shoes. (That was last week.) Thank you for giving me the shirt off your back. (The week before.)

I shiver.

"Oh, Macy," Alma says, "this isn't like the time when you freaked out because of your tongue, is it?"

My tongue felt too big for my mouth. I had no explanation. Alma didn't ask for any. She just sang me opera until I stopped banging my head against the wall and laughed. Singing opera is the *only* thing Alma can't do.

The bus is late. Alma gets up and paces. I don't like her being at the bus stop bench too long. Some guy is always bound to make a comment. I'm always bound to crack a skull. I hunker down in my Alma coat cave, shove my hands in her furry pockets, and scope out the area for scrubs. Clink. My hands touch bottles.

Alma turns when she hears me digging through her pockets.

"Carrots and peas?" I say, more to myself than to her, reading the label on a jar I've pulled from her pocket. I pull out more jars. "Squash? Bananaberry?"

"Give me those!"

By *those*, Alma means the half-dozen jars of baby food she has in her coat pocket. I stand up. "Are these the babies's's food?"

"Yes. But we get loads from WIC for free."

"A'ight. But why are they in your pockets?"

"This coming from the girl who eats napkins?"

Ouch. "Damn, Alma. I didn't mean nothing."

"Sorry. It's just I'm so tired of canned food. Spaghettios. Spam. What is Spam anyway?"

"Mmmmm. Spam. Canned ham and when you fry it up with a little rice and onions—oh! it's heaven."

"Yeah, if heaven were made of chemicals and fat."

"Chemicals and fat. Mmmmm."

"Macy!"

"You know what. It's all good. Just didn't know you were on the Disturbed Girl's Diet."

"I'm not *disturbed*!"

Ouch again. "A'ight. No offense."

"I'm sorry, Macy. Look, my mom has been coming down on me lately about the babies and me taking care of them . . . I guess I thought you were saying I'm selfish for eating their food. I love my babies. It's just sometimes, I just don't want Spagettios in my hair. I don't want to shove fast food down my throat because I'm too busy feeding everybody else. I don't want to be in charge. I'm—*annoyed*. Maybe it is a little selfish. But I just want to take a minute. Taste my food—even if it's mush. With the jars I can steal that minute for myself. . . ."

"Hey. You're the least selfish person on earth. Hello: *I'm wearing your shoes and your coat.*" I imagine her eating the baby food in Pepe's closet between classes. In a closet at home with kids pounding on the door.

When the next bus comes, I tell Alma to go ahead and I hand her her coat. She grabs it and climbs on, but just as the bus door closes she throws the coat at my head. That is the Alma I know. The problem is the Alma who eats baby food. The Alma I don't know.

I wear the coat but the cold hibernates in me. I get home. My mother's in the kitchen. Her back is turned. She's on the phone. "Don't cry, Daddy. You been doin good. You'll get out soon. I know it." She turns around. *She's* not crying. WTF?

My mother puts her hand over the phone: "Do you want to talk to him?" I freeze. My mother looks at me funny. "Augy, Macy's—What? Okay."

My mother to me: "He had to go."

She goes to the restroom and leaves her phone on the toilet like she always does. But my feet don't move to get it. My mouth don't know what to say to anybody about anything. What would I have said to my dad if I heard him crying? What should I have said to Alma? I know I didn't say any of the things I should have said.

I should have fucking said to my dad, *I love you*. But right now I don't know what *I* is. I don't know what *love* is. I don't know what *you* is.

Right now I would normally be breaking something. But I just feel broke down.

The counselor said if you don't know what to say, write it. If you don't know what to write, draw it. I take out a Sharpie and sit at the kitchen table. I draw a mountain and a sky on it. When I was a little kid I used to think mountains held up the sky. I liked to think my dad was the mountain when I rode on top of his shoulders.

But that's bullshit.

There ain't nothing holding up the sky.

I want my dad to call. I don't want to have to say the right things to him. I don't want to say I love you first. I want him to say all the right things because—he's my fucking dad, damn it.

I want to talk to Alma about not wanting to talk to Alma.

The phone rings. My mother runs out the bedroom and into the bafroom and picks it up. "It's for you. You have five minutes, then I want my phone back."

I grab the phone. "Hey."

Alma: "So, what's up?"

Me: "Uh, since the bus stop?"

Alma: "Shut up."

Awkward silence. Like the first one we've ever had. Me: "So—"

Alma: "So, I guess I'm going to get some dinner."

"Yeah." My stomach is growling.

"Listen, I'm not going to eat baby food anymore."

"Okay."

"I have to go."

She hangs up. For the first time I feel like she is gone. Like I can't call her right back like I always do, like I've done a million times.

That night, I burrow in the dirty laundry. I space out. I think about all the things I've eaten in the dark. I think about Alma. When did she start? Why didn't she tell me? How would I have acted if she told me? Alma's hunger scares me and I can't understand why. Any more than I could understand why my dad's tears scared the shit out of me.

But Alma is giving it up. The baby food. Because she don't need it. She don't want it. She's better than that.

Everything is back to normal.

QUESTION

Noun.

Am I disturbed?

READY—OR NOT

Adverbs. One for the money. Two for the show.
Three to get ready. And four to—

I think about writing a letter to Daddy in prison about what my mother is doing. More specifically, I think about writing a letter to my daddy in prison about *who* my mother is doing.

Instead I decide to write a letter to my grandmother. My mother's mother.

Dear Grandma,

I'm thinking about the day we met. It was sort of the day you and my mother met. You brought Mom the pictures of you two before you left. I always want to expand the picture. See all the things you cropped out, wanted Yasmin to forget. A daughter can never forget losing her mother. There's always a empty seat at the table.

As mad as I get at my mom, I get madder at you. Every time Yasmin does stupit shit, I think of the person who didn't do shit for her. YOU.

And why'd you finally show up? Because you needed someone to take care of you. You needed someone to love you. Yasmin wouldn't do it, and I know she still don't forgive herself. I blame you for that too. After she threw you out she spent hours, days, looking for you on the Internet. She still does sometimes. What sucks more than anything is she ain't never gonna find what she's looking for, but she can't ever stop searching for it.

I write this letter on Yasmin's behalf. To say everything even she could never admit. That you're a criminal. A thief steals shit but you stole the person Yasmin could've been.

Fuck you on behalf of my mother. You didn't even try. At least Yasmin gets credit for that.

I archive this letter in my dictionary. Next I write the letter to my dad. Put it in one of those envelopes the CPS worker left for us. Crumple it up. Uncrumple it. Keep it in my pocket.

SUPER

Adjective. Rhymes with Duper!

The history teacher is very excited. He has a *SUPER!* lesson plan. Tests are over so he can teach us something. We are learning about Pompeii. Pompeii is a Roman city from a long-ass time ago. Long-ass is to be defined as times when people write AD and BC. It got burnt down by a big-ass volcano. Big-ass. Not ginormous. I hate that word ginormous. Stop saying it.

I say to Teacher Man, "I do not get AD and BC. I do not get why the 1800s is called the nineteenth century. I mean why can't the 1800s be called the eighteenth century? We created daylight savings time, didn't we? *She-it*, if we could make day earlier and night later you would think we could call the 1900s the nineteenth century."

Alma draws me a diagram. She thinks she will explain AD and BC to me. She is even making it into some kind of game and folding loose-leaf into a dice. I ask her to hand me a dice.

Alma: "DIE!!!"

George: "Die? Die! No!"

Alma—rolls her eyes.

Alma! I want to shout. *WTF*?! I give her the eye. A first for us.

Me to George: "She said dynamic! Like Dynamic Duo."

This leads George to pretend he is flying with a cape. This leads the class to talk about when the X-Men will stop sucking so hard.

The teacher is mad. I don't think this is in his *SUPER!* lesson plan. I start thinking what would happen if a big-ass volcano exploded and the Super S got buried by volcanic ash.

So I tell the class to shut the hell up and they do. I motion to Teacher Man so he knows we all are going to listen now. He talks. He tells it like it was. Picture this.

Back then there are farmers. There are fishermen. There are potters. There are blacksmiths and carpenters. They are all waking up at the crack of dawn because they have shit to do. The fisherman has to catch the fish and sell the fish. He probably made his own boat. Can you imagine making a boat? You can't even make sense, let alone make a boat. There ain't no Super S back then. Everybody had to grow things. People built with their bare hands. George gets excited.

George says, "My uncle has hands!"

I say to the class, "He means his uncle builds things."

George nods so hard his helmet falls over his eyes. Everybody starts talking about their uncles that make things with their bare hands.

Me to Alma: "Back then I would be a blacksmith. I would work with iron and fire. I would get rich on rage. You?"

Alma: "I don't know what I want to be now. Let alone then."

Me feeling like I'm in a time-lapse, replaying her words: *I don't know.* "You don't know?"

Alma: "No. I don't."

Me: "Shit, if *you* don't know, who does?"

KABOOM!

Everybody jumps. The teacher has played a sound byte of a eruption. He's got our attention.

Teacher Man: "Imagine it. People are sitting in an amphitheater. Today's equivalent would be a movie theater."

Me: "Then just as they were about to say something to that rude motherfoe in back, they watched them turn to ash just before they did themselves."

Teacher Man: "Essentially."

"No, picture this," I say to George and Alma. "Your most embarrassing moment. The time you told yourself you wouldn't do X again, but there you are when nobody's looking, doing it again and—"

George: "Poof!"

Me: "Yup. Faster than a fart, all is turned to ash. A long-ass time later—"

Me to Teacher Man: "When did Pompeii erupt again?"

Teacher Man: "AD 79."

Me to Alma and George: "So a long-ass time later scientists dug around and found Pompeii."

Teacher Man to class: "You know what they found in Pompeii? They found buildings. They found houses and churches and schools and government buildings and theaters. They found art and pots and even an egg completely intact."

Me: "I'm the egg. You too, George!" I fist-bump George.

Alma is—doodling? Another first. WTF?

The class is paying attention. The teacher has them and that makes him SUPER excited.

I ask Alma, "What would they find if a volcano hit the Super S?"

Alma stops doodling. "Fake mustaches."

Me: "Yeah. A hundred for a dime! This makes you feel rich buying dozens and dozens of mustaches. You wear them once, you throw them out. There are mice running around somewhere wearing fake mustaches. The fun goes on and on."

Normally Alma gets mad at me at this point for running my mouth when she's trying to concentrate. But she don't. "You can buy earrings, ten for a dollar," she says.

Me: "For real! I mean, don't wear them in the shower. You know what gang-green is? You could buy a foot-long Star Wars pen—"

George breathing like Darth Vader: "Luke, I am your father."

Some joker: "At least that's what your mother told me!"

George coughs. And coughs. And coughs.

Teacher Man saving the joker from my wrath: "Take George to the nurse."

Joker hops on George's pretend motorcycle. George revs the throttle, coughs and drives to the nurse.

I ask Alma: "What would you want to be doing in your final moments?"

Alma shrugs, chews on her hair. "I don't know."

I don't know—again?

"Maybe I'd be a model. Maybe a famous artist would be painting me."

Me: "A model?"

Alma: "Yes. So? Models make money. In my final moments, I'd like to have some."

Me: "Okay. That's new. I don't know what to say."

Alma rolls her eyes. "That's new too. We're even. Anyway, what does it matter? One way or another we're all ash in the end."

I get a lightbulb. It matters. A lot. And it should matter to everybody's stupit ass.

Me to class: "Yo! Imagine a volcano erupted here. For homework I want you wack-ass cray-crays to write about what you'd want people to find when they dig you up. What you'd be caught doing in your final moments."

Teacher Man tells me, "Sit down."

Mistake number one. "Excuse you?" I say to Teacher Man.

The teacher presses the button. As my ass is being hauled away, Teacher Man says to the class, "You will write about what it would be like to have such an incident occur today. You will bring in an object of significance that you hope someone would find."

Super.

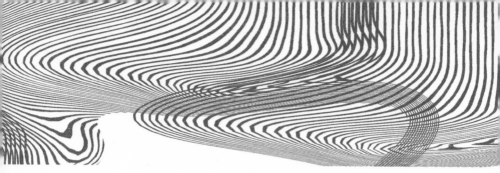

SIGNS

Noun. Synonym: symptoms—which is too many Ys (whys) in a row.

We're standing outside the gym waiting for the bell to ring and Coach to open the doors. "Whatever you coming down with, girl, you look contagious."

Alma pounds her chest to hold back a cough. "I'm fine."

She coughs again, but this time she goes in for a closed-fist chest punch. I block it before she inverts her boobs and has to wear a bra on her back. I guess her ears are feeling funny, because she starts itching like a ant colony crawled in there and then boxes her own ears until I grab her hands and stick them in her pockets.

"Alma," I say, smacking her in the forehead. "You have a fever. People get them."

"I'm not sick. I'm—*achoo!*—just a tad under the weather. I do not—*achoo!*—have a fever. I'm just—*achoo!*—overheated."

"Alma!" I snatch a box of Sudafed out of her hands before she takes another pill. "You're supposed to space out your doses. Have you been clocking when you took what?"

Alma is feeling her head. Tapping her foot and looking at the clock.

"Hello?"

Alma is not listening.

Shit, I think, does she actually believe she is going to get better just like that? I pull her toward me and put my hot head against her hot head. "Go home," I command. "It is a attendance award, not a Emmy."

"My mother always tells me to stay home," Alma answers, pulling a Benadryl box out of thin air.

"Where did that box even come from?" I say, watching her pop another pill like a Cheeto. "Did you rob the Super S?"

"If I sniffle because I have a booger, my mother says stay home," Alma says. "Once I stayed. I had the cold sweats. I knew the nurse would probably send me home anyway. I fell asleep. I had a dream." (See I for I Have a Dream.) "Then I felt a cold breeze. I saw a open window. Niko was standing on the windowsill. I ran over to him, caught him by the foot just as he started to fall. I tried to pull him up. All sudden, I felt all these little hands on me. Climbing past me, trying to jump."

She shuts her eyes. "It wasn't a nightmare. It was real. While I was asleep my mother piled all the kids around me and left. I was holding Baby Niko by the ankle because he had fallen off the bed. I had grabbed him in my sleep. The rest were just staring at me, watching me breathe."

Okay, I'm feeling her. At least if she drops dead at school no one would be standing on her corpse asking her to make a peanut butter and jelly sangwich. I leave her in the gym glistening like a pig because she claims the thermostat must be set "a tad bit high" and come back with cool paper towels from the restroom. I wrap them around the back of her neck.

"God, I just need to sleep!" Alma cries. She leans against the wall and hangs her head in her hands.

"God helps those that help themselves," I say. It's PE time and we have a substitute. I scope out the gym. I determine that the equipment closet would be a prime place for a cat nap. The one with all the nets would be perfect. The problem, of course, would be attendance. Once the sub counts Alma in he'll expect her to play or send her to the nurse. The nurse would most definitely send Alma home to slavery.

I go into the ball equipment closet. I hatch a plan. This is where I will wreak havoc.

Time-lapse to five minutes later . . . Thanks to me, the Master of Disaster, the basketball game is bombarded with soccer balls and baseballs and volleyballs and those little cone things you hit with a badminton racket and . . . There is so much commotion going on with kids sailing by on those little floor scooters kindergartners play on that the substitute counts fifty of us for attendance instead of twenty.

I have to give George some of the credit. During attendance he keeps saying things like: "What about Sandra? What about Martin? What about Diamond? What about . . ." All kids, mind you, that disappeared weeks, months, years ago.

I'm even able to check in on Alma and not be missed. Alma's hanging on a soccer net like a spider. She's going to wake up with a face like a fishnet stocking. She mumbles thank you in her sleep. Even in her sleep she's polite.

Closing the door on the equipment closet, I stand guard. I wonder how long a person can go without sleep. Alma looks ready for the NFL with the dark circles under her eyes. I wonder how long it took before Alma's mom stopped really looking at her.

How long did it take me?

STOP

Verb. As in drop and roll. Everything's on fire.

We are sitting at the bus stop. Alma inspects my hands. She starts filing my claws. Her hands are smooth and soft. With fake-ass hot-pink nails, all sudden. I flare my nose. "Why? I hate it."

Alma: "What?" She fans out her fingers. "God, Macy. It's JUST nails." She points at my stud. "I didn't pierce my own nose with a safety pin."

Me: "This is me. That shit is not you." I shut up because she stops filing. I lean forward and rest my head on my knees. Alma opens a bottle of peppermint lotion. She massages it onto my reptilian hands, and I shed my stress like a old skin. I try to think of anything that feels better than the way she holds my hands, but I can't.

GETTO BOYZ GET YRZ is graffitied on the bus stop bench. "To me, the ghetto is what what ghetto does. Just cuz you from the hood don't mean you're ghetto."

I close my eyes. Fall into a trance. We're transfused. My blood flows into her and hers into me.

"Is that right?" She massages my fingers and they feel like everything they touch could turn gold. "That's how everybody else sees it."

"Ow. My knuckle. Who's everybody? And why should I care what they think? Being poor ain't ghetto. Plenty of rich people is ghetto."

She lets go of my hand. "That's just how you see it. What you think isn't reality. Anyway, *this* girl's getting out of the ghetto. Or hood. Or whatever we're calling," she points at the streets, "all this."

"There was never a question, Alma."

The bus isn't here yet, but Alma stands up. She's trying to lift her backpack. It's full of library books. Textbooks. Color-coded notebooks. She hunches down to strap her bag on and stumbles under its weight. The bag rips.

I point at the tear. "Nothing a little duck tape can't cure."

Alma don't say anything.

"Alma. This is where you laugh." I can't see her face because of all her hair, but I see her pull out her cell phone, send a text, and shove it in her pocket. She's pacing back and forth now. She makes a visor with her hands and scans the street like it's going to make the bus come any faster.

"So," she says. "I've been meaning to talk to you." She looks down so her face is hidden behind the hair curtain, one hand in her pocket. "I'm not gonna hang out after school anymore." She brushes her hair aside and looks at me, biting her lip. "My uncle is going to pick me up. From now on. He got me a job."

"Your uncle? The one who gave you the pills?"

"He was just trying to help me out."

"Helping you to what? Become a crackhead?"

I look her in the eye, and she looks away. "You know what?" she says. "He's family."

Ouch. Like barbed wire ouch. "I'm just saying." No response. So I ask, "What's the job? Who's going to watch the kids?"

"I don't know. I told my mother I'm coming home late. My uncle said he has something good lined up for me. Something that pays a lot. Better than staying at home and working for free."

Working for free? That's cold. I mean no one could blame her, but that's not Alma's style. "So what exactly do you need the money for?"

She scrunches up her eyes, all agitated. "What do you mean?"

I admit it was a stupit question. Who don't need money? "Nothing," I say.

"My mother's not working her second job tonight anyway," Alma says and rolls her eyes. "She's not feeling well."

I lay my hand on her shoulder. "When is she due?"

She takes a step away and my hand slides down her back. "January is my estimate," she answers. "It's one of the only months when we don't have a fucking birthday."

I think this is the first time I've ever heard Alma drop the F Bomb.

"Going to save up. Going to get out." A shiny black car pulls up across the street. Alma says, "I gotta go."

Is this her uncle? The man driving looks at me but don't nod or open his window and say something. He just stares.

Alma turns her head toward me but don't look at me. She breathes in and pushes the air out her chest hard. "God, I'm so sick of birthday cake." She don't offer me a ride. She don't say good-bye.

I watch her cross the street. Her uncle rolls down the window. I don't like the way he is watching her.

She starts to climb in the back. Her uncle motions for her to sit in front. She walks around. Hops in the passenger side and buckles up.

"*Don't go!*" I scream. I run toward the car. "Stop! *Please!*"

They start to pull onto the street but stop, both of them staring at me.

She motions for her uncle to go and he does.

Maybe I imagine it, but I swear I see the word "disturbed" on Alma's lips.

SCRIPT

Noun. It's your line, Alma.

In snow, if you make footprints, you can just backtrack, carefully stepping on each of your own footprints, and nobody will know where you're at. Like you never happened. Like you went back in time. For every step I take toward home, I want to take two steps back in time before Alma stepped into her uncle's car. Before Alma talked about her family like employers who didn't give her her check. Before pockets full of baby food, and weeks with no sleep, and folded-up swans.

Nobody is home when I get there. Shit, my mother is probly out clubbing. That could mean she won't be back until Sunday when she crawls in around noon. And I might have no phone until Sunday?

I imagine every second from the time Alma stepped foot in her uncle's car, to what could have happened to her by the time it is Sunday. I want to smash a dish but all we have are paper plates. I wanted to smash a lamp, but somebody else already smashed it. There's nothing but the fucking TV. I turn it on and Ariana Grande is singing. I kick Ariana Grande in the face. I kick and I kick until keys turn in the door.

My mother screams, "What the fuck?!"

Her guest says, "Man, she really don't like that song!"

"Stop it, Macy!!"

I don't stop. Until I hear my mother running a baf and telling her guest to pick me up and throw me in the tub.

I stop. "You touch me and—"

"I don't want to touch you. But seriously," Mr. Guest says, grabbing a French fry out of a McDonald's bag, "you need to chill." He reaches into his shirt pocket and holds out a lighter and a joint.

"What?" my mother says. "Don't give her that!" She mouths, "We only have one."

"For real?" Mr. Guest says. "You don't want your TV?"

"Fuck yes. Help me move it."

She and her guest wheel it into the bedroom and slam the door.

Mr. Guest comes out one more time. "I always got a spare." He lays a joint on the kitchen table and walks out.

I pace around the living room. I have to make a plan. I can sneak into the bedroom and take the phone while they're—NO. There has to be a better way. The bedroom door opens. My mother comes out to use the bafroom. My whole body tenses up.

Please please please please PLEASE.

The toilet flushes. The bedroom door slams. I step into the dark bafroom and reach out my hand. YES! It's there!

I dial Alma. The phone rings. If I get more than two rings I hang up and start again. Because if it just rings and rings that means . . . But no matter how many times I dial, she don't pick up. This is nothing new, I tell myself. Get a grip. I know the script. Alma is just grounded again. Or her uncle picked her up from her new job and took her out for empanadas to celebrate. The more I ring, the more her mom knows it is me. I lean against the wall and lay down my head hard.

Bang bang bang. My mother and her guest . . . *Bang bang bang.*

My head! I close my ears with my hands. My head throbs. Like a heartbeat.

Bah bum Bah bum Bah bum Bah bum. A LOVE Supreme . . .

Fuck! Fuck! Fuck! *Bah Bum BAH BUM.*

I can't make it stop. I grab the phone and step outside onto the cold porch. I don't know what to do. *"WHAT?!!!"* I scream into a wind that just flings the words back into my face. But I have to do something. Could I sell Mr. Guest's spare joint for a ride to Alma's house? I pace like a animal. Kick the wall. This is how girls in my hood end up getting chopped up and stuffed into Hefties.

I storm back inside. NO. The difference between them and me is I'm the one who be doing the chopping. I grab my backpack, make sure my machete's still in it, and throw the phone inside.

That's when I hear the chirp of a text.

I fish the phone back out.

The text says: *I'm so sorry. DON'T*

Alma.

Please please please please please.

I text her, but she don't text back. This means she's at home in bed, right? This means she is taking care of the babies. DON'T means don't call and wake the babies. DON'T means don't get me grounded. DON'T means don't worry.

Not . . . Oh God. . . .

STRANGER

Noun. My best friend.

I think about volcanoes. I always saw myself as the volcano, not Alma. It's one thing to have a volcano that always erupts, like me. You get used to breathing in smoke—keep your sneakers laced. But it's another thing to look out your window and see a mountain. Marvel at how easy it holds up the sky. Then one day feel hot ash. Wonder how you missed all the smoke. After it erupts, what's left?

SPLIT

Verb. I used to tell Zane nothing could split us up.
Everyone wants to know why I'm such a bitch.
You try walking around with half a heart.
I ain't letting that happen again.

I know it is Monday morning because Monday the school serves breakfast tacos. Alma is always here first Monday mornings, patting her tacos with a napkin before she eats two bites and gives the rest to me. But Alma isn't here.

I face off with the clock on the cafeteria wall. I want to twist the arms off that clock and hear the crack of bone. Push the hour back to the time when Alma got in that car with her uncle. Take Time hostage. Tie a Hefty around his head. Shove his bony ass in a unmarked car. March Time back to every single moment when It should have stopped, but didn't. Scream: *Down on your knees!* and Time would know it better start praying. Make a shadow with my machete over the back of his scrawny neck.

Kids walk around me. "What's going on, Macy?" a teacher says all casual like she is asking about the weather.

I ask the teacher, "Is the clock broke?" She checks her watch and says no. I ask her if she's positive and she shows me the time on her cell phone. The bell rings for first period. I head to class, snatch a kid's cell phone, dial Alma's number. It rings and rings and I throw it. Knock over a desk. Go bang my head against the wall.

When God feels like I do—there are floods. There is fire. If God felt what I was feeling right now, the clock would explode. The windows would crack. The floor would split open.

But the windows show the same scene, like somebody hung a old dirty sheet on a line and never took the shit down. The floor is solid. Three million feet have passed over it. Three million more will pass over it. Floor don't notice when one girl—when Alma should be walking in out of breaf and late but hasn't, and maybe never . . .

Maybe this is just a bad dream?

My eyes happen to spot our health binders and the nutrition poster over them. I jump. The entire class jumps like the ring on a grenade just got pulled. I have had a lightbulb. Maybe, I think, I'm just feeling queasy about Alma's text because I'm hungry: exclamation point. For the past two days I've been living off that half-eaten box of stale French fries from Mr. Guest. (And yes, that included the box.) In health class I learned if you're hungry you can't think well.

I mean, shit, Alma apologized, right? This whole thing is in my head, that's all. Everything is always IN MY HEAD. But isn't everything in *your* head? What does it mean for something to be out of your head?

I hate thinking about thinking! I bite off my nail. It tastes like French fry. See! I *am* hungry.

I look at all the tasty foods on the food pyramid poster. When is the last time I had a carrot? You need carrots for good eyes. Alma is probly sitting right there at her desk, but I can't see her because my eyes are fucked up. In health we learned hygiene too. We learned that Q-Tip is not just a old-school rapper. It's something you use to clean the wack out of your ears. Maybe I can't hear Alma because my ears are stuck up. But that don't mean Alma can't hear me.

Alma! Alma! Alma!!

"Tell me about Alma," the counselor says. I jump. Blink.

"Maybe Alma is in the pyramid," I say to the counselor.

"Macy. Tell me about Alma and the pyramid."

"Well. Alma is . . . Wait. Don't condescend to me about Alma being in no pyramid," I yell at the counselor, who is magically leading me out the door. Alma is at home right now taking care of the kids. Tomorrow Alma will say that she can't be texting and changing diapers at the same time, and I should know that better than anybody. But she's sick. I'm the one who told her to stay home when she's sick, didn't I?

The counselor and I are at her office. I'm eating a cheeseburger. Oh! That was why I followed the counselor. The counselor pulls the wrapper out of my mouth. I do not stop eating. I almost bite the counselor.

I hear a ticking. I see the counselor's clock. It's 8:45 and I'm staring at the clock and thinking about everything I'm going to write in this dictionary after everything's said and done, and Alma reading what I wrote and dotting my eyes (my i's. MY EYES.) right before my eyes.

The counselor hands me a pickle, and I throw it at the window. It slides down the glass. I do not eat pickle, motherfoe. Any moment, Alma will be right before my i's and telling me to take a deep breaf. But Alma is still not fucking here.

The counselor asks, "How often do you eat paper?"

"What? What?" is all I can think to say for two minutes.

"What, you judgmental motherfoe, paper is from trees. You eat fruit from trees. Did you know syrup comes from trees?" Alma taught me that shit.

8:48. 8:49. FUCK in caps lock. Something is happening to me. My eyes can see. My ears can hear. I burp. I know I'm awake. I know I'm alive. I know I have to stop the clock.

I knock the drink the counselor is pumping into me like a I-V to the floor.

"I have to go to the *bafroom*!" I announce like I just found Jesus.

It is the perfect thing to say. Like I've said, teachers hate those seven words because it don't matter if they are true. You motherfoes have to let us go.

The counselor offers me her bafroom. "Not for what I got to do," I say. I hold my stomach.

The counselor gets on the phone and waves for me to go. I know she's calling for backup, so I know I have all of five minutes to pretend to go to the bafroom and sneak out a back door.

The back door is a door through time.

SECRET

Noun. Abracadabra.

If you've ever gone to a magic show you've seen a man in a top hat and cape. He can make pigeons disappear into his pocket. He can make rabbits disappear into a hat. He can swallow a diamond ring.

I'm standing in front of Alma's house. There is a long band of yellow plastic ribbon around the house that says, POLICE LINE. DO NOT CROSS. I'm late for the show.

The magician has been here. He took her couches. Her coffee table. Her kitchen table. The carpets. The curtains. The walls. Except for one with a window. Still has fingerprints on it. Somebody's smiley face.

A dude walks by laughing at his phone screen.

"Yo," I say, "you know what happened here?"

His eyes drop to the machete in my hand. He almost drops his phone. "Uh, the police don't know nothin. But my girl knows Giselle. Word is the kids were alone. Giselle thought her oldest daughter was watching them. Nobody knows where *she's* at."

He looks left, then right. "Kids got tired of waiting for the young lady to cook and decided to make something for themselves. Set the kitchen on fire. Older ones ran out the house, went to the park. By the time the fire department and the mother got there, three babies was dead. Cremated in their own cribs."

"Cremated? Our babies?"

I can smell the fire. I can hear the babies choking. Screaming for Alma, who for the first time don't come. Screaming when the fire touches their skin. I scream to outscream them. I slash at the air. The dude is gone. I have my machete but I have no one to kill. I can't kill fire.

I fall to my knees in white ash. Tanya, Alma's mini-me. Willy who liked to jump off the fridge, or was it Wally? Wally's Lambie. Or was it Willy's? Did he have his Lambie? My girl with her curls. She's here too. Wind stirs up dust and scatters Tanya, Willy and Wally, Lambie, Baby Girl into the air, over buildings, streets.

I stand up. Breathe in ghosts. Hold my breaf for as long as I can.

I would give up five years of my life if I could bring back Baby Girl. How is Alma dealing . . . Does Alma even know?

Alma. Alma is alive!

I use my machete to sift through the ashes. I want to find something of Alma's but there's nothing. The ground has probably been combed over by everybody and their mother already. I pick up three teddy bears clean as Canada snow. There's a pink one and two blue ones. These are the bears someone laid out for the dead babies. I make the sign of the cross and lay them back down in the ashes.

Alma is still alive. I glance back at the window. The magician was here. But magic is not about making things disappear. Any asshole can lose shit. Magic is about bringing things back. I'm the magician now. I will make her reappear.

SKY

Noun. Rhymes with Why.

I can't sleep because of Alma. I look up at the sky for hours, but I can't bring myself to ask. These are the same stars that I looked at when I asked for Zane. These are the same stars I looked at when I asked for my daddy.

Twinkle twinkle little star

A bunch of dust is all you are.

SWAN

*Noun. One time Miss Black told us this story
about a lady who's cursed to be a swan forever.
She only comes out at night to dance.*

If this was a movie I would hack into the school computers.
This would tell me if Alma is still enrolled at the school. I
would tap the school phones. This would tell me if CPS has
descended on her. I would know what I know now because I
bribed the school's secretary with a snack pack of Chili Cheese
Fritos, which I know she would sell her soul to El Diablo for.

This is not a movie.

It is Wednesday, and I'm not at school. I have things to do.
Because I have to do something. I'd rather do the wrong thing
than nothing. I'm not thinking. I'm doing. Moving. If I move
fast enough I can move faster than fate. Fuck fate. I got my
sneaks on, bitch! Eat my dust. I'll bury you in it.

Fill in the blanks: My mother is on the ___ with ___ .

Guest: Crunch.

Me: "Alma—she's gone."

Guest: Slurp.

My mother: "Gone where?"

Guest: Burp.

Me: "I don't know."

Guest: Scratch.

My mother: "Well, I'm sure she'll show up. She's a good girl."

Guest: "I'ma take a leak." Exit Guest.

Me: "Yes. She *is* a good girl. That's the problem."

My mother pausing her movie: "Yes. Her mom's problem. Just like you're mine."

Me: "So that's it?"

My mother: "What do you want me to do? It's not my business."

Me: "What is your business, Ma?"

My mother getting up from the couch: "Actually, my fucking business is none of yours, Macy. I don't know what you expect from me!"

Me: "Nothing, Ma. NOTHING."

I grab my backpack and run out the door. My feet are in charge. I'm just along for the ride. Five blocks later I'm standing in front of the Super S. It's dead in there. I walk in. I don't even care if the manager remembers me.

He looks up. The only difference between now and then is gray in his mustache. And I mean that is the *only* difference. He don't look like he's showered in the past year.

I pull out my machete and hold it where he can see it but the cameras can't. He falls back into a bunch of nudie magazines.

I file my nails on the blade. "Am I pretty now?"

Manager: "Who are you? What do you want? I'll call the cops!"

Me: "Because I want a stamp?"

Manager: "What?"

Me: "You're gonna call the cops because I want a stamp. Just one. NOW." Manager starts reaching his hands down under the counter.

Me: "Don't even think about the buzzer. I'm a expert on those things. Just show me where the stamps are."

He points at a case behind him. "Take em all."

Me: "I don't want them all. I want just one."

The manager nods and gets me my stamp. I pull the wrinkled letter to my dad out my pocket. Two kids come in for smokes, and I tell them to get the hell out. A kid comes in trying to steal a candy bar and I tell him to take it and get out. Three girls walk in and the manager eyeballs them.

Me to the manager: "You know, I heard in some countries if you do wrong with your hands they cut them off." Me to the girls: "He's a perv. Take what you want and tell everybody."

The girls stuff chips and soda in their backpacks, giggle, flip the manager the finger, and run.

I'm done. I lick the envelope and back out toward the door. "You can call the cops. And if they catch up to me, which they won't, I'll have a lot to tell them about you."

I run to the nearest mailbox. Kiss my letter, open the drawer, and hold it over the slot. My hand shakes. I start thinking. Shit. I change my mind but when I pull my hand back the letter catches on the edge of the slot and falls in. I stick my hand in the box but grab at empty space. I step back and run. I don't know where to, but I know it will take a train to stop me. My brain knows what I'm passing: the junkyard, the Dollar General. My eyes see only blur—

Whah! Oompf! because I think I just got hit by a train. I'm on the ground in front of where? Being murdered by who? Or what?

Me: "George? Get the hell off me. No offense but you're killing me!"

George cries.

Me: "Oh, man. I didn't mean—"

George: "No! No! No!" He stands up.

I look up. We're in front of that strip club, Hole in the Wall. Even my mother calls the girls in there skanks.

Me: "George? I mean. I'm not gonna judge, but—uh—whatchu doin here?" I nod toward the Hole.

George is pacing back and forth. "Earth angel! Earth angel!"

Me: "I hate to tell you this. But you ain't gonna find no halos and wings in there, baby. Unless it gets them more tips."

George: "No! No! Alma!"

Me: "What? What, George? What the hell?" I grab his Chewbacca coat and shake him. "WHAT?!"

I've scared him. His wide eyes are staring at the front door of the Hole. He whispers, "Angel."

My body tightens up. I can hear a mosquito breathe. The whole world disappears and it's just George and me and the Hole.

Suddenly George is banging against a blackened window. "Stop!" I say. He stops and turns toward me. I need time to think.

The door to the Hole opens. I see a table with a girl on it. She is crawling. A man is pouring beer on her. The door closes.

Out steps the tallest white man I have ever seen. His skin is red as a brick and his muscles as hard. Next to him and the gun I can see he's packing, my machete looks like Alma's nail clipper. I grip it anyway. I don't even care.

Brick Man talking to George: "What did I tell you,

motherfucker?" The man spits on the sidewalk. "What did I tell you if you stepped foot here again?"

I step up with my nail clipper. "Hey," I say, craning my neck to look up at him. "George no hablo inglés, okay? So you talk to me. Where the fuck is Angel?"

He adjusts his sunglasses. It's five in the afternoon and cloudy, but who am I to tell him? "Both of you assholes got sixty seconds to get out of here," he says, walking back into the Hole.

"George, come on," I say. Trying to make a mountain move would be easier than trying to move George. "C'mon, man," I beg. "We'll come back. We need a plan." A plan for what, I don't know, but I do know we have about thirty seconds.

"We'll come back, Angel!" George says after using up ten of our seconds, and I'm sweating like I pushed Mount Everest. We head down the street toward the bus stop. We're about halfway down the block when I hear a car stop back at the Hole. I stop and turn back. George does too. A shiny black car has pulled up in front of the Hole and parked in the fire lane. And what motherfoe should step out?

Alma's fucking uncle, that's who.

George gets in position like a linebacker. I jump on his back to slow him down. Uncle leans in and barks something at somebody in the car. My body knows what's going on before my mind can grasp it. It feels like somebody just reached into my chest, pulled out my heart, and showed it to me still beating.

Uncle walks into the Hole. *Hike!* George shakes me off and starts running toward his car. He tackles the hood. It dawns on me that this shit is not going to end well, whatever this shit is. Any hope we have of leaving alive will be gone if George fucks up Uncle's car.

I'm the running back. I catch up with George and grab him by his fur. I lose my grip but latch on again. I pull on him with all my might but all I end up doing is pulling down his pants. The club door opens again.

Holy shit. George is being picked up by his feet and dropped on his head into the gutter. Thank God for Ninja Turtle helmets. This bouncer is as wide as the other one was tall. All sudden I'm flying backward and snot is gushing out of my nose. It hurts like a bitch and when I touch it I discover I'm not covered with snot. It's blood. I'm about to ask someone to pick up the phone until I realize it's my ears ringing.

This is not a movie.

The car door opens. I can't see nothing because my eyes are tearing and I'm in the gutter now too. My baseball cap has fallen off. The bouncer makes another grab for me but then stops.

He didn't know I was a girl till now. My nose stud is gone. Possibly lodged in my brain. Blood is smeared across my cheek. I hear George screaming and pointing at the girl who has stepped out of the car. I can't really make her out—or anything else for that matter. I couldn't see two fingers waving in front of my face.

"Stop, Victor!" the girl says to the bouncer. "Stop! Just . . . I will make them go away!"

I don't need to see her. I cup my nose. I don't need to smell her. I'd know her blind, deaf, and dumb.

"You got five minutes, Angel." Uncle looks at the bouncer, nods toward the Hole, and the three of them go inside.

My vision is still blurry, but my ears have stopped ringing and I hear her. I feel her hand on my shoulder.

"You have to go, Macy."

I look up. George is stumbling forward. He throws his coat over her.

"Thank you, George," Alma says.

My brain is trying to come up with a way to describe what is before my eyes. Alma is wearing—Alma is wearing—Alma. NO. Alma IS NOT wearing. Kleenex has more substance than what's plastered on her body.

"Alma! Alma? What the fuck?" Remember this is not a movie. My head feels like a house fire. I think my nose is broke.

"You have to leave, Macy, okay? *Please!*"

"I'm not leaving you here," I say. I try to get up, but I can't. "Are you crazy? I wouldn't leave my worst enemy here, let alone my best friend."

"Then . . ." she stutters. "Then. Then I'm not your friend."

"Fuck you." I can stand up now. Suddenly I can think. "George," I command, "pick her ass up!" George picks her ass up just like that.

"Macy, please!" she says, wriggling, one of her white shoes dropping onto the street. They look like little-girl patent leather shoes, only the heels are six inches tall. "Macy," she says, looking back at the Hole and then at me, "They will kill you! Me! My family! Put me down, George! Please! *Please!*"

Oh Jesus Christ. Does she even know about the fire?

This is not a movie. There is no soundtrack. Only the sound of me choking on snot and blood and tears. The sound of George howling. The sound of Alma's heart beating—I swear I can hear it through George's coat, right through her chest.

"Put her down, George," I say. I'm standing up now. Barely. Alma is wearing a Kleenex and a Chewbacca coat. This is not a movie.

"I will never leave you," I say, taking out my machete. "If I leave you, I have nothing."

"Then, you've always had nothing," Alma says turning away.

"Fuck you," I say again. "Fuck that." The door cracks open.

"Macy! *Macy!*" she begs. "*Please*, okay? We can meet one more time. For a few minutes. 565 Broker Street. Apartment 3C. 12:15 tomorrow night. No earlier."

Two bouncers motion to Alma, and George and I get ready to run.

Alma runs for the door, trips on her heel, slips back into The Hole.

SCAR

Noun. How we're stitched together, George.

"Ma!" I yell, coming through the door. "George needs help!"

"Yeah, I can see that," my mother says. She is sitting on the—multiple guess:

Couch, packing a bowl

Bed, smoking a bowl

Toilet, eating a bag of marshmallows

Answer: All of the above, in that order.

While she is otherwise occupied, I grab my stash from underneath the floorboard—my dad's coke and my birfday money—and stuff it into my backpack along with Mi Machete.

My mother comes out the bafroom hiding a big-ass marshmallow in her cheek and turns her back to zip up her pants. George is standing in the living room scraping fresh marinara sauce off the wall. How did I miss that?

"What is he, we-tarded?" my mother says through the remainder of the marshmallow.

"Well, he's not deaf."

George shrugs.

"Listen," my mother says, licking her teeth, "I got a guest coming over."

"I should have known. You're wearing your *I'm having a guest* thong," I say. I see it sticking out of her whitewash jeans.

"I ain't in the mood for your shit. And your nose looks like shit. Damn, Macy. Really? What are you, gang-banging? Put some makeup on that."

"Help me then, and I'll get out of your hairs. George needs to dress gangsta." I wait for my mother to ask me to explain, but she don't. She just walks around George like you do a used car, inspecting his exterior.

"My ex, Nacho, was your size. I got a few things he left behind. That motherfucker ain't coming back."

I look at George. I know what I have to do before my mother gets back. I know what could happen to me too. "George," I say, pointing at his head. "George, the helmet."

George shakes his head. He shakes it harder the closer I get until the helmet falls over his eyes. "George, do it for Alma."

He hears her name and takes off the helmet just like that. I see what I think is a scar but he flicks his hair on it real fast.

I HEART George.

He pounds his chest and touches my cheek. His eyes are all red and I know he wants to cry—just not in front of my mother. I hold out my fist for a bump. He bumps back. I stick the helmet in my backpack quick before she comes back in and makes a comment.

My mother struts in holding up a outfit and eyeballing George. She's on a mission now. In a snap she has George stripped down to his tighty whities. George does not know how to say no to my mother. No man can.

Ever hear of pimping your ride? My mother pimps out my friend. In a matter of minutes, he goes from being a cream puff to a puff daddy.

"Hey, check you out," I say to him.

I can tell my mom wants me to say something to *her*. She wants me to tell her she did something good and she wants me to thank her. I would if I didn't smell the garlic from the pizza she ate on her breaf. She hates it when I do that: sniff around her face like a dog.

I back up. "Okay," I say, more to the walls than to any particular person. "We out."

"You know, your father spoiled you," I hear from outside the door. "Cunt!"

SISTER

Noun. This is for her too, George.

We hoof it for twenty minutes and soon we are approaching the Palace Apartments. *American Horror Story* could shoot their next season here. The ratio of cockroach to person is one million to one. Rats as big as dogs are kings of trash mountains. Shitty cars sit on cinder blocks. You get the picture. Ghetto in the ghetto. I feel George slow down as he takes it all in.

The only way I'm going to be able to walk up Broker Street and enter Palace Apartments alive is to have George stand up straight and put one gangsta foot in front of the other.

I stop in my tracks and look George in the eye. "What would Alma do without you, George? What would I do without you? You're our hero." I kiss my finger and lay it on that scar under George's hair. Look away. He don't say anything. We walk in silence for a minute. Then I realize I'm getting out of breaf trying to keep up.

George is walking tall. He's even got a little swagger.

Separately George and I aren't the strangest or scariest ass-holes ever seen, but together we are dynamite. Motherfoes just have better things to do than say something to a 250-pound gorilla and the sidekick with a foot-long machete sticking out her backpack. The key is to be a mystery. The minute people start getting too close and asking questions, we're dead ducks because, basically, George is bound to start quacking like one. And it won't take long before somebody offers us drugs or hookers and knows we don't belong.

"Just don't speak," I warn George before we get to the top of Broker Street. "Just pretend you're listening to music. Zone out."

George smiles. He's never needed a reason to hear music. He bobs his head up and down. He looks badass.

He raps like Ice Cube: *"Today was one of those fly dreams . . ."*

"Didn't even see a berry flashing those high beams." I can't help it. I crack a smile.

He cracks one back. "You look good like that, Macy." He taps my mouth and tilts his head.

He means: *When's the last time you smiled, Macy?* I don't have a answer.

We walk past a meth lab. Past hookers hanging in car windows.

When is the last time I smiled? When is the last time Alma smiled? I can't remember. But I do remember that time we stayed up all night on my mother's cell. I told her funny stories until she fell asleep. I could hear her sleep snores through the phone. It was like we were sleeping in the same bed. I heard her laugh soft in her sleep. She never saw the sunrise that morning but I did—for the first time. I had never seen a sunrise before. I say more to myself than to George, "I smiled when I saw that sun rise." But he hears me.

We stop. Not just because we're at the stoop of Palace Apartments. Because we are being followed.

George motions to me and I know to follow his lead. We spot some trash cans and walk behind them. So do our shadows: two guys in bomber jackets on our tail.

George reaches into his pocket. I'm thinking, what in the hell could he possibly have in his pocket that's going to do us any good? I debate if I should grab my machete.

George pulls out a needle. He drops his pants down right then and there and stabs himself. I'm thinking that this is a epic WTF moment when he motions for me to pull up my sleeve. I admit, I almost chicken out. But this was the guy who took his helmet off for Alma. I roll up my sleeve and shut my mouth as he stabs my skin.

George stands up to his full height and throws the needle into the grass like Agüeybaná. Our Shadow Men disappear.

George: "No worries. Just meds for me. No cooties."

I look at the tiny prick on my skin. He hadn't pushed the plunger on the needle down for me. George pulls out a Hello Kitty Band-Aid from his pocket, sticks it over the pinpoint, and rolls down my sleeve.

"I know, George. I fucking HEART you."

We climb up steps into Palace Apartments when there are steps to climb. We climb over people when there aren't. We hear a loud squeak that seems to be coming from—like—everywhere. "All sudden my mom's housekeeping don't look so bad," I say to George.

We reach the top of the steps. George and I review the game plan. He will play lookout and bodyguard on the outside while I work on Alma on the inside. When my mission is accomplished, George will carry Alma out caveman style.

The next stage of the plan is to rob my mother's guest-of-the-hour blind and use whatever money we find to get on a Greyhound. To go where CPS and Uncle can't find us. Till things cool down. Or forever—but I haven't told George this. George hearts his mother.

Leaving George on the landing with his instructions, I walk into the dark hall. I pull my hoodie on.

In front of 3C, I inventory my backpack. Cash . . . check. Coke . . . check. Machete . . . check. I stuff the cash and bag of coke in my pocket for easy access. Grip my machete. I push on the door and it cracks open, but I don't see nobody. I hear a whisper: "In here."

My Spidey sense tells me it's safe as it's gonna get, so I step inside. The only light is coming from a window with a lamp post outside it. I'm inside one large room. A king-size bed is in the center, a trunk in front of it.

"*Psst!*"

I turn my head and I still don't see nobody. A electric chair would look less scary than the stove yanked out of the wall. My nose finds the fridge before my eyes do. Nasty. A ghost stands behind a counter.

I run my hands on the wall trying to flip a light switch on. "No. Don't."

"Why?!" I squint. Walk toward ghost girl. Alma is wearing another costume. The robe and the nightgown are white. I can see through them.

I see why she wants me in the dark. I yank her nightgown. "What is this—?"

I shit you not, Alma says, "Stop! It'll tear!"

"That's your damn concern?"

"Tío bought it for me."

"You still call him Tío? Why are you crouching like that? Can we step out of the—uh—*kitchen*? My shoes are sticking to the floor!"

"No. Just stay here."

"Why?"

"Do it!"

"You know who you talking to, girl?" I'm getting loud. "I don't just *do* nothin."

"*Please!*"

I have a lightbulb. Look from floor to ceiling and wall to wall. "Oh shit. Alma? Is there a camera in here?"

She nods. "Just stay here. He can't hear us. I don't think."

I pull her toward me. Her hair smells like cigarette smoke. "No! No! Don't touch me!"

George pokes his head in and out, then closes the door.

"For real?" I hiss, throwing Alma against the wall. "Don't touch me? This from the girl who wrestled me in my sweatshirt?" I grab my mother's phone from my backpack and aim the flashlight at her face. "Oh my God. What are you on?"

Her eyes look too big, like she's seen something horrible and she's seeing it over and over and over again. I aim my flashlight over the room. Holy shit. Every wall is covered with mirrors.

"Put that down!" Alma reaches for my phone. Her hands are shaking bad. Like she wants to do something terrible and she just can't.

That's okay, I'll do it for her.

"What is this place, Alma? What did he do to you?" I grip my machete. "I will be waiting behind the door when Uncle comes home."

Alma reaches onto the counter. Pulls out a nail. Squeezes it in her hand until she bleeds. A crazy girl Jesus.

"Stop it, Alma!" I lunge toward her but she backs up until she hits a wall. She holds up a hand. It's firm. Steady.

"Do not come closer to me," she says. "I have to do this. It wakes me up. It brings me back. I've been taking them out of the walls, the counter. At first I burned myself on the radiator, but then Tío turned the heat off. I tried the stove too, but Tío pulled it out."

God, is this real? "What did he do to you, Alma? What is he doing? Did he rape you?"

"Did he rape me? Did he rape me? No! He raped *her*!" She points to a mirror, screams deep down in her chest. A scream so loud God could hear it, so deep her uncle can't. Her body has just caught up with her mind.

I'm frozen. It's not that she's told me something I didn't know the minute I saw her outside the Hole. But it is all hitting me at once. No matter what I've ever gone through, no matter how bad I thought the world was, I still believed there was good in it because of Alma. NEVER AGAIN.

"What happened that weekend? After you left me at the bus stop and went with your uncle." I cover my ears even though that don't make any sense.

"He was taking me to a photoshoot. I was going to be a model."

"ALMA!" I scream. "Why did you let him?!"

"*Fuck you*, Macy! Let him? *Let* him? He gave me pills. I couldn't even say no. But it was there. Those two little letters trapped between my teeth!" She groans. "Two letters. Two letters," she says over and over.

No.

Alma drops to her knees. She screams again. She screams a scream that should have been heard off every rooftop of the world but is stuck in this shitty room.

"Alma!" I drop to my knees beside her. "Alma, why?"

"I was just so tired! School was supposed to save me, right? But how was I supposed to do well at school when I couldn't even concentrate? And all the teachers kept asking me what was wrong. Saying that I was changing. What did they expect from me? For me to say something and get my mother in trouble again? So CPS could get me? I just thought I could make some money and get out of here . . ."

"Why didn't you ever tell me this?"

"Because I couldn't even tell myself."

"Alma, what happens when he gets tired of you? When he's got you dancing at the Hole? When he's pimping you out to—"

"He would never do that! He l—"

"*Loves* you? I love you, Alma. Let me help you."

"Help me? Save me? There's nothing left to save!"

"Alma, you're not what happened to you. You're the girl who walks out this door. Alma. Come with me."

Alma collapses on the floor. She tosses the nail in her mouth and chews on it. I pull it out. Her gums are bleeding.

"I can't," Alma cries. "I can't leave. He'll never let me leave. He will follow me anywhere I go. I couldn't leave him even if I left this room."

"I will kill him, Alma. And I won't just do it for you. I'll do it for every other girl. You tell the police it was all me. Just promise to visit me in jail."

"Macy, you can't just kill him. You'd have to kill his men. His boss. His organization. You could never kill them all. I can't go. They'll kill my family. What's left of my family."

Oh shit. She does know about the fire.

"Your family? Why aren't they here fighting for you?"

"My mom is fighting just to stay alive right now. She lost everything in the fire. Because of me. She thinks I'm better off with my uncle. At least that's what she chooses to believe."

"You aren't his. I see you, Alma. I know you. You ain't what's in these mirrors. In any mirror. Let's go." I climb to my feet. "Stand up!"

She kneels. "This is my penance. For my babies."

"Alma! That wasn't your fault! How do you even know your uncle didn't set the fire?"

She hugs her knees. "Please go before Tío gets back. He'll kill you."

I look at all the mirrors. Think about what Alma's been forced to watch. I know what her uncle will do. He'll think Alma let some dude (me) into the apartment. One of her neighbors is bound to say something, if they haven't already.

I walk to the door and stick my head out. I speak to George. He cries. I tell him not to come back in no matter what. I close the door. Tighten my hoodie. Grip the machete.

I face Alma. My stomach lurches. The only thing that holds my dinner down is Miss Black's pink roses. But the roses can't hold back my tears. I'm never going to see her again.

"You will never forgive me," I say to Alma.

"I'll forgive you, Macy. Get out!"

I step forward and raise my machete.

"Oh my God—What are you—"

For once I'm going to do something for her. Something she can't do for herself.

"Macy, *what*—"

Her words get cut off as I slash her face. Stripe her with

blood. Blood spatters bloom on her nightgown. I knock her on the floor and cut off her hair. Cut all the motherfucking petals off the rose.

"Now you'll be safe. Nobody gonna touch you now."

She screams into the linoleum. I stop. Wrap her in a blanket. I take the blow out my backpack and shake it on the floor like a blanket of Canada snow. In it I spell:

You're next Motherfucker

I tuck that hundred dollar bill from my fifteenth birfday into Alma's twitching hand. Then I go knock on the door. It opens and I slip out. Through the door I can hear her stumbling around the apartment, crying.

Out in the hallway, I wait a minute even though George is pulling on me. I want to see if someone is going to come. Is just one person going to open their door? At least yell they're going to call the police? All I hear is two doors shutting and someone turning their TV way up. Some girl screams but it's coming from the set. The moonlight glints off the tips of George's fur coat.

STAIN

Noun and verb. Rhymes with pain.

We go the Laundromat and use the pay phone to call 911 and tell the rude bitch on the other end to send a cop and ambulance to 3C at the Palace Apartments. George strips down until all he's wearing is his tighty whities. He puts the Ninja Turtle Helmet back where it belongs.

He holds up his Puff Daddy clothes and calls out over the washers and dryers, "Switch?"

It don't take two minutes before George swaps clothes with some fool and is wearing a giant red M&M T-shirt with camo pants to complete his crazy-ass outfit.

George walks up to another dude. He has forgotten to slouch. George says, "I want two quarters." He gets a whole dollar. He walks back and hands the coins to me.

My eyes stare at it. My hands throw the coins on the floor. Alma's blood is all over my hands.

George picks them up and pounds them into my hand.

Her blood is on his hands too now. I nod. I can't speak. He pulls my sweatshirt off. It's all soaked at the pits but I don't remember sweating. The washer starts. The water and soap mixes. I stare at the machine for thirty minutes. I think.

When you wash something, it changes. After enough washes, the color fades. Maybe that stain of barbecue didn't come out the way you wanted—but it fades. The size may change. That's the way most thoughts are supposed to be. Faded. Forgotten.

That is not how my thoughts work. They do not shrink or fade.

I don't just remember things. I'm there. I smell what I smelled the way I smelled it. I taste things the way I tasted them. I hear what I heard the way I heard it. Not the way you heard it, motherfoe. Not the way you think you said it. Not the way you meant it. I feel what I felt.

The spin cycle hypnotizes me. I'm going back. I'm about seven or eight and bitchin about my mom . . .

Daddy says, "You'll never believe this, Macy, but your mom would take bafs with you because she knew you was scared of the water. She would get you to lie on her chest and wash your hair. Once you fell asleep in the tub and she stayed in there for an hour because she didn't want to wake you up."

But I know something Daddy don't know. I woke up. I was underwater. My mother was sleeping, her hair floating like seaweed. Her body jerked. She choked and gasped and pulled us both out the water.

I swear I remember this too. *"Macy (gasp, cough), don't tell your dad."*

It wouldn't be the last time I heard that. Wouldn't be the last time when my mother, my dad, and me all chose what we wanted to remember about the past.

The suds and Alma's blood mix. George and I watch the patterns of soap. A melt of circles, spirals, flowers . . .

I wonder how many memories I have of our friendship where I thought Alma and I was hearing something the same way, smelling something the same way, tasting something the same way, feeling something together, when . . . when that wasn't it at all.

Watching Alma's blood mix with soap and disappear, I wonder if the way she and I remembered things was totally different. Wonder if every memory she has of me, or don't have, erases me completely.

I watch Alma's blood rinse, spin, disappear. After it's dry, George and I conversate. George says he'll meet me by the Dollar General in a hour. He wants to say good-bye to his mom before we make a break for it. I run home, leaving rivers of water and blood behind me.

My eyes are open but they are blind. Always were. Light don't help you see shit. It blinds you. If Alma and me wasn't seeing eye to eye, nobody ever would.

When I remember, I feel exactly how I felt. I see what I saw the way I saw it. You say you feel me, but you can't. All I feel is weightless. Empty. I run but I know I'm running in place. Trapped back in that room of mirrors forever.

SNOW

Noun. Let it.

Soon as I open the front door, my mother slams her bedroom door shut. She and her latest guest are laughing, horsing around on the bed. I fling the door open.

Mr. Guest rolls off the bed. "What the fuck?!"

I carve the air with the machete.

My mother: "Oh my God, Macy! What the fuck are you doing? Is that blood on your face? On the . . . ?" My mom trips over her guest. "Macy!?"

I walk toward the bed. "Macy? Who the hell is that? Cause I'm no one. Nothing."

I hear: "*Fuck this!*" Mr. Guest barrels out the house buck necked. My mom runs out after him in a sheet, screaming. I hack at her bed until I hear the clang of steel springs. Cotton fills the air like snowflakes.

The police come. I watch myself get Tased in the mirror.

I'm in Canada. I fall onto snow. Make a snow angel.

TO BE OR NOT TO BE ME

Quote. That is the question.

I stare at myself in the blank TV screen. A stranger stares back. I can't have piercings because I might "engage in self-harm." I've looped strands of thread through the holes in my ears and my nose. I look like I am unraveling. My hair is growing back in patches. My furry legs make me think of George's coat. Can't use a razor here unless a nurse supervises you. I'd rather become George's coat. A nurse eyeballs me when I start to scratch my scalp. He takes a note and waits. Says he clips my nails or it's the Quiet Room.

Jesus is on the carpet playing Scrabble with a bipolar heroin addict named Suzy. The difference between here and home? All these crazy motherfoes is wearing fuzzy slippers. You can't have laces here. Could hang yourself. Or you could run away on a smoke break. I choose being barefoot. Another difference between here and home? These motherfoes smell better.

In some ways this is the sanest place I ever been. The couch I'm sitting on is a couch. The bed is a bed. But daylight never ends. At night the flashlights shine right in your face every fifteen minutes. The White Coats are here to re-suss-itate, revive, force-feed you back your life. I choke. Can't keep none of it down.

VAGINA

Noun.

I'm in a mental institution. We are watching the news. Other people are not in a mental institution. They want long eyelashes. They want pudding. They want war. They want peace. We see clips of Nigeria and something about the election there.

I turn the volume up. "I remember the kidnapped girls from Nigeria. Where they at?" But nobody's talking about those girls from Nigeria.

"Those girls are not being raped and tortured," I tell Jesus, man who misspells *damnation* on the Scrabble board. "Maybe they tucked their legs into their vaginas. Folded themselves up like origami. Back into their own wombs until it's safe to be reborned."

Jesus chucks letters of D-A-M-N-A-S-H-U-N at me.

I kick over the board. "Jesus says I came out his rib. I say he came out my vagina."

Jesus stands up. "And he made a scourge of cords and drove them all out of the temple!"

I grab my puss and sing, "My Cuntry Tis of Thee!"

Jesus is escorted to a Quiet Room. Doc ups my dosage of pills.

I'm in a mental institution. We are watching some celebrity. She needs to eat so she can get fat so we can watch her get skinny. She wears different outfits. In all of them you can see her vagina. I was wrong. Vaginas can talk. We watch her vagina go to restaurants. It goes on vacation. We think about whether it is pregnant. Everyone knows where her vagina is all the time, except when she shits. Even then, people have a fairly good idea.

"Where are the girls?" I ask and ask. "Somewhere there are 200 missing vaginas." But no one here can tell me where the 200 missing vaginas are. The doctor gives me what is called a cocktail.

VISITORS

Noun.

I'm in a mental institution. I'm sitting on my bed. My armpits are spiky. My transformation into George's coat continues. The holes in my eyebrow and lips are closing. Knock. Knock. I have visitors.

Black and purple bruises wrap around Velvet's neck. She is wearing her fur coat.

I ask, "Is it your turn?"

Knock. Knock. Alma holds her hair, dripping with blood. She lashes her hair at the wall, at the bed, at me. Droplets spray in the air and rain down. It is raining blood. Alma kneels down and stares at her reflection in a puddle. Screams. Melts. Evaporates into a crimson cloud that hovers over me. Drips. Storms.

Shoes. A nurse trip-traps into my bedroom. Hands me a folded piece of paper. On it are names that she wrote down. Lots of names. Hundreds of names. Deborah, Awa, Hauwa, Asabe, Lugwa, Kauna, Lydia, Hannatu, Filo, Hijara, Rejoice,

Nguba . . . I read and reread them over and over. By the time the nurse comes back in, I have half of em memorized.

Nurse says, "You have a visitor." Blood sprays on the back of her stockings as she wades out. The smell of roses parts the blood as my visitor walks in. The rain stops.

Miss Black pulls up a chair and sits beside me. I don't say anything. She don't say anything. She cracks open a book. The turning of pages is the last thing I hear. When I wake up, I'm tucked under the covers like a little kid. I pull off the covers and plant my foot down beside a grocery bag. In it is muffins. Records. Miles Davis. John Coltrane. The rain starts up again.

I stuff the bag under my bed and go to the TV room. The nurse walks in. "You're popular today. You have another visitor."

It's my mother.

"I forgive you," she says, plunking on the couch. I freaked her shit out, but she gets it. She once tried LSD and did some crazy shit. "What were you on, girl?"

I open my mouth like I'm about to sing, then shut it.

The Purple People Eater Lady the staff insists is called Florence flips from the food channel to the Kardashians eating cupcakes. I see myself on the screen eating from out the couch cushions, chiseling the fridge, chewing on a McDonald's French fry box. The crumbs, crusts, runaway Skittles, the accidental button, the cardboard still sit in my stomach. I'll dissolve and they'll be all that's left.

"Whatchu been eating? You lookin like a skeleton."

"Not hungry."

"Your shrink says if you don't start eating more they gonna make you."

"Good luck with that."

"That's my girl." She reaches into her handbag. "Brought you these." Doritos. A bottle of Big Red.

"Thanks."

She opens the bag for me, lays it on my lap.

A nurse walks in. "Dinnertime, friends. Fifteen minutes."

"Check you out. Getting served. I saw the menu. Salad, meatloaf, potatoes, bread. Dessert. Ain't you fancy?"

I hold up a Dorito. Throw it back in the bag. Turn the bag over and read the ingredients like Alma would: maltodextrin, monosodium glutamate . . .

"Saw your room. Do they lay little chocolates on your pillow too? Can me and Fred get a room?" Fake laughter. "By the way, where'd you get your hands on—"

Fred? Fred, sodium caseinate, disodium phosphate . . . "Poison."

My mother scooches to the end of the couch. "What?"

"POISON."

I launch the Doritos at the television. Purple People Eater stomps them to crumbs.

An alarm goes off. My mother is escorted out. I'm surrounded by White Coats. Purple People Eater and I lead a parade down the hall to the Quiet Room. When I wake up, I'm led to the Nurse's Station.

I hold out my medicine cup. "What's this green one? And this other white one?"

"Honey, here's your water. The doctor decided to adjust your cocktail."

"TOO MUCH COCK!" I shout, hurling the cup against the wall. "That is the problem!"

I am back in the Quiet Room.

VANISHING

Adjective. I *am* the *magician.*

I grind my teeth to salt. They wrap me in the cocoon. I can't move. I can't breathe. The nurse brings out the snake. It bites. I sleep. Wake up in my house. Jump through a window. Walk through the television screen. I walk past that newswoman reporting on the dead foster girls, only this time I see them do the dead man's float—past the Nigerian mothers protesting about their forgotten girls, the ghosts of their girls trailing behind them. Missing white girls and brown girls stepping out of posters on telephone poles, falling into step, making a timeline. I just stand there, a fool, angry at everybody but protesting nothing.

How long have I been in the Fun House? Thinking I'm looking out the window, but all this time all I was looking at was mirrors of myself. Only now I'm realizing my world was so small. Fuck, my world is a snow globe.

I'm out the Quiet Room. I'm the magician now. I make my pills disappear in my mouth. Reappear in the trash.

My mother comes to visit me. She takes one look at me and knows. She whispers, "How long?"

I keep my eyes glued to the TV. "How long what?"

"Don't even play."

"Why do you care?"

"Where are the pills?"

"Are you kidding me?"

"What difference does it make if you don't want them?"

A White Coat starts circling. Too much whispering.

Me all loud: "Ain't none of your business."

My mother on the downlow: "It's *their* business."

I nod and sit back. "Tomorrow."

We have a deal. I give my mother the pills and she don't tell the nurses I been skipping. This goes on for a couple of weeks.

At the top of the third, I'm back at the couch waiting for my mother. My mother don't come.

Where she at?

Where is Alma?

I sent EMS to Alma's door. I assume they have her. That she's checked out the hospital, living—in foster care? Where is she now? Where is everybody?

I stand up. "I have to call George!" George and I got to figure this shit out. If we don't take care of her, no one will.

"Phone. I want a phone!"

A nurse: "You'll earn phone privileges in due time. We can talk to your doctor—"

"NOW!"

Back to the Quiet Room, where I fall asleep sending telepathic messages to George.

WHITE COATS

Noun. They're coming to take me a-w-a-y.

It is visiting day. My mom does not come again. Instead Nokia comes. I can tell from her pants and shoes and badge that she is CPS.

I snatch a peek at her clipboard before she flips it over. "Where is my mother?"

She plants herself on the couch beside me. I move and sit in a armchair.

Nokia: "Can we introduce ourselves first?"

Me: "I'm crazy. Is you crazy too? Then there's a pair of us. Don't you know? They'll never let you go."

Nokia clears her throat. "Well. It's . . ." She flips through her clipboard. "It's Macy, right?"

I say, "Your mother named you after a phone, right? My mother named me after a department store. Could've been worse. I had a friend named Velvet. Speaking of my mother: Where that bitch at?"

Nokia: "You are a character. I have been looking forward to meeting you. Let's watch the language, Macy, okay? I'm not your enemy."

Me: "Because you're not my enemy don't mean you're my friend."

Nokia: "Maybe we can become friends."

Me: "Okay, friend, where is my mother at?"

Nokia: "She's been arrested, Macy. That's why I'm here."

Me: "Arrested? For what? Those guys are her boyfriends," I say without thinking. Oops.

Nokia takes out her laptop and beings to type. "I see. Well, that isn't why. She's been dealing."

I speak carefully but I feel like all my private thoughts are on a teleprompter. "Am I going to be arrested?"

"No. We know she took your pills but she's been into other things too. That's why—" Nokia gets a ring on her cell and excuses herself. I guess she knows I'm not going anywhere anytime soon. She's gone a long time. Long enough for me to sing along with Leonard Cohen. But two renditions of "Waiting for a Miracle" later she don't come back into the room. I start to wonder if she was ever here.

Next thing I know my doctor wants to talk to me. I know something is up because there are two White Coats tailing us as me and the doctor head to her office. I fucking hate being predictable.

The doctor closes the door. She folds her hands. She leans in close. She sighs. The words about my mother being in the hospital. The words that keep flashing in my head: *Daddy got your letter. Daddy got your letter.*

Dear Daddy,

I love her. I don't know why those are the first three words I want to tell you. It makes no sense that I'm telling you and not her. I mean we fight. But this letter isn't about that. Okay, it started that way. Revenge. Keeping that promise I made to you, to tell you if anything was going on behind your back—if she was cheating on you. As if you didn't know already. But the second my pen stabbed the paper I knew this letter was about something else.

You went behind bars but I feel like we're all in prison. Zane's prison is foster care. Mine is my brain. Mom's is—her body. I can't picture Mom old.

Last time we talked you said you wanted things like they was before. But the more I think about it I don't want anything to be like it was. I want everything to be new. When you get out you're supposed to start a new life. Is something new possible? Are we possible?

I love you. Macy

"Can I go now?" I ask the doctor. The doctor says I can.

I open the door. The workers waiting outside jump up. "Sorry," I say. "No freak show today."

WORDS

Noun. Everything and nothing.

I ain't spoken in months now. My words are trapped in the same black hole with Alma's *NO*. The only ones that get out escape to blank paper. The only place they are safe. The only place everyone is safe from them.

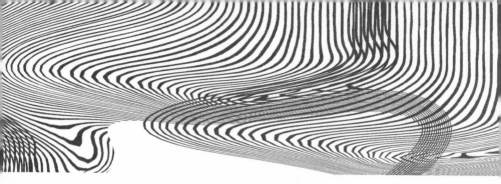

WHY

Noun. Reasons 1 and 2.

Why do I hate? ~~Because it's so much easier than love.~~ Because hate is reality. Love is a fantasy.

Why do I write? Let me break it down. Teacher Man taught us about something called haves and have-nots.

I have not a bed
I have not a room
Got nowhere to go
nothing to do
I have not a choice
I have not a door
I have not a lock
I have not a place in this world
I can't make it stop
All I have is this blank paper
and these lines
and
they are

MINE MINE MINE

WILMA

Noun. Wilma's been to Washington. I been to a mental institution. This gets me to thinking.

Music therapy. They play a lot of things I never heard of. Makes me think of being back with Miss Black. I go get her record and hand it to the music lady. She knows what I want without me having to ask.

"Well, as a matter of fact." She pulls out a damn record player. It has a handle to carry it around like luggage. The brown leather has survived many trips. It got stickers from Alabama to Wyoming on it. I don't touch it. I don't want to ruin it.

Music therapist: "Wilma is tough." She points to the record player, which apparently has a name. "Feel that leather. Go ahead." I do real quick.

She teaches me how to work it. I set Miles Davis's'sss "Kind of Blue" in motion. I feel like whoever put the planets where they go and watched them start to spin. But I can't move. Nobody makes me, even after music therapy. I get up when the sky turns into the record, the moon a silver needle scratching each track.

X

X is where I sign my name on my release papers from the hospital. X is where I sign my name to prove that I know why I'm being taken into the custody of CPS and to a temporary shelter. I'm being taken because my mom was caught dealing my pills and her boyfriend's drugs by none other than 3211. I'm being taken because my dad got my letter, then got on probation, and when he got home he beat the living shit out of my mom.

YOLANDA

Noun. A PERSON.

Music therapy. Last time before I leave. I bring John Coltrane. "Ascension." It sounds like every instrument I ever heard of falling down a flight of stairs. Like my life. I want to play it again but a lady dressed as a Christmas tree—with like bulbs and shit—starts to scream because the music is so weird. "No! No! *Feliz Navidad*! No!" Her ornaments shake back and forth.

I'm about to say something. For the first time in months.

Music Therapist catches my drift. "Macy, I'll tell you what. Why don't we set you on the computer. I've been meaning to tell you, but I might as well right now. I have an iPod and a gift card for you, for a going-away present."

Me, voice gravel and glass: "How?"

Music Therapist: "How? Uh. I just got them?"

"You rich?" My voice cracks like I'm a thirteen-year-old boy. I look down at her shoes. Basic. "You don't look rich."

Music Therapist laughs. "No."

"What's your name?"

"It's Miss Yolanda."

I write her name down in my dictionary. Start working on my playlist. My fingers hit the keys like they're pressing the button for a nuclear bomb. Time to set it off.

YASMIN

Noun. My mother. Me?

I want to see her. CPS takes me to the hospital. I walk in. There's a bed hooked up to machines just like in a movie. She's asleep. I stand close to her for longer than I probably have in years. The only way I can tell the woman laying in the bed is my mother is by the red lipstick. I put some on. Go into her bafroom and look in her mirror. There is my mother in the mirror.

Her hair is growing back in, thick on one side. The other side is freshly shaved. All her piercings have been replaced. She has pierced her nose like a bull. She is . . . She is beautif—she is me.

I walk to the sink. I look in the mirror and say, "I will make it up to you, Mom. And to Alma."

I face her. "I'm sorry."

"You . . . *YOU!*"

My mother is trying to sit up. She can't scream right because her mouth is all swollen. Her eyes are all swelled up so she points all over the room trying to find me.

"YOU!"

A nurse runs in. "What's going on here?"

"YOU!!!" She holds her face with the tips of her bruised fingers.

She knows what I did. And she will never forgive me for it.

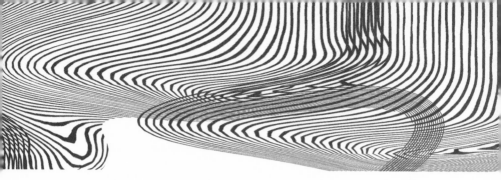

YOU

Pronoun. Anti-noun.

She meant: *YOU* did this. It's *YOU*r fault.

I never want to see *YOU* again. *YOU* are dead to me.

Z

Z is not for zebra, motherfoe. Z is for Zimmerman. No, not that Zimmerman.

Zimmerman is the name of the family that's taking me in. I'm sitting in a car stinking of McDonald's on the way to their house. I take the bag and stuff it through a open window. I open up my brown bag, carefully move my records, and grab my muffins. No, stupit. Not those muffins. Those things is like three months old. Nasty. (Okay, I still have them but like not to eat them.)

Miss Black came back with her husband. She's going to have a baby. I hate the baby. (What? You thought I was cured? Puhlease. There is no cure for me. I'm the cure, bitch.) Anyway I hate the baby only cause it's not me.

Z is for zip. As in I'm not going to say zip to any Zimmerman or anyone about anything. As in, every word that CPS has been saying to me for three days has gone in one ear and *zip!*

out the other. As in, that name I signed on the dotted line don't mean zip and the minute I have the chance I'm out the door.

Z is for zero, which is what I have to my name. I don't have any money. I don't have any clothes accept the sweatshirt, my dad's boxers, and the flip-flops on my feet. One of my flip-flops is torn. Got just this brown bag with the records and the lipstick I took from my mom's hospital bed.

Z is for the bolt of lightning that is my life. Z is for the crack in my broken heart. Z is for the little boy I left in a hospital bed a year ago who is now standing on the Zimmermans' porch. The boy who has his hair cut and combed. The boy who smiles with white teeth. He looks at the Zimmermans and they nod their heads and he runs right toward my car. He opens my door and reaches out his hand to help me onto the curb. This boy who I once walked like a dog walks me up the steps arm in arm.

Z is for Zane.

ZOMBIE

Noun. Look up the Cranberries. Trust me.

I tell Mrs. Zimmerman if she don't give me access to a computer and a phone I will set her house on fire while she sleeps. Just kidding, stupit. What am I, loco? They keeping a bed open for me at the nut house. (But I do tell her I will piss her floor at her next dinner party.) I think of negotiating for the newest iPhone, but I got my dignity.

Miss Black added me to a group of kids she keeps in touch with on FB. I see George's name.

I message her: Yo. Miss Black. Because my life. I can't even. But. Yeah.

Miss Black: I feel you, Macy.

Me: Thanks, Miss B. Cuz it's like that. You and me.

Miss Black: No question.

Me: How is George?

Miss Black: Macy, girl. I can't even.

Me: I'ma be cool, Miss B. I can handle it. (But it's the first time I want to sit down.)

Miss Black: Who's with you?

Me: Zane.

Long Pause . . .

Me: Please. (I hold my breaf.)

Miss Black: George told the school counselor he kept cutting school because of a zombie. Turns out his mom had a stroke. Child was trying to take care of her on his own.

I breathe. I HEART George.

Miss Black: His mom's in a state facility now.

Me: And George?

Miss Black: George disappeared after CPS showed up. He was spotted a couple of times. Working at a gas station. Sleeping at a shelter. I left him a message at the shelter once—left him my number. He messaged me a dancing bear. LOL.

I type in hearts around a dancing bear.

Miss B sends me two numbers. One for her. One for the shelter.

Me: Thanks, Miss B. I'll be in touch. I'm out.

To the man taking a message at the shelter: "Tell George March 15." I give him the Zimmermans' address.

And I wait for the dancing bear to show up in my FB inbox.

AGÜEYBANÁ II

Verb. Here comes the Sun, motherfoes.

Agüeybaná's name means Great Sun. He ruled over all the tribes of Puerto Rico. One day Ponce de León and his squad shows up. The Taino people think they're gods. Agüeybaná II plays it cool and tries to keep the peace. But Ponce de León's got goals. He makes all the Tainos slaves to work the gold mines. Most of the Tainos die. Agüeybaná II says eff these motherfoes. He and his squad rise up against them. His macana is no match against Ponce de León's guns, but he goes down fighting.

I still have my machete. It took my lawyer going to court for me to keep this bitch in my possession. I have it in a lockbox in a bank. The Zimmermans had the account number and ID. Yes, *had*. Zane wrapped the info in foil and gave it to me for my birfday. No matter what's his last name, Zane is on Team Macy 4eva. My machete will see the light of day again soon.

The Zimmermans are fighting in the next room. They fight funny. They do it in whispers like pissed-off snakes. They fight when they wash the dishes because they think I can't hear over the running water. The first time I figured out they was fighting I thought—oh shit, and those are some nice dishes too. But not one china cup or dish flew. They was mad, though. It's kind of like a boxing match with no boxing, just walking around the ring and pushing each other against the ropes.

"She didn't flush the toilet again," Mrs. Zimmerman says to Mr. Zimmerman.

"Now, Sylvia," Mr. Z says.

"I mean that log, just sitting there, it's disgusting! And it's no wonder, she's eating enough for two grown men!"

"Now, Sylvia," Mr. Z says. "She's only been here three months . . ."

Mrs. Z says, "Three months too long. I can't live like this. She's nothing like her brother."

"Well," Mr. Z says, "that may be true, but he was barking like a dog when he first got here. Just standing on two feet was an improvement for him . . ."

My brother. What a small fucking world. He was about a hour away the whole time. I think about that a lot. How close and far away Zane has always been. And not just Zane. My dad, Alma, Alma's uncle.

Alma's uncle's on FB. He tweets. His sick ass is actually from New Jersey.

Alma? I know she made it to the hospital. George finally messaged me last week. Told me he went back to the Palace Apartments alone to check up on Alma.

I HEART George.

He found out what hospital she was at. Tried to visit her even though the nurses wouldn't let him through. By the time he was able to sneak in, she was checked out. A nurse told him

326

her uncle brought some of her friends and took her home. The nurse was like, "That girl, what a shame, what happened to her face. It made me cry to look at her. But when she saw how scared and nervous her friends looked seeing her scars? She stood up and took those girls' hands. Told *them* it was going to be all right. I'm praying for her."

Her friends. More of Uncle's girls. I dreamed Uncle locked Alma way up high in a apartment like a treehouse. She dresses the girls for their johns. Puts ice on their bruises when they come back. I call out to save her, to let down her hair, but of course, she can't.

Fuck hair. Fuck using the stairs. I'ma cut that motherfucking tree down.

From my bed, I watch Zane reading a newspaper. He's definitely a Zimmerman. He goes to a special school. He speaks French and . . . drum roll, please . . . Yiddish.

Now the Zimmermans are talking about the vacation they're taking this summer. They're going to *Canada!*

Mrs. Zimmerman: "We've got to put her in respite, Arty. Are you kidding?"

(Respite, for all you ignorant motherfoes, is when you send your foster kids to another foster home when you're sick and tired of their ghetto asses and you have somewhere to go.)

Mrs. Zimmerman: "She spit on my Oriental carpet yesterday. Just like she was standing in the street!"

Sorry! Dang! Spit happens.

Mr. Z: "Sylvia . . . Take Zane and leave Macy? How would that look?"

The Zimmermans are going to officially adopt Zane this May. I'm happy for him. Mrs. Zimmerman said they were worried he was retarded—she uses the words *intellectual disability*—but then they found out he had Asperger's and were so relieved. I guess here in suburbia, Asperger's is in style. Obviously having a emotionally disturbed kid ain't.

I hold up my pen between sentences. I'm writing with Mrs. Zimmerman's pen and I'm sure it's a antique. It's silver, and the tip is sharp enough to cut out someone's heart. It slips nicely inside a pillowcase or in the pocket I sewed inside my sweat-shirt. Nobody even needs to know I carry it. Not unless they deserve to know. Nobody knows what a girl like me can do with a pen.

Agüeybaná II, The Great Sun, had his macana. My great-grandmother had her machete. I laugh and stick my secret in my pocket. I check my backpack. iPod (thanks, Yolanda). Play "Point of No Return."

Hit Repeat.

Listen for a motorcycle horn. Look for the Ninja Turtle helmet. I'm ready. I have my map of New Jersey . . . and Canada. And my pen against my chest like a arrow shot from my heart.

MACY CASHMERE'S DOPE PLAYLIST

"The Ghetto" by Donny Hathaway
"Mi Machete" by Grupo Niche
"Straight Outta Vagina" by Pussy Riot
"A Love Supreme" by John Coltrane
"The Lonely Ballerina" by Michele McLaughlin
"Funeral" by Band of Horses
"Darkness" by Leonard Cohen
"Back to Life" by Soul II Soul
"The Day Women Took Over" by Common
"We the People" by A Tribe Called Quest
"The Revolution Will Not Be Televised" by Gil Scott-Heron
"Renegades of Funk" by Rage Against the Machine
"Point of No Return" by Immortal Technique

SHOUTOUT

To the Woman Who Always
got My Back
Miss Black
One day I'ma give you more
than M&M's to pay you back.

ACKNOWLEDGMENTS

To my seventh- and eighth-grade English and history teachers, Ms. Brisson and Mr. Phelan, from St. Dominic's Elementary School in the Bronx, now closed down: Oh, what I would give to find you and tell you both in person how much you meant to me.

Thank you, Gabriel Garcia Marquez, for rescuing me from the Dead White Men's Literary canon, for awakening the voices and cultivating the soil for future works. Everyone needs diverse books, and we need them written by diverse writers now and forever.

To the University of Notre Dame MFA program that changed my life, with shoutouts to William O'Rourke for helping me put an engine in my airplane and to Steve Tomasula for not caring if my airplane had an engine.

Props to Emily Keyes, my agent extraordinaire at Fuse Literary, for finding the perfect home for our Macy (and her machete). Thank you to Amy Fitzgerald and Alix Reid at Carolrhoda Lab, for choosing my project. To Amy Fitzgerald, my brilliant editor, thank you for your expertise, insight, and guidance.

Much love to Titi Matilde for the entire set of Little House on the Prairie books that I pulled all-nighters to read, and to

Titi Jessica for interviewing me about my poetry and my love of dictionaries (LOL) on Elizabeth Seton Hall College radio.

Thank you, my dear Uncle Joel, for reading works I wrote in my twenties, perhaps the absolute worst children's books of all time.

To my mother for Coliseum Books, *Jane Eyre*, *Alice in Wonderland*, *The Little Princess*, and *Heidi*, and Greek Mythology. I keep the candles lit.

Eternal gratitude to those who have loved, rescued, and empowered me to write throughout my life: shoutouts to Titi Carmen and Titi Clarissa, my godfather Richie, and my godmother Susan.

To my Michael/Mickie/Miguel: genius, brilliant professor, phenomenal Chief-of-Staff, gifted poet and writer, bestest dad, soulmate. You have provided me ten MFAs with your knowledge and expertise of the craft and everlasting faith. You are the antecedent to my pronouns, the spell check to my Teeshirt and TV, my Cliff Notes, My SparkNotes, my EVERYTHING.

Dear Dad, thank you for never doubting that I would be in *THIS MOMENT.* You treasured my Post-It-Note metaphor quilt and bought me my first (and second) Smith and Corona. Thank you for the Christmas gift of every Stephen King book you could fit in the Macy's box. Thank you for always having a book in hand wherever you go. I have the confidence to talk to any rabbit I please now. ;) "No defeat! No surrender!" XO Your gold, Sugar Bear

TOPICS FOR DISCUSSION

1. School is sometimes portrayed as an antagonistic place and sometimes as a safe haven for Macy. Compare how Macy behaves in Miss Black's class and how she behaves in Miss Black's lunchtime detention. Why is there a difference? What sort of classroom atmosphere might help students like Macy do well?

2. Hunger and neglect are recurring themes in many of Macy's experiences. How is Macy affected by her hardships? Why won't Macy eat the food her mother offers her? In what ways do you think Macy would be different if she hadn't gone through these experiences?

3. Why does Macy decide to tape her breasts? How does Macy feel about her body? In contrast, how does Alma feel about hers?

4. How are the male characters (such as George, Macy's dad, Mr. Guest, and Alma's uncle) portrayed in the book?

5. In the "Blessing" chapter, Zane acts like a dog and Macy treats him like one. Why do you think he does this and why do you think Macy goes along with it?

6. What does Macy mean by "I'm still somewhere between today and yesterday"? Discuss an incident in Macy's life that you think relates to this quote.

7. Macy knows that Zane may have a better life with his foster parents, but she insists that he should stay with their family. Why does she think he should stay? How does Macy cope with her brother being taken away?

8. What does the machete represent for Macy? Why does she refuse to let the police take it away?

9. Macy's encounter with the police reminds her of other, fatal encounters between police officers and people of color. In what ways does Macy identify with the victims of these incidents? What do you think would have happened to Macy if Velvet had not distracted the police?

10. Compare the first time Macy meets Velvet with when Macy finds out about Velvet's death. Why does Macy care about Velvet? In what ways do events in Velvet's life have an impact on Macy?

11. How would you describe Macy's relationship with Yasmin from Yasmin's perspective and from Macy's? In what ways are Macy and Yasmin similar? Why do you think Macy is loyal to her mother despite their antagonistic relationship?

12. Discuss Macy's feelings about her father. Why does Macy initially keep her mother's cheating a secret, and why does she eventually decide to be honest with her father? What would you have done in her position?

13. What do you learn about Macy's relationship with her mom from her poem "Daughter to Mother"? Does it change what you thought of their relationship before reading the poem?

14. Macy is extremely protective of Zane, George, and Alma. What does this say about Macy as a person? In what ways does it backfire, and why?

15. Macy thinks she knows Alma better than anyone and is stunned to realize Alma has kept many secrets from her. What did Macy miss? What clues throughout the story reveal that Alma is less perfect and put-together than Macy believes?

16. What forms of sexual violence has Macy experienced? How do these experiences influence what she does to Alma? What goes through Macy's mind when she learns about what Alma's uncle is doing to her?

17. When Macy is getting treatment, how does her experience differ from her life before? In what ways is it similar? What aspects of the experience are healing for Macy and how?

18. Macy memorizes the names of the girls kidnapped from Nigeria. Why are these girls so important to her?

19. Why do you think Macy writes her story in dictionary format? What does this format tell you about Macy as a character?

20. What do you think will happen to Macy, George, Alma, and Zane after the end of the book? How has Macy changed since the beginning, and in what ways has she remained the same?

UNEXPECTED.
ECLECTIC.
ADVENTUROUS.

For more distinctive and award-winning YA titles, reader guides, book excerpts, and more, visit *CarolrhodaLab.com.*

ABOUT THE AUTHOR

NoNieqa Ramos spent her childhood in the Bronx, where she started her own publishing company and sold books for twenty-five cents until the nuns shut her down. With the support of her single father and her tías, she earned dual master's degrees in creative writing and education at the University of Notre Dame. As a teacher, she has dedicated herself to bringing gifted-and-talented education to minority students and expanding access to literature, music, and theater for all children. A frequent foster parent, NoNieqa lives in Ashburn, Virginia, with her family.